Myth Dawning

Molly C. Gross

CHAPTER 0

When the stars were nameless and the winds still, there existed two universes.

The two universes collided, creating an explosion like none ever seen before, and chaos was born. She was unstable, elements free and unbound throughout the new world that had formed. As time went on, the exact amount of time forever a mystery, as there becomes a time when the past is too much the past for anyone to recall, certain elements stabilized and mutated to form the first beings.

These were the Protogenoi.

Though the world was stabilizing, there remained powerful energies from the initial collision. The Protogenoi were exposed to these residual energies, giving them powers, magical abilities. From the Protogenoi came others, but none as powerful as the firsts, so the Protogenoi ruled over everything and everyone. With such power came madness and misuse. There was a rebellion that morphed into a war. The war lasted for years, nearly destroying everything, but eventually the Protogenoi were defeated and forced back into their elemental forms.

The victory led to a divide between the victors. Those who blamed the magic for driving the Protogenoi insane decided to outlaw magic all together. Others believed it was the power given to the Protogenoi by the people that drove them to such extremes and cruelty and wished to keep magic alive. The two groups separated, agreeing to live without any connection, so to not interfere with the other's way of life.

Over the years, those who lived without magic lost their ability to wield it as they no longer had use for it, not unlike a vestigial organ. They forgot about the world as it was, when there was magic and it was united. They forgot their origins and came to see history as myth. These people called themselves humans and the land they lived on Earth.

CHAPTER I

1773

"And that makes 342," I say, brushing a long strand of hair the ocean breeze has blown into my face out of my line of sight. "There's something calming about watching a rebellion from afar, but I do hate to witness good tea go to waste."

Priscilla sits next to me, looking less than delighted, and I am not sure whether her mood is a result of me dragging her out of bed to come to the harbor or because of my commentary on the events occurring down there at the moment. Perhaps it is both, judging by the way her eyes droop with fatigue and her mouth twists with disapproval.

"It is madness," Priscilla says.

She lies on her stomach next to me, peering over the edge of the roof at the wharf below. Our breath mingles with the cold air around us.

"Without doubt. It is a statement nonetheless."

"I mean it is madness that we are here, Abby" Priscilla says. "Mother will see to our deaths if she finds out."

"Nonsense. She will not find out, and this is important. We must see what is happening, what we will be fighting for," I say, watching one of the crates bob in the water.

Priscilla sits up on the roof, attempting to smooth out her dress, all the while shaking her head on what seems to be an infinite loop of reproach.

"Abigail, there is no fight. You are letting your mind forgo with your sense again. Regardless, if there was a fight, you would have no part in it," Priscilla says.

"Priscy," I say, using the nickname she abhors, just as I prefer the shortening of my own. "There is no fight yet. Merely because it is not presently occurring does not mean that it will not. And, who is to say whether or not I will fight?"

I sit up to face her, not bothering to straighten out my dress. She reaches out a hand to help me up, and I accept.

"Society is to say," she says.

I frown at my elder sister and make to follow her down from the roof, but a loose tile catches my foot. Priscilla's pristine dress is the last I see. I hear her yell, but my own heartbeat thrumming in my ears and pounding against my chest drowns out her words.

1832

Hearing the click as the vault unlocks, I smile and jam my hands into the large pockets of my oversized, navy jumpsuit. The outfit is comfortable as far as disguises go. It helps me not only pass as maintenance, but also as a man.

"Smart as a steel trap, truly you are," John, my accomplice, says from behind me.

I hear a familiar sound and the surely proud smile drops from my face. I knew I'd have a better chance attempting this on my own. I turn, slowly, coming to face him, with my hands raised above my head in surrender.

"Evidently not smart enough," I say, more to myself than him.

He offers me an almost apologetic smile, the type that's easy to see through to the completely insincere apology underneath.

"No hard feelings, but I don't intend on sharing this money with you and especially not with all the others that blue-blood skinned, as you planned to do."

I hear the gunshot, and then everything goes dark.

1926

"This is your captain speaking with your midday announcement— Shoot," I say, as a bug flies into my ear, and I lift my hand up to swat it away.

I take a moment to be grateful that my swatting hand was the one holding down the intercom. The passengers were, thankfully, not gifted with my cursing. I don't understand what flies are doing out in the middle of the ocean. The rest of the crew on the bridge looks over *at me oddly, having not seen the bug and only my spastic reaction to it. As if they didn't already question me for simply being a woman. Now, my sanity is in question, as well.*

"We are on course to Le Havre, France," I continue, turning the intercom back on, "set to arrive an hour earlier than originally scheduled, which will allow you to disembark at 9 tomorrow morning. Calm seas are expected until we reach our next port, and the weather forecast predicts a rain free rest of the day. Have a swell day!"

I set the intercom down and look around the bridge, with its large windows making up the entirety of the walls in order to ensure a full view of the surrounding ocean.

"Early again," says Jeremy, the watch keeper.

"I'm also going to take an early lunch," I tell him, smiling politely, before making my way to the door.

I walk through the long hallways of the top floor, where all the nicest suites are on this cruise ship. Being surrounded by windows all day is not the same as actually breathing the fresh air of the outdoors, so I head out onto the deck before retrieving my lunch from down on the lower decks. It is expected to be a rain free day, or so I hear. As I walk, I pause to look over the railing and watch the white crests of the waves, small from this distance, crash and smooth over.

Something shoves me, the weight of hands pressed flat against my back. I lose my balance, toppling over the railing. I reach out to grab onto something, anything, but I'm falling head first. The only thing to reach for is the water below.

1989

It's summer, and for once I have an open schedule. I had thought it would be a great idea to spend some time with my mom, so I asked her what she wanted to do. Paddle boarding. I agreed but had to add in that I heard that the odds increase that you'll be attacked by a shark when using a board in the ocean because, from under, it looks like a seal.

At that, my mom blanched and was ready to back out of what was her own idea, but I'd actually been wanting to try paddle boarding so I convinced her that I was sure it was perfectly safe. Plus, she had gone paddle boarding without me before and survived to tell the tale; so, here we are, paddle boarding.

The sun is beating down on us, and the heat seems to be rising off the surface of the water in waves, which adds to the feeling that hot air is coming at us from all directions. Apart from the heat, however, it is relaxing on the water.

"The water is normally much clearer," the guide is telling us. Of course, the water is always much clearer the day you're not there. And, normally there are dolphins leaping out of the water by the dozens, performing professional choreography. Just not today, I think to myself, hiding a smile.

"It's nice and calm, at least," my mom tells the guide, keeping up polite conversation.

My mom smiles in my direction, and I return her smile before looking back down at the water. There's some movement below, and I squint my eyes to try to make out whatever fish there might be in the opaque water. It's coming up, closer to the surface, and I realize I'm looking into the wide mouth of a shark, its white teeth standing out in the murkiness of the water.

"Shark!" I yell, to warn my mom and the guide.

I jump off the board. Hitting the water, I don't look back and swim as quickly as possible towards the shore. My mom and the guide have made it a good distance away, but my mom hesitates, looking back for me.

"Keep swimming," I manage to yell, already out of breath. Or, perhaps I'm hyperventilating.

Something touches my leg.

2006

A bright light shines in my eyes, and I reflexively flinch away.

"Wow, is that your natural eye color?" the security officer, standing outside my car with the assaulting flashlight, asks.

Shauna, my best friend since three years ago when we met freshmen year in high school, also the birthday girl, leans across my lap from the passenger side to look at the officer. She is the reason *we are in this predicament right now. We were driving around her neighborhood, listening to music, and she thought it would be a good idea to stick her head out of the sunroof as they do in movies. I didn't disagree, and now here we are.*

"Yes," Shauna says. "She gets asked that a lot. They're amber. Cool, right?"

I push Shauna off my lap and back into her seat. The officer seems to reorient himself and moves the flashlight away from my face.

"Are you aware that you were driving recklessly?" he asks.

"Was I?"

The question comes out in a British accent, something that tends to happen when I'm put in uncomfortable and potentially stressful situations. I hear Shauna hold back a laugh and truly hope the officer doesn't think we are mocking him or, worse, drunk.

"I stopped at the stop sign," *I add, thinking that might help the situation and am at least relieved to hear that the accent is gone.*

"You had a person standing out of your sunroof."

"I did."

"I'll let you off with a warning."

"Thank you," *I say, breathing a sigh of relief.*

The officer walks off back to his car. Shauna stares at me, smiling.

"We're lucky your neighborhood security couldn't care less," *I tell her, and the goofy smile remains.*

"Alice, I think he liked your eyes," *she says.*

"Get out."

Laughing, she gets out of the car, and I yell after her through the open window, "Happy Birthday!"

I pull out of her driveway and search the road for other cars before rounding the corner.

The crash is quick. I turn the corner and feel the jolt of another car slamming into the passenger's side. A sharp pain pierces my head, the breath leaving my body, but then any and all physical sensation ceases—

I don't know how normal deaths occur.

But, when I die, before I leave this world, everything around me slows...

...The windshield shatters from the impact, and I watch the slivers of glass explode around me. They reflect the pale light from the street lamps, standing out like stars against the black night. The car's digital clock reads 11:00. The small, antique clock hanging from a chain on the rearview mirror appears suspended up in the air, frozen, even the second hand not moving. A pearl of blood appears on my right arm, the bleeding staunched by the lack of forward movement in time. My brown hair barely moves, floating in the zero gravity air. A piece of the broken windshield is a hair's breadth away from slicing across my face.

The antique clock drops, yanking the chain down against the rearview mirror. The car's digital clock clicks, switching to 11:01. The glass shoots around me like confetti released from a cannon, and the nearest shard flashes across my vision as it scratches my face, leaving behind a cut I can't feel the sting of. And then it's all gone.

We are born, and there's light. We die, and it's dark. Darkness comes after those last few, frozen moments on Earth. There's not meant to be anything left for us on Earth after that darkness because there's another part of the world meant for life after mortal death.

Havcire, the dawning of your immortal life.

It's a nice slogan, right? I came up with it, partly because my name is Dawn. I've had different names, but the first I can remember is Dawn. Ironically, I don't actually get to live in Havcire. I get sent back to Earth, or Vestigium as they call it. Only in those last few minutes of life do my memories of past lives and Havcire's existence come rushing back, when I remember that death is not the end.

I inhale deeply the second I can once again sense my body and open my eyes to find a familiar hallway. The floor and walls are made of tiles of varying shapes and sizes. Each tile shows different scenery. The one I stand on is an ocean, the water moving beneath the floor. The sun reflects off the waves, sending the light away in different directions.

Another tile on the wall to my left shows what would look like an ordinary town, at least from this view, if it weren't for the fact that the quaint, oddly shaped houses are levitating, most likely the homes of Incanters.

As I step toward the single bench in the hallway, made from white marble, the tiles on the floor ripple like a pond disturbed by a raindrop, making it appear as though I'm walking on water. Without warning, the places through the tiles disappear, and the tiles become solid white marble to match the bench.

I look down at myself, beginning to feel a bit more normal. It can be disorienting to die, no matter how much practice one has. I'm wearing the same clothes I'd been wearing in the car. The rip in my sweater's sleeve remains, from where the piece of glass cut through. My blood stains the fabric around the tear, but my skin itself is completely healed.

Sitting down on the marble bench, I have to be careful not to slide off it and onto my bony butt. A high-pitched ding, which I swear should only be detectable by a dog's ear, echoes throughout the hall.

"Here we go again," I say, as I lie down on the bench, the marble not the most comfortable, but the cold does feel nice through my clothes, a good reminder that I can still feel something in this time of death. "Hi, Jenna."

"Hi, I'm Jenna," an overly joyful, disembodied voice says. "Welcome to Havcire, my home."

I clasp my hands over my stomach and try for my best impression of Jenna. I raise my eyebrows, plaster on a large smile, and imagine I have no care in the world as I say, "You're dead."

"Your mortal body has passed on," Jenna continues, "but your immortal soul has made the journey from Vestigium, or as you probably know of it, Earth."

I learned a long time ago that this hallway could be used to travel to different parts of Havcire. However, it only works for Celestials and even then it only works when the tiles feel like transforming into the doors. It also requires for the Celestials to make direct contact with the marble, which is helpful to avoid accidentally falling through one of the doors while merely walking in the hallway. Unless, of course, one is careless enough to walk through barefoot.

I push on the bench with my feet so the rest of my body slides more towards the end, where I let my head dangle off the side. I'm not a Celestial, so escaping through one of the portals to rid myself of Jenna's cheery voice is not an option. Perhaps if all the blood rushes to my head and fills my ears, I won't be able to hear Jenna anymore.

"In Havcire, new souls are either classified as Citizens or Subjects. Citizens live out their immortal lives however they desire, all their basic needs provided for by the Celestials. *I* am a Citizen."

"Hoorah for you, Jenna," I say, wishing someone could hear just how ecstatic I sound for Jenna.

Everything looks better upside down, more interesting. Less real.

"Subjects have misdeeds to pay for. They are granted the opportunity to serve under an Experimenter, a special type of Citizen, to right those wrongs and earn their place as a Citizen. Experimenters strive to aid those alive on Vestigium. As a Subject, you could be part of this honorable mission," Jenna says.

"Honorable my ass," I say, groaning as I force myself back up into a seated position. My head feels double its size. I can still hear Jenna, though.

"May your immortal life begin!"

The large, heavy doors of the Council Chamber open. Unlike the rest of the hall, the doors are made of a dark wood. Not even polished, they stand out against the shining marble, looking like they'd be more fit to function as a gateway into an enchanted forest. Although they open rather gracefully and without sound, there's something loud about the action, something that makes me feel like even if I were a few turns around the corner, in a separate hallway, I would still sense these doors opening.

Another Subject walks out through the doors. She looks to be about seventeen but looks aren't exactly a reliable measure of age around here. She has dirty blonde hair, with a bit of a wave to it, that falls to just above her elbows, about to where my own does.

She's nervous. As she spots me in front of her, she jumps, startled, but she quickly recovers, smiling kindly. If her nerves weren't enough of a giveaway, her smile would have confirmed that she's early on in her lives. This could even be the first experimental life she's been assigned, for her smile conveys hope.

I smile back because I hope she can hold onto that hope for as long as possible. Even a hopeless situation is better with hope. And, maybe she'll have more luck than I've had. The girl walks off down the hallway to meet with her Experimenter, to start another life.

I enter the Council Chamber. For me, this is where hope goes to die.

CHAPTER 2

Meet the Council, the head of Havcire. Seated in the middle, on his throne of gold, we have Barnabas. Maybe you've heard of him if you've read that little book known as the Bible. Although, it's not the most accurate account of the man, if one could call him that.

The Council is made up of three Celestials. Barnabas, like the others, has been known by many different names throughout history and among different cultures. However, none of the accounts are completely accurate.

He is about seven feet tall, every foot filled out with muscles like a body builder. His white, button-down shirt looks molded to his chest and arms. With a matching jacket, along with his nice white pants and dress shoes, he'd look ready to attend a wedding. His blonde, almost silver hair flows around him in long locks but somehow manages to stay out of his face, as if there were a permanent, invisible fan placed strategically in front of his face for that exact purpose. In reality, it must be magic behind the hair. I have caught him with his hair pulled back into a bun before, so maybe it does get tiring to keep it out of his face.

On Barnabas's left, we have Minerva, who at first glance could pass as a normal human being. She wears a white halter-top that twists at her chest and ties back around her neck. Her white boots come up just above her knees over her tight, white jeans. Her long, black hair flows straight down her back, like needles of silk, against the back of her throne, which is made from actual spider silk.

Her throne used to give me the creeps when I first realized what it was that gave it its gossamer sheen, but now I just wonder what it'd be like to touch its smooth surface. Minerva's warmly toned skin gives her a natural beauty. She is slim but not without strength, as can be seen in her defined arms and seriously set face.

On Minerva's shoulder, as always, is a griffon. It is small for its kind, the size of a barn owl, but it also differs from others in a more drastic way. It has the ability to hear and see everything on Vestigium while still remaining in Havcire. With the head and wings of an owl and the body of a lion, including a tail of fur, it's the Council's little spy. However, I've only ever seen it report to Minerva... and that other person I don't think about. The griffon simply favors the two of them. The former I can understand. The latter, obviously, not so much.

Lastly, on Barnabas's right, is Lucifer. Lucifer has the power to control the souls of the dead. His affinity for souls is a large part of the reason why he has a place on the Council. And, no. He's not the fallen archangel, the devil... not exactly. Like most other Celestials, he chose his name based off of Vestigium stories, which *were* based off of them to begin with. It sounds very circular, very chicken and egg, but the Celestials were around before us, the humans.

Lucifer, like Minerva, has dark hair, but it is cut short and curls at the ends. It stands out against his pale skin. Although Barnabas is taller, looking at the two of them seated next to each other gives the false impression that Lucifer is actually the taller of the two, with his slim features and the way he holds himself, as if elongating every limb. His plain white, V-neck t-shirt brings attention to his sharp collarbone. The shirt hangs loosely, gathering at the waistband of his white pants. He sits on a bronze throne. The armrests form blades, the ends sharp to the touch, which surely sends a message about getting too close to the Celestial.

"A total of approximately 460 years of life. 26 lives and counting. You are still not a Citizen, as you have not decreased your sentence significantly enough as a Subject," Barnabas reports.

"I'm aware," I tell them.

"We like to make it clear to you that you are a failure," Lucifer says, smiling cruelly.

Lucifer pokes the tip of his finger against the end of his armrest, instantly drawing blood, and holds it out in front of his face to inspect. He watches a spot of blood pool to the surface before disappearing back under his skin, the small wound healing in a matter of seconds.

In case I were to forget, Lucifer's little act is a reminder that the Council members are Celestials, which means they are much stronger than I am and cannot be harmed. I, on the other hand, am merely a Subject. Well, I do not need the reminder. I smile good-naturedly at Lucifer.

"Speaking of failures, Luce—"

"Don't call me that," Lucifer interrupts.

"We're such good friends, though."

Lucifer looks to Barnabas and Minerva.

"I'd like to kill her. Let me kill her," Lucifer pleads, and it's not completely clear whether or not he's being serious. Regardless, I work to suppress a smile. Perhaps I have a death wish or...

"No," Barnabas answers, as Minerva points out, "You already did."

That's it. I either have a death wish or I just no longer have a fear of dying. I've done it plenty of times, enough so that it no longer seems like a viable threat.

"Speaking of, Lucifer," I continue, emphasizing the Celestial's full name, "I was trying to say that killing me in a car accident wasn't your best. Has that not been done before?"

"Your Experimenter—"

"Max," I say. My turn to interrupt.

Lucifer doesn't think it worth his time to learn the names of the different Experimenters, or really anyone for that matter, especially anyone who was originally a human.

"Your Experimenter, as I was saying, informed me of his need for your demise too late. I normally require at least a two-day advance notice."

"How inconsiderate of him. Of course, not as inconsiderate as killing me every time my life gets on track, but it sure is right up there," I say, and I catch Minerva's sympathetic look. A lot of good her sympathy has done me. As in, no good, just to be absolutely clear.

Lucifer betrays himself, cracking a smile. *That* is something. To get a genuine reaction out of Lucifer, it can almost make me believe they see me as a real person, as if once I walk back out those doors, Lucifer might recall this moment, recall me when even I no longer can. But, that's just me clinging to the little I can, wishing that, for once, something I did left a mark. In reality, I'll leave and won't be a second thought.

Barnabas, per usual, looks uninterested, as though he's currently pondering another matter entirely.

"You are aware," Barnabas states, coming back to the matter at hand, "that Max's experiment tests his theory on nature versus nurture. Once he gains the necessary data, that life ceases to be of importance."

"I got that much. It is my life. I meet with you, get memory wiped, reborn, killed off, and then I'm back here. The circle of life—"

The screech of the griffon cuts me off.

Oh no. Its head swivels, causing the brown feathers around its neck to ruffle, revealing purple skin beneath. The doors to the chamber open.

"And it moves us all," I hear a familiar voice say.

The other person the griffon favors. It's hard not to think about someone when they've just entered the room.

Phoenix, dressed in a white sweatshirt and white jeans, walks in confidently and not as though he just interrupted a private meeting. He looks the same as I remember, appearing to be in his early twenties, which makes sense since Celestials are immortal and don't age, unless they want to.

He pushes dark, brown hair back from his face but it still falls wavily back over his forehead. His seafoam green eyes find Minerva, and he blows a kiss to her. He comes to a stop, standing slightly behind me. I look away quickly and back toward the Council, avoiding eye contact with him.

"What is it, Phoenix?" Barnabas asks, irritated.

"I come with news," he replies, as the griffon lets out another screech, lifting off Minerva's shoulder and flying over to perch on Phoenix's.

"News that could not wait until after this meeting?" Barnabas asks.

"Max sent me to inform you that he has to redo one of Dawn's previous lives because there were too many confounding variables," Phoenix says, managing to simultaneously ignore

Barnabas's question and answer it by proving the news could not wait.

"And would that be because you were the confounding variable?" Lucifer asks Phoenix.

There was a time when I actually liked Phoenix. I resented the Council for sticking me in the Subject System. I still do, especially because I still don't know what I did in my first life to deserve this. At the very least, I think I should know why it is I'm being punished. I digress.

I used to think Phoenix was my ally. In hindsight, the reason for that was he wanted me to see him as an ally.

Phoenix is infamous for interfering with other people's plans. He appeared in many of my lives, trying to invalidate Max's experimental results. In this attempt, through his many appearances, he became a kind of anchor whenever my memories were all returned to me, something that was constant throughout the majority of my lives. But then, he stopped showing up.

Normally, he'd make some surprise appearance for at most a day in each life but, during Life Twenty, he stuck around for *three years*.

Max was testing what effect extreme isolation would have on me, so my years were meant to consist of no friends and absent parents. But, Phoenix showed up as my classmate later on and became my close friend. That was, until he suddenly didn't show up anymore, and I wasn't only lonely but also deserted.

Thing about never having something to begin with is you have no way of knowing truly what you're missing. Well, Phoenix showed me exactly what it was I was missing, leaving me feeling empty and— Whatever. Moving on.

Point is, I later found out that, for once, Phoenix had actually been working with Max and the other Celestials to manipulate my life. It was all part of the plan. The desertion, that is. When he disappeared from my twentieth life, he disappeared completely, until now.

My dislike for Phoenix has grown in his absence. I have a talent for holding grudges, which is the kind of thing you learn about yourself after twenty-six lives.

"No comment," Phoenix answers, if you can call that an answer.

"I assume it's one of the first nineteen lives you showed up in without Max's blessing. It's good to see you after... how long has it been now?"

Those words just came out of my mouth.

My plan was to keep my mouth shut. And worse, I'm looking at him and posed a question. I can't look away now. A question sets up the expectation for an answer, a continuation of conversation, which is not something I would have intentionally caused if only I had been thinking a moment ago.

I hold onto my anger and force myself to hold his gaze. His eyes look colder than I remember, pools of frozen green water. Maybe even his physical appearance was a part of the lie.

"About a century," Phoenix answers, voice low and tone uncharacteristically serious. He quickly turns back to the Council, and I can breath again.

Minerva looks uncomfortable on her throne, something I've never seen before. It's a big change from her usually perfectly postured form and—

Never mind. There it is again - legs crossed, back straight, shoulders down and back, and head held high. She once again somehow looks perfectly comfortable in a position I would think should look stiff.

"I am slightly offended everyone thinks I'm the reason this redo is needed," Phoenix says, carefree tone back.

"Phoenix," Minerva says, all scolding older sister-like.

Technically, I don't think any of the Celestials are related, even though they claim to be part of one generation that descended from the same few beings. But, they weren't exactly produced in the same way that humans are. My Havcire history is a bit rusty, though, with bad foundations and what little I know buried under lifetimes of memories.

"Minerva," Phoenix replies frivolously.

An exasperated grunt escapes Barnabas.

From how they act alone, I would question why the Council puts up with Phoenix, even if he is the only one who can easily travel between Havcire and Vest. However, they not only use

Phoenix, they also entrust him as their messenger, which seems much like relying on a game of Telephone to relay information.

Phoenix nods his head toward Minerva and the griffon obeys, flying back over to perch on her throne.

"What life? Just spit it out," I tell him.

"Spit what out?" Barnabas asks, as Lucifer asks, "Did we miss something?"

I forget most in Havcire aren't familiar with Vestigium figures of speech.

Phoenix looks at me slightly shocked. Sure, I'm not in a rush to be sent back to Vest for yet another life, but my curiosity beats both my hesitancy to be sent back and my hesitancy to interact with Phoenix.

I've never needed to redo a life before.

"Don't look so surprised," I tell Phoenix. "Most of the time my life is controlled by an experiment. I like to make good use of the time that's not, and you are wasting it right now. You'd probably know this about me if you were around more."

"I've been around," Phoenix says.

"So just avoiding me then."

I hear Minerva doing her best to explain what it means to figuratively spit something out to Barnabas and Lucifer.

Phoenix looks like he has something to say, but I don't need to hear it. I look away.

"All right," Phoenix says, finally speaking up, and silencing Minerva's explanation, "if you insist on knowing what I was specifically sent here to tell you, then the life she will be repeating is her twentieth life."

"Hell no," comes out before I can stop myself.

"Hell is a myth. One would think you'd know that by now," Lucifer says, helpfully chiming in.

"I won't redo that life. Everything went according to Max's plan," I continue, ignoring Lucifer, "even if I didn't realize it at first," I add under my breath.

"Apparently that's not true if Max feels the need to spend time redoing it instead of going onto another life. Regardless, you know you don't have a choice in the matter so this is a moot point," Barnabas says, closing the issue.

"Now that everyone is informed, shall we adjourn this meeting and send Dawn to be processed?" Minerva asks. The other two Council members give nods of acquiescence.

"I—"... would like to know the reason I'm redoing Life Twenty. I would like to know what is going to be different in this new redo version. I would like to have a minute more to exist knowing who I am before my memories are erased again.

"Phoenix, would you take her to the processing room?" Minerva asks, interrupting me.

"Yes, my pleasure," Phoenix tells Minerva. He motions for me to follow him out the door.

Well, damn them.

CHAPTER 3

The tiles in the hall have returned to their true states as portals to areas of Havcire, and I imagine being able to escape from yet another life as a lab rat.

I would jump through one of the tiles and emerge on the other side as a free Citizen. I could live in an Incanter town, studying magic. Although I could never actually learn to wield such power, they would accept me as they do other Citizens. Some Citizens even acquire some minor psychic abilities after a time.

Or, there's always the Graveyard, where no one would think to look for me and for good reason.

But, only Celestials can control the portals by touch. For me, this is a hallway with boarded up windows through which I can only glimpse lives I could have but will never obtain.

My actual future involves reliving a life I have already lived where I made a complete fool of myself. To give myself more credit, more accurately, Phoenix made a complete fool of me. I didn't do it to myself because I couldn't have known any better. Now, I'm going to have to go through that again. Except, this time, it will be even worse because I will have fallen for his whole friendship act for a second time and won't even know there was a first time. Fool me once, shame on you; fool me twice, shame on me.

That saying shouldn't apply when memory wiping is a factor in play.

"I do know the way," I mumble.

Phoenix leads me down another hallway to our right, this one purely and truly made of marble, but the processing room is down the opposite one. I look at Phoenix ahead of me and back behind me towards the correct path. I open my mouth to question Phoenix's navigating skills.

He grabs my arm and pulls me through a doorway I hadn't even seen.

I trip from the abrupt change in direction and fall into him, his arms instinctively wrapping around me to hold me up, as the door to the room closes behind us.

I quickly push him away once I regain my balance, ignoring the warmth spreading through me from the brief source of contact. Or, trying to.

It takes a moment for my vision to adjust to the darkness of the room but, once I can see, I realize it's more a broom closet than a room. However, instead of brooms, there are weapons and armor.

Unlike the rest of the building, it smells like wood and dust in here. It seems to stretch on forever, like a never-ending hallway, complete with copper lanterns hanging down from the ceiling, providing dim lighting. This isn't the main armory because I have passed by that room before and seen how large it is. The weapons here look more archaic than functional, like a display for a museum exhibit.

"What are we doing here?" I ask.

I bump into something shaped like a pole but made of what feels like a heavy metal. Pivoting, I catch it before it can slide further down the wall and clang against the floor.

Oh wow. I'm holding what looks to be a trident. Carefully, I place it back in its precarious position, leaning partially against the wall and partially against a chair.

Sitting on the chair is a large shield, which glints bronze in the yellow lamplight. Beside the shield, something flashes like a spark of electricity but it disappears within the second. I'm tempted to stare at the chair until the spark makes another appearance, but I turn back to Phoenix.

Further back in the room is a table that looks as though it could break from one more speck of dust. There are two items placed on it. In the center is a scale that seems to be made at least partly of gold, the rest onyx. To the right of the scale lies an amulet. Its golden chain rests on the table, while the amulet hangs over the edge of the table. Though the amulet must be heavier than the chain, it remains hanging in the air, defying gravity. As the light from the nearest lamp glints off the eye depicted on the amulet, an unnatural blue hue reflects off it.

Again, there's a flash behind my right shoulder, and I turn quickly enough to make out the bolt of lightning before it disappears again.

Zeus's Thunderbolt. Except, I think it actually belongs to Barnabas. Ancient Greeks once took the stories of Barnabas and reinterpreted them to represent their god, Zeus.

My mind makes sense of the other objects in the room, identifiable from Vest mythology.

It all clicks into place - Poseidon's trident, Minerva's Aegis, Anubis's scale, the Eye of Horus amulet, Excalibur, the Staff of Moses, and many other weapons and objects I don't have the knowledge to identify. Not to mention, all those I cannot see that extend on throughout this endless room. As Phoenix shifts in front of me, I gasp, noticing an item I'd missed on the floor behind him.

"Is that... Thor's hammer?" I ask, practically stammering.

"Mjollnir," Phoenix says, "though it's technically Barnabas's. Thor is his Norse interpretation."

Zeus *and* Thor? Barnabas does not live up to the hype.

"To be honest, Barnabas is a bit of a letdown," I say, to which Phoenix shakes his head.

"And you're making this judgment based on what? A fictional superhero? We're not movie characters, Dawn."

"Okay, *Loki*," I say, knowing Loki is one of the Vest interpretations of Phoenix. Unfortunately, Phoenix, judging by his current expression, actually seems pleased by this comparison. Of course he'd enjoy being likened to a god of mischief. Moving on. "How many weapons does Barnabas need, anyways? This is kind of an odd place for the Council to store all of this, isn't it?"

"Dawn," Phoenix says, shutting me up. "We don't have much time because if you don't show up to processing soon, the Council will be informed and they'll start questioning where you went..."

I open my mouth to ask again where this is exactly and why we are here, but he holds up a finger to silence me before any words can leave my mouth. I glare at the finger but remain quiet.

"...so I need you to just listen," Phoenix continues, emphasizing this by raising an eyebrow skeptically to question whether I truly understand and probably whether I even know how to just be quiet. I nod my head slowly to prove that I comprehend the concept.

"You're going to have a lot of questions, and none of them are going to be answered until later when I can answer them for you. Until then, however, I'm going to need you to act like everything is normal for everyone's sake. What's going to happen is that you will be sent back to relive Life Twenty but this time you are going to remember everything, as in all your other lives, the existence of Havcire, and who you are in general."

"And I'll remember how the last time I lived this life you betrayed me by working with Max?" I ask.

"Yes, you'll remember that."

"Great."

"What happened to keeping quiet?"

I mime zipping my lips closed, but I slip the imaginary key into my pants' pocket for storage.

"No one else will know that you've kept your memory," Phoenix continues. "Let's just say I've messed with the system a bit. Don't waste your time questioning my motives. I convinced Max this life needed to be redone because it's the only one where I have an excuse to be in Vest for a long period of time, but that doesn't happen till later on so you'll have to wait till then for any more information."

He stops talking abruptly and turns to open the door, while my head spins. I agreed not to ask any questions but, as if in rebellion, they keep popping up in my head at an alarming rate.

"Wait up," I say, grabbing onto his arm to stall his escape. "I'm just supposed to go along with this?"

"I figured you'd be satisfied with what I promised, a chance to be aware of your situation this time around. If anything, at least when I show up this time, you'll remember you hate me. Is that not enough?"

I know we're out of time. I release his arm.

Phoenix reaches toward me, and I resist the urge to take a defensive step backwards. He takes the imaginary key from my pocket. Though he doesn't actually touch me, I swear I can feel exactly where his hand goes. Next I'll be feeling the metal of the imaginary key.

Phoenix backs up and tosses the key in the air toward me. I can't help myself from snatching it out of the air. Thankfully, I can report that I don't feel the ghost key.

"It's enough," I tell him, "for now."

CHAPTER 4

Through the large, glass doors of the processing room, I see Max pacing, waiting for my arrival.

In Havcire, Vests can choose to look however they would like. You can't transform into a completely different person, but you can look like any form of yourself, as in the seventy-year-old you or the seven-year-old you.

Max looks about sixty, with mostly gray hair and a face that has aged fairly well. I'm certain he enjoys the sense of authority that comes with looking older than the average age people choose to appear in Havcire.

Unlike Max and the rest of the Experimenters and Citizens, Subjects don't choose our age in Havcire, as we aren't here long enough for it to matter. Rather, we appear as whatever age we average out at, based on the ages we lived to in Vest during our various lives. I, for instance, usually average out to somewhere in my late teens, early twenties.

Max stops pacing when he hears the doors close and turns to face us, relieved. Max doesn't love the whole processing process, as he prefers to just sit back and record his observations of the experiment rather than actually deal with his Subjects in person. Any time spent with me here is time spent away from recording data about his other Subjects currently in Vest.

"Well, shall we get this show on the road?" Max says, while motioning for me to follow him as he walks to the tub.

The tub is the machine that erases my memory and transports me back to Vest. It uses science and magic, and I'm still not sure where the science ends and the magic begins when it comes to how the tub functions.

It is a large rectangular, glass box filled with water. Hence the name. Extending from it are cords, some attached to computers and some connected to IV bags.

The Experimenter labs look extremely out of place compared to the rest of the rooms and halls in the Ziggurat. The labs are the only rooms that are modern and filled with up to date technology. Technology is hard to come by in the rest of Havcire, as magic makes its use mostly obsolete.

"Dawn," Max says, drawing my attention away from the tub and to the suit he's holding out in front of me. I take it from him and go behind the panel screen to change in private.

I part with my destroyed sweater, neatly hanging it on top of the screen. No doubt, these clothes will be trashed, but I can't help treating them with some care. When I reach to pull my leggings down, I see the leaf tattooed on the inside of my wrist.

I'd actually forgotten I even got the tattoo. It's a struggle in the short time I'm in Havcire to remember all the details of my past lives, many of them becoming somewhat lost, submerged in my subconscious beneath other memories.

I don't think the mind is designed to store multiple lifetimes of memories.

I'd gotten the tattoo only a few days before my death. It was meant to mark my decision to study environmental law. Now, I realize that decision must have been significant enough to set up the rest of my life, allowing Max to finalize his conclusions and kill me off. Again, without allowing me to actually live out that life.

Apparently one decision is enough to decide the whole rest of one's life. Or, at least that's what Max thinks. Sometimes I wonder if he's really interested in finding answers or if he's simply determined to have a completed experiment, no matter the validity of the results.

It's something I wonder generally about the Experimenters. How many of them decide to be Experimenters because they truly are invested in the work and motivated to help others, and how many merely want to taste success for their own benefit?

Although, I'm one to talk. All my lives are about trying to make up for my first mess of a life, whatever it was that I did. I'm all for success. If only I could successfully complete my sentence and finally become a Citizen.

"Any breakthroughs in your research recently?" I ask Max.

"Actually, I have found significant data to disprove my hypothesis."

I don't need to see his face to sense his excitement over having the opportunity to discuss his experiment. I can hear it in his voice, his reluctance to deal with other people dissipating.

I know Max studies nature versus nurture. He wants to test whether one or the other has more of an effect on one's behavior in life, but there's much I don't know about his experiment. I'm merely a Subject, and he doesn't have to report to *me* about his findings. Although, that doesn't mean he won't if I ask.

"What *was* you initial hypothesis?"

"That one's environment has a larger impact on their behavior than their DNA," he answers.

So, he favored nurture over nature. But, if he's close to disproving his hypothesis then—

"It appears as though," Max continues, the flood gates opened, "nature's and nurture's impact may vary greatly based on the individual. For example, with you, the environment we put you in doesn't appear to change how you act. With other Subjects of mine, though, there is more variability."

I place my folded leggings up on the screen as I listen but Max pauses in his explanation.

"We're just going to trash those clothes," he says.

I glare through the screen, guessing at Max's location on the other side of it. I take off my socks and deliberately fold them neatly before placing them on top of the leggings.

"So does that mean you're nearing your conclusions?" I ask Max, bringing him back to the topic, as I pull on the suit.

"It means it may be time to move on to another hypothesis, a new experiment."

My hand falters as I try to zip up the large zipper on the front of the suit.

"And new Subjects," I add, not loudly enough for anyone else to hear.

I might be trash like these clothes sooner than I thought.

I tell my hand to chill and focus on zipping. It's not over yet, and this life won't be like the others. No matter Phoenix's motivations, he's given me a chance to take control of the Subject System. I know how the Subject System works, and I can use that to work on my sentence. Every little bad behavior increases a sentence, while every single good act decreases it. I can use that. I can be very, very good.

I yank the zipper the rest of the way up. The suit was designed specially not to travel between the two worlds. Consequently, when a Subject is born again in Vest, he or she is born like a normal baby, not in some very over-sized piece of clothing that would definitely create complications in the birth. The suit looks just like a wet suit, but the material is specially designed for this purpose.

I take a deep breath and step back out from behind the screen to find Max sitting at the computer that controls the tub.

Phoenix glances briefly in my direction but quickly finds something of more interest on Max's crowded desk. I don't miss Max's poorly veiled annoyance directed at Phoenix for touching his equipment and notes.

"Phoenix, you can leave if you would like. I have it handled from here," Max says.

"Actually, I'm curious and would like to see the tub in action. Plus, Minerva told me herself to ensure everything goes smoothly so I'm going to stay."

Max looks like he's searching for any good reason for why Phoenix should leave but gives up because he can't say anything that would conflict with a Council member's direct orders. Whether those orders are fact or fiction, I don't know, but I wouldn't make any bets on their truth.

"No worries, Max," I say, trying for a kind smile. "We'll both leave you to be with your preferred company soon enough."

I gesture to the surrounding computers. Max looks unamused, so I busy myself with getting in the tub.

"Your life data always indicates high levels of amiability," Max says, as if puzzling through a scientific problem. "Personally, I've never observed that in you."

Ouch. I don't believe he meant for that to be an insult, but it oddly stings. Phoenix leaves Max's desk to come lean against the tub. Max practically jumps with anxiety over Phoenix's proximity to the tub, but he turns away to set up the computers for the process.

I feel sweat drip down my back, despite the cool material of the suit. I tell myself that this isn't like all the other times. But, what if Phoenix doesn't follow through on his end? What if he is lying about it all?

While I wait for Max to tell me he's ready, I eye a certain IV bag warily. It's filled with a bright, blue liquid. I know it's the bag that contains what erases my memory. It's still full, still ready to erase all that I know once the process begins.

"How do you plan on helping me keep my memories if that erases them?" I whisper to Phoenix, indicating the bag.

An empty bottle appears in Phoenix's hand, the PowerAde symbol clear on its label for a moment before the whole bottle disappears from sight.

"That's not the memory potion anymore," Phoenix whispers back.

"Ready to go," Max says, and that's my cue.

I lower the rest of my body under the water, taking a deep breath in as I submerge my head. The water begins to ripple from the slight vibrations the tub emits whenever the process begins. The contents of the IV bags begin to flow and enter into the tub. I close my eyes.

CHAPTER 5

Fifteen years later

My alarm seeps into my consciousness, but I don't rush to turn it off. The song I set to play is the theme song of the show I'm currently watching, and it lets me imagine for a few seconds that I'm the heroine in a sci-fi adventure.

These past years have been nothing but a montage of extreme normalcy, so the fantasizing is a necessity. One might think I'd welcome normal.

One would be wrong.

Of course, there's still the fact that I have been conscious of my 460 years of memory since about the age of one, when I found I could begin to process my past lives and memories.

It was somewhat unusual pretending not to know how to talk during the terrible twos and having to find normal two-year-old methods to communicate.

Since, however, life truly has been normal—ish. The whole point of this experimental life is to see how I turn out when completely socially isolated.

When I started school, I realized I was practically invisible to my peers. I think if I hadn't known Max was manipulating my life, I would never have realized to what an extreme my invisibility extends. Knowing what I know, however, I do realize that I could scream in someone's face at school and they would show no indication of seeing or hearing me. This, I say from experience.

Even when I make physical contact, Max has a system that immediately and automatically covers it up, erasing it from the mind. It's like a highly efficient, magical clean-up crew.

It hasn't been too bad having no one around my age notice me, though. It's given me the chance to focus solely on the Subject System. I've done my best to decrease my sentence by behaving well. It's the best plan I have. The only plan I have.

It wasn't only friends. Max also ensured my parents' careers took off soon after I was born, so they weren't around much either.

But, it's fine! I've adapted to a life of minimal social interaction. That adaptation may involve a lot of talking to myself.

I helped a bird once. Its wing was broken, so I kept it till I could release it safely. And, when I was old enough, I started volunteering daily at a dog shelter. Turns out Max can't make animals ignore me, too. Plus, it helps with my Subject System points.

You know when you pass by a dog and their owner and you say hi to the dog but forget to acknowledge the owner? Well, in this life, I have an actual valid reason for doing that. There's a bright side, right?

Life's been good. Really. Truly.

On the surface, my life seems natural and not orchestrated by an Experimenter. After all, growing up with absent parents isn't in itself considered too abnormal, nor is being a loner.

More importantly, if I had been able to keep my name, I would now be Dawn Dawson. Missed opportunity there. Instead, I am Haley Dawson in this life, not that I hear my name used too often because of that whole I have no friends thing.

I reach over and turn off my alarm. My phone reads 5:30 in the morning, an hour earlier than I normally get up.

Every day is the same. I wake up and rush to school, missing Harry and Gene Dawson, who are already at work. I barely listen in all my classes, instead doodling or writing stories in a notebook. It's not like I haven't been to high school before. East Olympic High is no special place. I come home, do homework for an hour, and then I'm off to the dog shelter where I volunteer. I pick up dinner for myself and eat at home, watching television and waiting for Gene and Harry to come home. But, most of the time, it gets too late, and I give up and go to bed.

Last night, however, I was restless and promised myself that I would wake up early and go for a run, a real radical change to my schedule. It seemed like a better idea last night than it does now, but I must hold myself to my word.

I head out the door and run into Harry and Gene leaving for work.

"Wow," Harry says, as I narrowly avoid walking into him and Gene. "She's alive."

They stand outside on the porch, as I pause in the doorway.

"That I am," I say, smiling.

Gene gives me a quick hug. Her light brown hair, coincidentally almost the identical shade of my own, flows down her back, still warm from being blow dried. Against the chill of the morning, it's oddly a comfort, and I find myself wishing for a moment that it all could be real, without the manipulations of an experiment.

Pulling back, Gene looks down at my sneakers.

"Going for a run?" she asks.

"I'm surprised, too," I say.

"Gene!" Harry yells from their car. "Have a good day, Haley," he says, throwing me a kiss.

Gene smiles and waves goodbye before heading after him. I watch their car pull out of the driveway, feeling hollow. No, none of that. Instead, I shall think of how I got these few minutes of interaction past Max and consider it a small victory.

"Take that, Max," I say, looking up towards the sky, as if I could spot Havcire through the clouds. "I win this time. I'm a winner. Winner," I say, taking my good ol' time saying the word like a really bad sport and... "I'm talking to myself."

Grimacing at my own lack of sanity, I duck my head and put my earphones in. Music pulses into my ears, and I begin my run.

Ten minutes into the run, well more of a jog, I realize that I should really do this more often. I am entirely out of shape.

Physical ability does not transfer so easily from one life to the next. While I started off feeling light on my feet, now I feel like the ground is pushing back at me with every step, my feet slamming into the sidewalk. I try fixing my posture so I don't just collapse, but that takes way too much effort. I take deep breaths in through my nose and exhale out of my mouth, trying to focus on my breathing to push myself on, but my throat starts to burn from the cold air.

As I sprint for the final minute, the bushes around me form pretty green clouds, which make me feel like I'm spinning, my eyes unable to focus. When the minute runs out, I stop to catch my breath.

Leaning over, I rest my hands on my knees and try to return my heart to a normal rhythm. As I recover, the sun begins to come out to the East, and I lean over to stretch my legs.

Upside down, I can see the house behind me. I almost lose my balance, reaching my hand down to the ground to steady myself, when I see a hand sticking out from the dirt on the lawn.

My breath hitches, but I quickly realize it's fake and accompanied by a styrofoam R.I.P. gravestone and other Halloween decorations.

Relaxing, I laugh at my own irrational hysterics and quickly finish stretching before turning to jog the rest of the way back to the house. A nagging feeling sticks with me as I jog back, though, as if I walked into a room and instantaneously forgot what I was doing there. I really need to get into the habit of running more often.

My failed run affords me some extra time, so I blow dry my curly hair that I usually just pull into a bun every morning. Showered and feeling refreshed, I decide against wearing one of the two pairs of leggings I rotate between on a daily basis and put on some nicer jeans, as in my favorite pair with the rips. Real nice. Over my gray t-shirt, with the depiction of a plane on it, I throw on a green jacket.

Fun fact: In all my lives, I've actually never been a passenger on an airliner. I have piloted a plane before, though.

The green jacket is new. I got it because I liked how it looked against my hair, bringing out the natural, gold highlights. But, looking in the mirror now, I realize maybe it makes me stand out too much. Except, that's ridiculous. I can't stand out. Max has made me invisible to everyone anyways.

I stare myself down in the mirror, resisting the urge to grab my black jacket, my go to jacket. Nothing can hide the bright amber of my eyes. I tried colored contacts once. Didn't work. Pulling the jacket tight around my shoulders, I leave my room.

A slight breeze rustles my hair, blowing a stray piece directly into my face, when I open the front door. I grab the hair tie off my wrist and quickly pull it out of my face and back into a ponytail with the rest of my hair before leaving the house.

I've never been too good with letting my hair down, despite many attempts to style it differently, and I mean that literally. It just gets in the way.

Climbing in, I pat Peter on the steering wheel and pull out of the driveway. Peter is my car. He was Gene's old car but he didn't have an identity till I got him. Peter's a black Jeep Wrangler named after Peter Parker, my favorite superhero consistently across my lifetimes.

Maybe Max has a point. I really don't change much even across different lives. Is that bad, though? Objectively, I guess that would depend on whether changing would make me a better person. Considering I'm a Subject and not a Citizen, maybe a little change would do me good? Or, maybe the system is just unfair and I should already be a Citizen... Yeah, that seems right. After all, I like me.

Anyways, yes, I am only fifteen technically and only have my permit. But, when I proved to be an oddly experienced driver after my supposed first driving lesson with Harry, Gene and Harry agreed to let me drive to school and the dog shelter on my own. I'm not supposed to drive anywhere else on my own, but it's not like I go anywhere else.

I pull into one of the extremely small spots in the East Olympic High parking lot, where no one can ever manage to actually park in between the lines so there's no choice but to just park in the area left between the two cars adjacent to you, which is most likely right in the middle of a line.

Parting with Peter, I grab my bag and take out my earphones.

I've learned to make the best of my supernatural invisibility. Selecting Elton John's "I'm Still Standing," and turning up the volume on my phone, I enter through the doors of the lovely hellhole. I swing them both wide open for a dramatic entrance that my fellow students wish they could see.

The familiar scent of mold reaches me, and I breathe it in like fresh daisies. The sounds of high school students chattering fills my ears before the dancing beat takes over.

CHAPTER 6

By the time the doors have shut closed behind me, I'm gliding on my feet through the hallway, bouncing my shoulders up and down to the beat. In the second before Elton's voice begins singing the lyrics, I drum excitedly against the locker doors lining the hall.

Shooting out my arm, I point to some football player, whose name I believe to be Ryan. He just so happens to be looking in my direction even though I know he's not looking at me. Consequently, he gets the honor of my lip syncing being directed towards him with the first line, "You could never know what it's like..." to die repeatedly and stay so nice, I add along in my head, shooting an enthusiastic smile to the other surrounding, oblivious teens.

I proceed through the halls dancing. Some girl holds up her arms in question, and I slap her hand in a high five, the clap going along nicely with the song.

Undoing my hair from its ponytail, I flip it like a rockstar in Vanessa's face, a particularly rude girl. She swats the air, as if a bug had buzzed by, but otherwise seems unbothered.

I grab a pen out of another girl's hand. It makes for a great faux microphone with the puffy pink ball at its end. The pen girl looks at her empty hand in confusion for a moment before returning to her conversation, pen forgotten.

Still, I return it to her, taking her hand and placing the pen back in her palm.

"Thank you," I tell her quickly between lyrics.

As the chorus approaches, a group of students head towards a classroom, and I rush to get the door for them, shooting finger guns at a random girl along the way.

Little good deeds help to decrease my sentence. However, the girls I hold the door for pause right in the doorway when someone else calls to them from the hallway. I guess I'm hanging out here for a bit.

The boy hurries up to talk to them. I wonder if the amount of points I get increases the longer I hold the door. I also wonder how exactly they think the door is staying open for them right now.

I continue to lip sync to the girls standing in the doorway. The boy holds a flyer out for the girls to see.

I stop mid-chorus, the silent words dying in my throat, as I catch a glimpse of the flyer.

"May I borrow this for a second? Thanks," I say, absentmindedly, even though I know they'll take no notice of me anyways. I grab the flyer out of his hand.

The flyer is for a Halloween party, as I had thought. The decorations earlier. Halloween... It says the party is on October 31st, as Halloween falls conveniently on a Friday this year. Today is Wednesday, making it the 29th. Today is October 29th! How could I not have realized what day it was?

This is the thing I came in the room to get, but forgot the second I entered the room to get it. The nagging thing. And damn, it's so much worse than just having forgotten to retrieve a pen or something.

I turn off my music and place the flyer back into the boy's hand, which is still in the exact same place it was when I took the flyer from him.

Hurrying over to my locker, I leave the door to close on them. I feel a bit guilty but brush it aside, the point system not being my top priority right now. Plus, they shouldn't be having a conversation right in the middle of a doorway anyways. People need to get in and out of that room. It's a fire code violation. I'm practically saving lives by not allowing them to stand in that doorway for any longer.

I make it to my locker and slam it open, blindly shoving books into my bag, probably filling it with all the wrong ones. In Life Twenty, it was a few days before Halloween that Phoenix appeared in my life. It was October 29th to be exact.

So far, everything that could be the same in this life has been the same as Life Twenty. I tell myself it's fine and take a deep breath.

If he shows up, that's good because it was part of his plan, and he can finally answer my questions like he said he would. But, then why do I feel like I'm about to be pushed onto a stage to perform a one-woman show for which I didn't learn any of the lines?

I look down at my bag and see that I have in fact stuffed it with the wrong books. I take them out and put the correct ones in for my morning classes.

"Oh god!" I yelp when I close my locker and find someone standing right behind where the door had been.

"So the masses claim, but my friends just call me Phoenix. Happy Halloween," Phoenix says, as he holds the flyer up to my face.

I yank the paper from his hand, crumple it up into a little ball, and throw it back at his face. It bounces harmlessly off his forehead and lands on the floor between us.

"It's not Halloween yet," I respond.

"Rude," Phoenix says, looking down at the crumpled up paper on the floor as if the paper itself has offended him.

I'd forgotten how well he pulled off the just another teen in high school look. He wears a blue *Queen* t-shirt with black jeans and converse. His dark hair is more ruffled than usual, probably to help distract from the angelic-like perfection of his face, but it's not working too well. On the bright side, no one would look at a Celestial and immediately come to the conclusion that they were ancient, magical beings.

Instead, my fellow classmates would be much more likely to look at Phoenix and simply think, "He must be the latest foreign exchange student, who may or may not professionally model."

The odd accent Celestials have would help support that theory. Of course, it doesn't fit any nationality specifically but I don't think anyone but a linguist would be able to recognize that identification issue. To me, it sounds somewhat like a British accent, but there are also times I hear hints of a more Slavic or even Irish accent. Clearly, I fall into the non-linguist group.

Although, Phoenix does seem to be pulling off a fairly accurate American accent at the moment, with only small hints of something other.

"You're the one who had to do the cliche move of popping out from behind the locker. You couldn't have just walked up and said hi?" I say, as his attention turns back to me and away from the assaulting crumpled paper.

"It's Halloween..." Phoenix begins to say but then sees my face. "Okay, it's almost Halloween. I thought I'd get you in the spirit by jumping out. At least I didn't say boo."

I roll my eyes at him. Pulling my bag onto my shoulder, I start walking towards my first class. Phoenix follows.

"Don't you have questions for me?" he asks, catching up.

"Oh, of course," I tell him. "I have many. I'm just working on mentally organizing them first."

What are you doing here? Why did you return my memories? Why did you work with Max? Why do you now seem to be working against the Council and Max? Why are you even involved with my life?

Yeah, it's gonna take some time for me to even figure out what to ask first. Why couldn't he just show up and explain, since he's the one with all the answers? Oh look! There's another one.

When a whole second passes without me making any attempt to continue conversing with him, he speaks up again.

"My name is Phoenix, and I just moved here. I don't know anyone and was hoping you could help me find my way around. I have English with Mr. Green first. Do you know where that is?" he says. After seeing I'm not going to play along, he continues.

"Phoenix? Like that mythological bird?" he says, in what I assume is supposed to be an impression of my own voice but is way too theatrically high to be accurate. "The majority of my family took on the names of gods, bit of a god complex issue," he answers, in his own voice. "But," he continues, "is it really a god complex if there are those who truly believe you are a god? What do you think?"

"Definitely," I say, giving into the conversation.

I look to the girl walking closest to us in the hallway, definitely close enough to overhear our conversation; well, more accurately, Phoenix's conversation with himself.

"You should really stop," I say. "People can hear you."

Intrigued, Phoenix raises an eyebrow. The expression is concerning. It also makes the scar that runs through his eyebrow stand out, a feature of his that only makes him look more like the trouble he is.

"Do you think so?" Phoenix asks, sounding genuinely curious. "Because, personally, I was wondering if my noticeability would win out over your invisibility."

"Why don't we not test that?"

"Please, even if someone were listening, they wouldn't take me seriously. People don't want to believe something that makes their perception of what's possible seem impossible. Watch."

Before I can stop him, Phoenix turns to the girl walking next to us.

"Hi. I'm Hermes, the Greek God of travelers, thieves, and so much more," Phoenix says, topping it off with a wink.

The girl laughs, clearly charmed, if not by his words then by his looks.

"Hi, I'm Aphrodite," she responds with a flirtatious smile.

"Of course you are, love," Phoenix says, returning her smile, before turning his back on her and walking away, leaving her with a slightly offended, slightly irritated expression to which I try to offer an apologetic look before remembering there's no chance she'll see it. I give up, walking after Phoenix.

"Really?" I ask Phoenix, as I catch back up to him, shooting him a glare.

Phoenix shrugs.

"Merely proving a point, successfully by the way."

"Well, my invisibility stayed intact in case you were wondering, so you better hope it spreads to you at this distance or else people might think it strange you're talking to an imaginary being."

Phoenix flashes that type of charming smile that tells me the next words out of his mouth are going to be something he's oddly very proud of.

"I don't need your help seeming strange." And there it is. "So, English?"

I open the door to the classroom we just stopped outside of and gesture inside.

"After you, oh mighty Greek god," I say.

Phoenix grabs the edge of the door above my head and motions for me to go first. I roll my eyes but enter the room.

I go to sit in my normal seat in the back, right corner of the room so I can easily not pay attention during class and not get in trouble for it. The problem is, however, today there is someone sitting in my spot.

The culprit has a face with very sharp features. His onyx hair is slicked back with what looks to be a whole bottle of hair gel, and his pale skin lacks any blemishes unlike the rest of the student body, including myself, who has the pleasure of dealing with the whole body of a teenager thing again. In addition, the guy is wearing a suit.

So, in conclusion, he doesn't exactly fit in here. Unless, the drama club is doing a dress rehearsal today for a play that stars the love child of Dracula and James Bond. As there is no drama club here at East Olympic, it makes this scenario highly unlikely.

I reluctantly accept that my seat has been stolen and sit down in the one in front of the new guy. Phoenix settles himself down in the seat next to the new guy.

Not long after I sit down, I feel a tap on my shoulder. When I turn around, a pale hand is extended straight out to me, expecting a handshake. I reach out hesitantly. If I didn't know better, I'd say the kid was actually a vampire. But, I do, and I know that vampire lore stems from a sect of Incanters.

More strangely, however, than this boy potentially being a creature that does not exist, is the fact that he is looking directly at me, shaking my hand in a formal greeting. He *sees* me.

CHAPTER 7

Part of me acknowledges the fact that my wrist looks boneless, flopping in this stranger's grip. Am I in shock? Or, am I not surprised by the fact that something else unusual is happening? Seems to be expected whenever Phoenix is around that shit will get wonky.

"Hello, I am Poindexter Harrington," he's saying. "I just transferred from Crestpines, a private school not far from here. You may have heard of it. Anyway, it's a pleasure to meet you, Dawn..." Poindexter hesitates when Phoenix clears his throat loudly but then continues, "...son. Dawson, Haley Dawson."

Apparently, I'm Bond, James Bond in this scenario. I take my hand out of his grasp, rediscovering my bones, and offer up a smile.

So he knows my name. He covered it up well enough for anyone who might have overheard, but I can recognize my own name. That clears that up. He must have come with Phoenix, which means he must be from Havcire. Plus, if the fact that he knows who I really am isn't enough evidence that he's not from around here, then the fact that he can notice me at all is evidence enough.

The bell rings.

"It's nice to meet you, too. We'll have to talk more later," I say, directing that last part at both Poindexter and Phoenix.

On my desk, what I hadn't noticed before, is our new book for the class. The cover portrays a golden depiction of a muscular man with a seriously set face, holding in his hand a bolt of lightning. Three guesses as to the topic.

Our new reading assignment is a collection of Greek myths. What is this craze over Greek mythology? There are loads of other myths.

"Haley," Phoenix says.

I don't look. He says my name again. And again.

"Shush!" is my mature response.

My "shush" accidentally comes out louder than the offending calls of my name, attracting the attention of my teacher, who, by the way, can actually notice me because he's not considered my peer... to some extent.

It's actually more complicated. Max has this whole thing set up that Mr. Green can call on me in class but not notice me outside of the bells that mark his class period. The same goes for all my other teachers. I guess that ensures that I can't form any true connection or mentorship with my teachers, as that would get in the way of me being a complete loner. Max really covers all his bases.

"You don't want to hear the quote of the day, Haley?" Mr. Green asks.

"Who's Haley?"

"Your classmate, Josh," Mr. Green answers, shaking his head. "Weren't you just the other day bragging about how you know every single person in this school? I still don't understand why that's something of significance but apparently you were wrong."

"I *do* know everyone." Josh sounds sincerely offended.

"What about Haley?"

"Haley who?"

"Dawson."

I watch this exchange, seated only a couple seats away from Josh. I wave at him as he looks right through me.

This conversation could loop around forever, with Josh repeatedly forgetting who I am every time my name comes back up. It would be comical and, don't get me wrong, I've let it run its course before. But, we don't need to do it today.

"Who?" Josh is asking again.

"Sorry, Mr. Green," I interrupt. "I do want to know the quote of the day."

"Thank you. We should get back on topic. Aristotle said, 'Knowing yourself is the beginning of all wisdom.'"

Well, I know twenty-seven different versions of myself. I wonder what Aristotle would think of me.

"I forgot your teachers could see you." And then, "Sorry."

That word out of Phoenix's mouth is enough to get me to turn around and face him. The jerk is smiling, like he knew exactly what would happen if he said it. Because, he did. I roll my eyes and go to turn away from him but—

"I put up an illusion. We look like diligent students."

"Get rid of it. I want to actually be a diligent student."

"Doesn't Barnabas look great here?" He points at the cover of the class book, wiggling his eyebrows in a way that makes me want to laugh, but I don't dare show that.

"What?" he asks, innocently. "I actually had nothing to do with this, but I am always up to learning more about part of my history."

"Says the person always claiming myth was written by those trying to forget history," I say. The marker squeaks on the white board at the front of the room.

"That's true, of course, but it doesn't make all of the stories fiction."

I turn back to the front of the class, shaking my head, to find Mr. Green... in the library with the candlestick. I can't help but always think of Clue. He finishes writing the topic of the class today up on the board.

"This is going to be the next book we read," Mr. Green begins. "Although it contains a lot of myths, it doesn't cover the whole history of the Greek gods. So, today, I will briefly go over some important background that will aid you in understanding the myths, and your homework assignment will be to read the first two chapters, as each chapter is a new story."

As Mr. Green continues with his lesson, a desk drags across the floor behind me. A few students peer back for a second but then turn their attention away, unbothered.

Phoenix isn't wrong in this case. I should really test out what type of proximity to myself is needed to be part of my Max-credited invisibility. It'd be an interesting little experiment.

Phoenix now sits practically over my shoulder, having dragged his desk into what should have been the row between desks. Fire hazard. Looking back slightly, I see Poindexter is the only one who is paying any attention to him, and he looks fairly amused.

"All accounts of the world before the beginning, before there were people and living things, report that there was darkness, a nothingness," Mr. Green lectures.

Isn't darkness technically something? Or, maybe not, as it is the absence of light. If light is something, then darkness could be considered nothing. Unless, nothing is something in its own right. That's a very positive outlook I think. If nothing can be something, then anyone can be anything. Maybe I was always meant to be a motivational speaker.

"According to Greek myth, there was Chaos," Mr. Green says. "Chaos is referred to as a void from which everything originated, including the Greek Gods. Over time, Chaos has been perceived differently, sometimes even being interpreted as a female being. Chaos was thought to reside in the place between Earth and Sky until the Gods' war with the Titans, during which the Titans were banished into Chaos."

"Should I tell him how much of that is true?" Phoenix whispers.

I tilt my head back a bit to look at him. "And what? Claim that you're an expert on the topic because you were there to heroically fight the Titans?"

"There were no Titans. And no, I could just say my father is a world-renowned mythologist."

"True, and putting on a facade would be nothing new for you," I whisper back with a sarcastic smile.

"What's with all this sass? I think you've become too much of a teenager again," Phoenix says.

"Gotta socialize into the culture to survive."

"Except, you don't because you're a loner anyways."

I shrug. "You're right. Oh well, I guess I've just always been this way, teenager or not." Or, it's a necessary defense mechanism against someone I don't want getting too close again. Either one's just as likely.

I turn away, my ponytail whipping behind me. I hear Phoenix exclaim when it hits him in the face. Oops, happy accidents.

"Because of the unknown nature of Chaos, little is actually known about her in mythology other than that Chaos was present before anything else," Mr. Green is saying, as I start to pay attention again. "Because of this, Chaos is not mentioned in your book, but you will be tested on her so I hope everyone is taking notes. Now, I'm going to bring up on the projector a family tree showing how all the gods are related in order for you to have a better understanding of who all the characters are when reading your books."

CHAPTER 8

"What are you doing?" I ask Poindexter.

He crouches on a bleacher, his head lowered to look in the gap to see underneath the bleachers. He lifts his head up to answer me.

"Checking under the bleachers," he says, before looking back under.

My stomach growls. It's lunchtime, and we had agreed to meet here so that Phoenix could finally inform me about what was going on and who the hell this kid dressed in a suit and crouched on the bleachers is. Of course, Phoenix is late and hasn't graced us with his presence yet.

"Yes, I can see that but *why* are you checking under the bleachers?"

Poindexter gets up. His clothes are a bit ruffled from bending down to examine the suspicious bleachers, the top few buttons of his white shirt having come undone. I can make out a red and gold figure depicted on the undershirt he wears. It's Iron Man. He's wearing an Avengers graphic tee, seemingly out of place with the rest of his look. It's not Spiderman, but a close second.

I smile, as he busies himself with straightening out his suit. He sits down on the bleachers a couple rows below from where I'm sitting and lastly refastens the top buttons of his shirt, covering up what's beneath.

"In movies, whenever someone has a conversation on bleachers, there's always someone else who overhears it from below the bleachers, and no one ever checks to make sure that they're not being eavesdropped on. So, I am checking," he explains.

I start to laugh but stop when he lifts an eyebrow in question. He's being completely serious.

"This isn't a movie, though. Nothing like that ever actually happens. Everyone is in the cafeteria or somewhere else on the main grounds eating lunch right now. Definitely no one cares what we're going to be talking about. At least, not in this world," I say, and Poindexter smiles, a challenge clear on his face.

"I wouldn't question my ways. Better safe than sorry. Plus, fiction can be more reliable than a variety of other sources."

He is talking to someone who has died many times and come back to life each time. Perhaps he's not wrong about fiction being closer to reality than we realize. Or, more accurately, fantasy.

"But," he continues, "then again, I've been homeschooled for most of my life so the majority of my social interaction knowledge comes from television and time spent with my parents and their friends."

I've never gotten to stay in Havcire for more than a day. Last time I checked, though, watching television wasn't a very common pastime.

"Are you a—?"

"Subject," Phoenix says, and I almost jump out of my skin for the second time today. How does one walk up metal bleachers silently?

Phoenix walks right on up past Poindexter and me to stand at the very top of the bleachers.

"You're late," I tell him.

"Am not."

A gold pocket watch appears in Phoenix's hand. The light shines off its surface as he swings it around by the chain, catching it in his palm. He glances at the face.

"Oh, guess I am," Phoenix amends.

He gives the watch one more swing, and it disappears.

"I am a Subject," Poindexter confirms, "or so Phoenix told me yesterday. Apparently we have the same Experimenter."

Phoenix volunteering information? He found another Subject and willingly told him a truth?

Phoenix thrives on keeping others in the dark as much as possible. It's like how he measures success. Success equals the amount of secrets one has control over. They're his currency; and yet, he shared information with Poindexter. There has to be a reason. I just have to get it out of him.

"No offense," I tell Poindexter, to which he shrugs indifferently, "but why is he here?" I ask Phoenix.

Now, I know that when, just a moment ago, I was thinking I've got to get the truth out of Phoenix, it seemed like my plan would be, well, a plan. Something that didn't involve just outright asking Phoenix for the truth, as it has been established that Phoenix does not offer up that kind of thing willingly. However, bear with me, I have to start somewhere, and that entails asking some outright questions. The key to getting the actual answers is listening for what Phoenix will not say.

Phoenix steps down and sits on the bleacher just above Poindexter.

"I came across Dex's information in Max's lab and saw that he was surprisingly close in location to you. I figured it wouldn't hurt to have some extra help," Phoenix answers.

Dex. They're on a nickname basis. That doesn't bode well for my likelihood of trusting "Dex."

"You may call me Dex, also, by the way," Dex says, as if reading my mind. "My friends do." Dex pauses, seeming to recall something. "Well, if I had friends, they would call me Dex."

"Wait. You brought *Dex* because he was conveniently close by?" I ask.

"I was on the way," Dex provides helpfully.

"When you can teleport, anyone's on the way. And, Dex, you just agreed to leave with this stranger?"

Dex smiles. Even though he looks as if he could still be among the undead, with his extremely pale skin, I notice some lightness in his dark eyes, bits of hazel in the iris. Though his smile is restrained, his eyes look like they're laughing. I don't get him, and normally I get people.

"My life was pretty dull. Sheltered and really, very dull," Dex answers. "Did you say teleport?" he asks, that curious excitement sneaking into his voice, though his face remains neutral. Again, odd. Why is he holding back?

"Yes, it's one of Phoenix's powers as a Celestial," I tell Dex. A card has appeared in Phoenix's hand. He flips it over and over again between two fingers. It's a tarot card. The Magician, the card that represents deceit when it's reversed.

I'd think he'd be more low key about his tendency to deceive, but maybe he's lost his touch. One could say he's showing his hand. Haha. Or, for some reason he wants me to see and know that he's being deceitful again. Somehow me believing he's being deceitful could be part of his trickery... somehow.

"Also illusions," I add. "Can't believe what he says or shows you."

At this, Phoenix looks at me. He tosses the card off the side of the bleachers. It spins away, slicing at the air, before disappearing.

"You wound me," Phoenix says with mock offense.

Dex stares at the spot where the card disappeared and then turns back to us.

"A Celestial? Like an angel?" he asks.

The second the words leave Dex's mouth, a shining halo appears above Phoenix's head, an angelic smile to match plastered onto Phoenix's face. Dex looks at the halo, wide-eyed.

"Did you tell him nothing?"

The halo above his head pops away like a burst thought bubble. He ignores me and faces Dex.

"Not an angel," Phoenix says, "but it is where we got the name from, as Vests interpreted many old stories of us as angels later on. The Council, which I told you about..."

At this, Phoenix looks pointedly at me. What? Does he want a cookie for telling Dex the most basic thing about Havcire?

"...is made up of three Celestials," Phoenix continues.

"Wizards," I say, and instantly regret it when a wizard hat appears on top of Phoenix's head as the halo did. "Stop that."

"We're not wizards," Phoenix explains to Dex, while still wearing the hat. "Incanters are more wizard-like. They use spells. We just have certain abilities."

The wizard hat pops away.

"*Magical* abilities. He did tell me he had magic," Dex supplies.

"Yes, see. I also told him all about the Subject System," Phoenix says, and then he's sliding across the bleacher, ending up directly in front of me with one bleacher between us. He puts his foot up on the bleacher between us and leans toward me, his forearm resting on his bent knee. In short, he's in my personal space. "Speaking of, what have you been up to?"

His eyes still seem cold. I swear they're the same color as I remember them, a bright, seafoam green. I question how I could have ever seen that color and thought of warmth because, like those years ago in the Council chamber when Phoenix broke the news about this life, I feel chilled to my core staring into them. Or, maybe the chill is just the feeling of betrayal seeping into my bones when face to face with the source.

I hold his stare, which is harder to do than it should be, and then try for my most innocent expression. I stand up and make my way up to the top of the bleachers to put some much needed distance between us.

"I don't know what you're talking about," I answer, convincing even myself.

"I, along with Max, have noticed your steady decrease in sentence. I don't think he's suspicious yet, but that wasn't part of the plan."

"You mean it wasn't part of *your* plan. I couldn't just sit around and wait for you to show up. This was my chance to try and actually beat the system knowing what I know. You're not the only one who can have plans."

"My plans never get figured out," Phoenix says. "Unless, I want them to. You, on the other hand, have not done the best job at staying under the radar. I believe I had mentioned something about acting normal until I arrived."

"No, doesn't ring a bell."

"So, Phoenix, what *is* your plan?" Dex interjects, and I wonder about whose side he's on.

"Thank you for asking," Phoenix says. "The—"

"Please, no fancy delivery," I interrupt.

Dex isn't wrong. I need to hear what Phoenix is up to. I happen to have waited fifteen years to hear what the hell is going on, but I need to hear it as it is.

"All right," Phoenix says, as if accepting a challenge, and then he dives right into it, no fancy delivery indeed. "Someone other than the Council started the Subject System. They accomplished this through mind control, which they're still using on the Council to prevent them from interfering with the Subject System. I also believe this person never intended for the system to actually be fair."

I look to Dex. He's nodding his head, taking in the information.

"I don't believe you."

Phoenix looks at me, eyebrows raised. He doesn't look the least bit surprised.

"And that's why I normally opt for the fancy delivery," he says.

The fancier, the less factual, the more room to add in persuasion and lies. Now that I've got the supposed facts, it'll be easier to fact check.

"Look," Phoenix continues, further taking note of my skepticism, "whenever the Council is asked about the Subject System, they just shut down. I plan to discover who is behind the mind control and give the power back to the Council, consequently fixing the rigged Subject System. I have contacted an Incanter and am waiting to hear back about ways to identify such persuasion."

The Subject System might actually be corrupt.

Sure, it's always seemed unfair to me that I wasn't permitted to remember my past lives. I could have learned from them and actually had the chance to better myself. It especially has never seemed right that I can't even remember my original life, the life that got me into this mess to begin with.

The possibility that the system really is completely corrupt, though? If it were true, would that even be a relief or just another thing to add to my list of ways I've been wronged? It would mean all these lifetimes really have been a waste. Twenty-six lives and, throughout all of them, I never stood a chance.

"Dawn, stop pacing," Phoenix says, yanking me out of my thoughts. Not to mention, I hadn't even noticed when I started pacing. I feel like I need to go on a run and, considering how my run went this morning, that's saying a lot.

I make myself stand still. The Council is being mind controlled, according to Phoenix.

"The Council seemed perfectly fine last I saw them," I point out.

"That's because you didn't ask them any questions about the Subject System."

"I am *in* the Subject System," I counter, but Phoenix shakes his head.

"They're only affected when asked about the system's creation and specifically about how it functions," Phoenix explains. "Even if you don't want to take my word about this, you know that the system is corrupt. The fact that no Subject has ever completed their sentence should be evidence enough for you that I'm telling the truth."

"Never?" Dex asks.

"No," Phoenix confirms.

The way he just assumes I know the system is corrupt. Sure, I might have claimed something along those lines in the past but mostly out of frustration over the fact that it seemed unfair I'm still a Subject and not a Citizen. It's a natural thing to do, when things aren't working out for you, to claim it's the system's fault and not your own, a sort of self preservation thing.

But, it's not as if I truly believed that. I'm no less in the dark than any other Subject, minus of course the whole memories being returned to me in this life thing. Still, it's news to me that not a single Subject has ever become a Citizen *if* that's even true.

Just because I can't find a motivation for Phoenix lying about this doesn't mean there isn't one. I need to focus on what I do know is true and prioritize what I need to find out is true.

"So what happens when a Subject fails?" Dex asks.

"We continue on like this, living lives under the control of an Experimenter," I answer.

"Forever?"

It may be time to move on to another hypothesis, a new experiment. Max's words from before I started this life come back to me. Alarm sets in, but that's not a now problem. I still have time before that has to become one of my top of concerns.

Phoenix was there, too, when Max admitted as much. I glance at him briefly, wondering if he's thinking the same thing, but Dex is waiting for an answer.

"Or until the Experimenter decides their research is complete. Then we'd stop coming back to life," I answer Dex, honestly.

"You'd die a final time," Phoenix adds, "and be classified as a SWOR, a Subject Without Redemption."

I try not to glare at Phoenix. Now he's all full of information of course. Nice, unpleasant information. Dex looks between us, absorbing this. No need to tell him that the end might come sooner rather than later for the both of us.

"I'd prefer to avoid that," Dex says.

"I want proof that what you say about the Council is true," I tell Phoenix.

"Such trust issues."

"I consider them my greatest attribute."

"Always better safe than sorry," Dex chimes in.

I nod toward Dex and shoot him an appreciative smile. He may be hard to read and possibly guilty by association, but he just took my side so he gets the benefit of the doubt for the moment.

"I'll get you proof," Phoenix agrees. He looks like he's already scheming about how exactly to do that.

"Just one question—"

"Doubtful," Phoenix interrupts.

I sit down on the top bleacher and take my time getting comfortable, which isn't so easy to do on a hard, metal seat but I think I pull off at least looking as though I am. I leisurely cross my legs.

"How are you looking into this without the Council's knowledge?" I ask. "Can't the griffon see everything and report it back to Minerva?"

"That's technically two questions."

"The griffon?" Dex questions.

"Magical bird, owl, lion thing. It can see every part of Vest from Havcire," I explain.

"Yeah, sure. That makes sense."

I raise my eyebrows at Dex. Does it? I want to say he's being sarcastic but, honestly, something about how he says it sounds oddly sincere.

"The griffon is loyal to me," Phoenix says, pulling my attention away from Dex. "He won't reveal anything, even to Minerva."

The bell rings, signaling the end of lunch. My stomach feels neglected.

I'll just have to eat in class, where eating is not allowed. Fortunately, my Algebra II teacher likes me and will let it slide.

I jump up and step down past Phoenix and Dex to grab my backpack. Dex also gets up, swinging his bag onto his back, but not before making sure his suit jacket is sitting properly on his shoulders.

"Dawn," Phoenix calls after me, "meet me after school. We'll go on a field trip for your proof. And, Dex, you can go volunteer where Dawn normally does so you can start decreasing your sentence, as well. It's worked so far for her."

Dex nods, agreeing, and waves goodbye to both me and Phoenix before walking off toward the main building.

I jump off the bleachers and look back at Phoenix.

"Why do you have to make my idea sound like an order of your own?" I ask, to which Phoenix smiles.

"It helps my ego."

I shouldn't have asked.

CHAPTER 9

Teleporting first feels like shrinking to the size of an atom. Then, as a microscopic being, you experience a death drop. Thankfully, the death drop is so fast that it doesn't seem to last very long.

The last part reminds me of how professional stuntmen jump from really high platforms and land on the ground safely by somersaulting to go with the momentum. My head and feet switch places, as I seem to spin in space, growing back to my correct size. And...

My feet hit solid ground. Somehow my hand is still in Phoenix's. Familiar white, marble walls surround me, the door to the Council Chamber just a few feet to my left.

Yes, I had asked for evidence that the Council was being manipulated, but I didn't expect Phoenix to bring me right to the lion's den for that evidence.

If I'm caught here, a Subject who's meant to be in the middle of a life with no knowledge of Havcire, I don't even know what they'd do but I definitely could not just resume my life.

"What are we—?"

Phoenix's hand slips out of mine and quickly covers my mouth, smushing my lips. His other hand holds a finger up to his own mouth to shush me. Either would have been sufficient to shut me up, especially since I now hear voices coming from the slightly ajar Council Chamber doors.

How Phoenix's hand manages to smell like a fresh winter day, I'm not sure, but I manage to glare at him so he drops it. I ignore the sensation of his fingers sliding off my lips and focus on the conversation going on beyond the doors.

I recognize Barnabas's deep voice but it's too muffled to make out.

Phoenix steps to the side and motions for me to get closer to the crack in the doors. Carefully, I step forward and angle my head so I can be as close as possible without being spotted.

"We have been informed of a potential problem with your experiment, Georgina," Barnabas is saying.

"Watch the Council," Phoenix whispers from my side.

"Informed by who?" I hear, who I assume to be Georgina ask.

"Anonymous tip," Lucifer replies.

I look at Phoenix.

"I'm the anonymous tip," Phoenix whispers, seemingly proud of himself. Then again, when is he not? "Now, look inside."

Oh well, hopefully they're all too preoccupied with Georgina to notice me peering in. I look through the crack in the doors, which is really only wide enough to look through with one eye anyway.

"My experiment tests emotions," Georgina says, "specifically which emotions provide the most motivation. In order to test this, I have to manipulate what emotions my Subjects feel."

It's unnerving. Georgina actually looks about my age. Well, the age I appear to be right now. She actually could be even younger, possibly as young as thirteen. One couldn't tell from her voice, though. She sounds like she could command an army of middle schoolers, the scariest army of them all.

"Your experiment threatens to endanger an innocent life on Vest," Minerva says this in a way that makes it sound as though the matter is closed. The answer is no to whatever it is Georgina planned.

"My Subject, Helen Akers, needs to feel a strong sense of guilt, and being the cause of her friend's death is the most effective method," Georgina goes on.

I have to resist the urge to turn away and look at Phoenix incredulously. I have to stay focused on the Council. I'm here for my evidence but who does this Georgina think she is?

She talks about killing an innocent person like Vanessa talks about cutting some nice girl from the cheerleading team just because she's looking a little heavier. Actually, Georgina kind of reminds me of Vanessa.

Georgina stands tall as she speaks, all five feet of her, showing no remorse.

"Is anything I plan to do against the Subject System rules?" Georgina asks.

I expect Minerva to say something. She'd been about to before Georgina asked her question but none of the Council members say anything.

A minute passes, or at least it feels like a whole minute, and no one answers. Lucifer's normally bored expression looks vacant. In fact, all three of them look this way, as if their minds have been wiped, not a single thought roaming around within.

"You may proceed with your experiment."

The words are startling. It's Barnabas who speaks, except his voice comes out monotone, and he still holds that blank expression.

"Ensure your actions don't alert any Vests of our existence."

Phoenix was telling the truth about at least one thing. I know these Celestials and the three in there right now are not themselves, and they definitely don't know to what they're agreeing.

"Of course," Georgina says. "I've ensured no one is near them in Central Park."

"Come on," Phoenix whispers, taking my hand to teleport us away.

I back away from the doors and BANG. I cringe. My foot hit the side of the door. I swear it was just a tap but it might as well have been a bomb going off in this echoing hallway.

"Oops," I whisper, freezing in place.

"Who's there?" Barnabas asks, his alert, demanding voice back. They couldn't have stayed out of it for just a bit longer?

Phoenix pulls my hand, unfreezing me. I follow him away from the doors. He presses me up against the wall.

Why aren't we making a run for it? Why hasn't he teleported us away?

Above my shoulder, he pushes his hand against the white, marble tile. Under his touch, it becomes translucent and then an image starts to form. The portals.

"Stay put," Phoenix orders and his hands are on my shoulders, pushing me right through the wall.

I stumble backwards but steady myself, thankfully, on solid ground. Some of these portals deposit right into open air.

"Phoenix!" I yell, irritated, even though I know for sure he can't hear me anymore.

I consider for a second throwing a tantrum but my surroundings distract me.

Beneath my feet is limestone, and it completely surrounds me. I'm in the center of what appears to be an ancient amphitheater, except it looks completely new, the limestone polished and in good condition, forming the rows upon rows of seats. The amphitheater is so large I can't even see the surrounding land from where I stand.

I turn around and almost bump into something. Levitating about five feet off the ground is a spherical rock the size of a bowling ball. I wave my hand above and below it, but it stays put.

I don't know why I would question a levitating rock at this point but it was worth testing out.

Phoenix said to "stay put." He didn't mention not touching anything. I tap the rock and quickly withdraw my hand.

You're not going to believe this, but it feels like a rock.

A rushing sound fills my ears. The rock glows a light blue and images appear. It shows Vestigium, every country and ocean.

That sound, it's not in my head and the wind did not just pick up. I look up and find that above the very top row of the amphitheater, a wall of water encircling the entire place has risen up.

Oh no. No no no no no.

I take a deep breath, thinking I'm about to be completely submerged, but the walls hold steady. An image forms on the water, like a movie projected on a screen.

I let out the big breath slowly. It's Times Square. People rush by on the street, while others, clearly tourists, stand in place, trying to capture the experience with their cameras. People sit on the red stairs below the bright billboards on the skyscrapers.

I look back at the rock. A red dot covers the location of Times Square. It's a live recording, showing the place in Vest.

Central Park. Georgina said her Subject would be in Central Park. I drag my finger across the surface of the rock, locating Central Park, and zoom into the location like I would on any touch screen device.

It works. I can see Central Park close up in more detail and... the lake is frozen? The lake is frozen in October. Yes, because that's normal.

"Seems you've got the hang of it."

I whip around to find the source of the voice, no doubt looking like I've just been caught with my hand in the cookie jar.

A man stands on the top row of the amphitheater, the wall of water rising up just behind him.

Even from this distance, he looks tall. His hair is so white it looks blue with the water reflecting off it. It might actually be blue. I can't tell. He looks to be about forty and in really great shape, which is made clear by his tight-fitting clothing. It's a white wet suit, made entirely out of what appears to be fish scales but it looks as strong as body armor.

Some of the water separates from the wall and slides into his open palm, forming a trident made purely of water. It's not a huge leap for me to guess who it is I'm facing.

"Poseidon?"

Poseidon smiles. He really looks like he means it, too, so I smile back politely. I'm not sure I've quite wiped the guilty look off my face, though.

Clearly he's a Celestial, but he seems much more laid back than the members of the Council. Perhaps, he'll just look past this whole thing, forget I was here.

"It's a pleasure to meet you," I say.

"Likewise, regardless of the fact that I do not know who you are," Poseidon says. "You are touching the Omphalos."

Ohhhh. I look at the rock behind me, the Omphalos, and back to Poseidon. I've done a lot of research this life on mythology. Sure, a lot of it isn't true, but it is based on the history of the Celestials and Incanters so I've done my best to study.

"The rock Cronus swallowed in place of Zeus uh... Barnabas," I say, correcting myself at the end.

Which means, I'm in Havcire's Delphi. According to myth, Zeus placed the Omphalos in Delphi as a symbol of their victory over Cronus, as he determined it to be the center of the universe. Those details probably aren't true, but the amphitheater is in Delphi, and here I am in an amphitheater.

"You know your myths. See, unfortunately, only Celestials and Citizens are permitted to be here, and I can sense that you are neither. I must activate the security measures. They'll probably kill you. My apologies," Poseidon says.

"Wait." Poseidon actually does wait to hear what I have to say. I scramble to think of something. "I'm not supposed to die this way."

That sucked.

"Then maybe you won't," he says.

The walls of water collapse. I turn to the Omphalos and press frantically on the Central Park location. The red dot appears anew there. The water crashes down. The Omphalos turns hot under my hand.

CHAPTER 10

This is different than teleporting. It's not fast. It feels like being folded into a paper fan, my body being pressed down flat like a crease in the paper.

1966

Fingers curled, elbows locked, shoulders strong, core tightened, legs straight, feet and toes grasping. I cling onto the bar above me with my hands and feet, my body bent in half. I swing up so that I'm now above the bar. I unfold my body, straightening my legs up into the air.

I'm a perfect line, reaching up to the ceiling above with my toes. My fingers loosen for a second, signaling the rest of my body to let go, before tightening once again, as the bar slides under my grip like we are one machine. The momentum from the swing down gives me the power for the dismount.

Away from the bar, I fly into the air, turning and turning.

There's a moment when it feels as if I'm frozen in the air like a weightless particle before the ground rushes forward, and I bend my knees in preparation.

My feet reach for the ground, sticking the landing. As I raise my arms up and face the surrounding crowd, the end of "Wild Thing" plays out in my head, my own internal soundtrack.

Maybe I should look into rhythmic gymnastics rather than artistic now that it, too, is contested in the Olympics. Then, I could actually work songs into my routines. I'm not sure the judges would appreciate my taste in music, but anything would be an improvement over silence. There isn't silence now, however, as the crowd cheers.

"I thought I told you to add an extra twist to your dismount."

My coach's voice erases the smile on my face as I step off the mat. Her face, on the other hand, looks as though it's never smiled.

Despite being in her fifties, she has not a single wrinkle, her skin pulled too tight across her face to allow for such a thing. I imagine she stares in the mirror every night and wills herself into looking as stern as she acts.

"It doesn't appear as though I needed it," I say, indicating the displayed score overhead.

"Casey, what have I told you?" she says. "You cannot win on confidence. You must do your best and more—"

"And I did," I say, before she can go on. "I could not have done the extra twist and still landed perfectly."

"You must do your best and more because," she continues, while giving me a chiding look, "your best may not be good enough to win the gold."

I land smoothly on the grassy ground but reach for the nearest tree. I'm not dizzy so much as disoriented. I feel like I just traveled through time rather than space. Human minds really are not made to hold separate lifetimes of memories.

I'd forgotten just how fun Life Twenty-Four was, with all the environmental pressures of being an Olympic gymnast, courtesy of Max. He wanted to see if I'd break under the pressure, if I'd give up on my dream after a plethora of failures. When it was clear that I would not, I was killed per usual. Of course, before I could actually fulfill that dream. The story of my lives.

I'm in Central Park. It's cold, too cold for October. Plus, I only live about an hour away from here and it surely can't differ this much, but it does explain the lake in front of me. It's frozen as I'd seen it on the Omphalos. I guess the Omphalos does more than just show places on Vest.

I hear laughing. Stepping out from behind the tree, I see two girls, who look to be about seventeen, standing on the frozen lake. The one laughing carefully runs and slides across the ice on her sneakered feet, her short, orange hair swinging in her face.

The other girl looks more hesitant, not to mention cold. She wears a knitted cap over her long, brown hair.

The orange-haired girl spreads her arms out to regain her balance. As she successfully slides to a stop, knitted cap girl noticeably relaxes and even lets out a relieved laugh. Orange-haired girl waves her friend over.

"Come on, Melanie! Try it," she yells over.

If she's Melanie, then that makes the other girl Helen Akers, Georgina's Subject.

Now, maybe it's the fact that these are the girls Georgina was referring to regarding her plan to kill one of them in this very park, but I have a bad feeling about this.

Melanie takes a step forward, beginning her careful run on the slippery ice.

"Wait!" I shout. Helen looks over, but Melanie appears too focused on not falling to pay me any attention. "You guys should—"

There's a deep, echoing crack and a splash that quickly follows. Panicked, Helen looks away from me and toward the source of the sound.

There's a life I'm glad I remember in detail, merely because it means I don't need to fully relive it through a vivid flashback like I had of my Olympic days.

I watched a friend die. It's not uncommon to be confronted with death in war. To watch a friend die, however, is the same no matter the circumstance. I felt useless; but even worse, I felt I could have done more to save him if I were just smarter or faster or something, which leads to a lifetime of replaying the horrible moment and going over scenarios where you react differently to see if there really was anything that could have been done. The answer is always a miserable, "I don't know."

"Melanie!" Helen screams.

The cold melts away. Every bone and muscle in my body unfreezes, as I sprint for the lake.

I leap onto the frozen surface as fast as I can. In the air, I just pray I come down smoothly despite the speed and power at which I've jumped. My feet find purchase immediately, and I run across the lake.

Helen has fallen to her knees where Melanie went through the ice and into the water below. She's blindly reaching into the water, searching for Melanie. Some part of me is aware of the fact that she still screams her friend's name in desperation.

I feel a vibration beneath my feet and stop running. There, under the ice, a few feet away from the hole where she fell through, is Melanie. Her hand hits the ice from below.

I drop down and slam my fist into the ice. It splinters. I hit it again, thinking only of getting through to grab onto Melanie's hand. The ice is the only thing in the way. Melanie is right there, right through it.

The ice breaks easily, my fist passing through, but it makes the sound of a small explosion. I open my hand and reach for Melody, finding her arm. With one heave, I pull her out of the new hole in the frozen lake.

Back on the ice, she turns over and coughs up a mouthful of water. Helen rushes to her side, kneeling down to pat Melanie on the back.

I feel like I just forgot to breathe for the past five minutes. I look at the two girls, the fear and relief clear on both their faces. They're okay. Melanie lost her hat, though.

"Thank you," Helen says.

"Yeah," I say, and mentally hit myself. I'm really not good with gratitude. "We should get off this lake. And, you should get her inside somewhere warm as soon as possible."

Melanie catches her breath, through with coughing, but she's clearly shivering. Who wouldn't be after taking an impromptu swim in a frozen lake?

Helen looks down at my words, tears threatening to fall. She looks ashamed. Of course she does. This whole thing was meant to make her feel guilty for her friend's death. While death was avoided, it still almost happened.

"What's your name?" I ask her.

Eyebrows scrunched, she looks back up at me. Her name is Helen Akers. Clearly I know this, but it'd be a little odd if I revealed I already somehow know her name.

"Helen," she answers.

I shouldn't say anything. Even if I did say something, it'd be a bit difficult to prove to her by myself that what I told her was true. It'd be right off to a mental institution for me.

Plus, it wouldn't benefit her anyway to simply know that she's a Subject. She wouldn't have her past memories, and she'd still have no control over how Georgina manipulated her life. She would know, though, that there was at least a reason for why her life was so messed up, that it's not random, that there's someone somewhere actually controlling what happens to her.

I would want to know.

"Helen, this wasn't your fault," I tell her. "Some things are just out of our control. All we can do is decide how we react and learn from what happens."

I am such a hypocrite. That is one thing I've never been able to accept. Maybe I should just tell her the truth, mental institution or not.

A tear escapes, rolling down her cheek, but she smiles. It's a small smile, but genuine.

"Thanks," she says.

"You're welcome," I manage this time.

Melanie shivers, her teeth chattering, and manages to say, "I'm cold."

"I know," Helen says, helping Melanie up. "We're going."

I go to leave, carefully making my way back over to the grassy ground, while also keeping an ear out just in case the ice decides to break again. They should be safe, as we ended up fairly close to the edge of the lake, but you never know how motivated certain forces at play are.

"Wait," Melanie shouts after me. I'm one step away from being off the lake, but I turn back around. "How the hell did you punch through the ice like that?" she asks.

"That's a good question," I hear Phoenix say from behind me.

CHAPTER 11

Phoenix grabs my hand for the third time in the past minute. To be fair, I yanked it away the first two times he took my hand, which wasn't hard to do because by "grabbed" I mean he, as gently as possible, placed my hand in his to examine. I let him get away with it this time because I figure he'll just keep trying until he does anyways.

"How's your hand?" he asks.

"You're looking at it."

He looks away from my hand long enough to shoot me an unamused look.

My hand is fine. There are no cuts and no bruises. It's not even slightly red from where I slammed it into solid ice.

Phoenix lets go.

"You're fine," he declares, although he doesn't sound like he believes it.

"Of course I'm fine. Where were you?"

"I was covering our tracks with the Council and then making sure Poseidon didn't look into who you are," Phoenix says, distracted. He looks back over to the frozen lake we haven't taken more than a few steps away from. "You punched through the ice, and you're fine?"

I shrug my shoulders.

"It must have been thin."

That's what I answered Melanie also, and it's true. The ice must have been thin where I punched through, plus the adrenaline of the whole situation must have helped.

Of course Phoenix was off making sure everything was good. The Council is still oblivious to what he's up to, what I'm up to also I guess, and Poseidon is in the dark, as well. He's got everything figured out, everything under control.

Maybe I'm just jealous of Phoenix. The real reason for my dislike of him. Maybe I should start lying to everyone, and then I'll finally be in control of my own life. My god. It's been a long day.

Phoenix shakes his head and walks on, away from me, further away from the lake. Okay, bye! Except...

I look around at my surroundings. There are a lot of trees here. I haven't been to Central Park enough to even know exactly where I am in it. I also have no way home.

I jog to catch up with him.

"Do you have any idea what kind of problems you just caused?" he asks the second I catch up.

"Excuse me? You mean by helping a Subject not experience unnecessary trauma? Not to mention, preventing an innocent from dying," I say.

"Exactly."

I stop walking. I'll stay stranded here if need be. Phoenix stops and looks back at me. So, he won't just leave me here. A smile forms on my face despite everything.

"Let's try something," I say. "A little empathy exercise."

I keep walking. Phoenix follows.

"This should be good," he says dryly.

I shush him. He raises his eyebrows but stays quiet.

"Imagine life is a buffet," I begin, "but instead of going up to fill your own plate, others do it for you, others like the Council and Experimenters. Sure, you get to choose what it is on your plate that you want to eat, but what about the rest of the buffet? What if you have no vegetables on your plate? None at all?"

I wait for Phoenix's answer. He seems to be thinking it over.

"Do you really like vegetables that much?" I reign in a grunt of frustration.

"That's not the point."

"I'm losing your point."

"I just want my life to be my own. Helping that Subject experience a win for once wasn't supposed to be on my plate," I say.

A chunk of broccoli appears in Phoenix's hand. He offers it to me like it's a beautiful bouquet of flowers. I glare at him. Where do these things even come from? Unless, it's just an illusion.

I slap the underside of his hand, and the broccoli flies up into the air before falling down onto the ground. Thump. Not an illusion.

"Fair enough," Phoenix relents, "but you've still messed things up."

"And here I was thinking you liked messing things up."

"I do, but you're messing up my messing up of things."

"That makes perfect sense," I tell him.

We come upon a clearing. Phoenix leans against a tree, tilts his head back against the trunk, and looks up at the sky. He reaches out, grabs my arm, and pulls me against the tree next to him before I get the chance to protest.

"Now, so that we can get back, please look up at the sky," Phoenix says.

I look up. It's actually a fairly nice day. The few clouds in the blue sky are white as porcelain, the lack of wind making them look more solid than usual today, rather than stretched out like pieces of cotton.

"What about teleporting?" I ask, keeping my eyes on the sky.

"You'll like this better." Interesting. Almost as if he cares what I'll like or not like.

That's the thing about Phoenix. He's so good at making people think he listens and cares. He gives you his full attention. If someone were to attempt to interrupt you, he'd outright tell them to wait a moment, that you're speaking. And, he'll do it politely. He doesn't just respond vaguely but with real sentences that make it clear he's truly heard what you said *and* thought about it beyond the bare minimum. These seem like small things but if you know, you know.

Regardless, it's all fake as hell. In the end, he'll disappear and leave you to die.

I heard once, in another life, that if people spent less time staring at what was right in front of them and instead more time looking up, a whole other world could be discovered. Hello, Havcire.

One can't actually just spot Havcire by looking up at the sky. It's not hidden among the clouds like some heaven. Still, the concept of a whole other world existing somewhere out there is nice, especially when you don't know what that other world is. Then, it can be anything you want it to be.

"Do you have a private plane?" I ask, about ninety percent joking. Phoenix doesn't even bother answering, so I take that as a no.

There's something oddly grounding about staring up at the sky.

Speaking of down here on the ground, Phoenix is standing real close, too close. The simple brush of his arm against mine feels like a fire in this unusually cold weather. And, is it just me, or is he intentionally brushing his arm gently against my own?

No. This is the type of thinking that's gotten me in trouble before. Blame it on the hormones. He probably doesn't even notice. Unlike me, who's—

"What do you see?" Phoenix asks, distracting me from my attempt to casually lean away from him.

It's a nice day out, as observed, but there sure is nothing that warrants commenting on.

"Sky. Clouds," I say, looking back at Phoenix. He pulls his attention away from the riveting sky to look back at me.

"Creative. Do any of the clouds look like something specific to you? And, do not just say clouds again."

Well, there is a nice blob. Something gives me the idea that's not the correct answer either. The cloud just above the blob does look to have some sort of shape.

I tilt my head to the right. It appears as though part of the cloud forms the head of a bird dipping downwards toward the ground. The beak is almost as long as the rest of the bird's head, which extends further back behind its eyes, feathers elongating the head's shape like a mohawk.

The head now clearer, I can also make out the bird's legs and wings. It has long tail feathers and wide wings, wings that stir the previously still air around it, blowing the other clouds further away, including the blob. As if awakening, the bird shakes its head, the mohawk feathers ruffling.

I feel Phoenix's hand on my shoulder, urging me to step back, as the cloud bird soars down directly toward us.

CHAPTER 12

T he trees whistle and leaves break off, swirling in the air from the gusts of wind that blow through the previously still clearing. The bird thrusts out its wings one last time to steady its landing before going still.

Up close, it's about the size of a van with the wings tucked in. The body still looks to be made of cloud. When the sun hits, the rays shine through, illuminating the bird from the inside out. It's amazing.

"You saw it," Phoenix states, and pulls my gaze away from the bird to look at him. He's smiling, which I always find suspicious.

"How do you know?" I ask. My voice comes out quiet, afraid to startle the bird. It seems like it doesn't even know we're here.

Phoenix walks forward, around to the front of the bird.

"If you hadn't, she wouldn't have come," he says, not any quieter than usual. "She's a Kaeli, made from air and magic. They can't survive long in Vest without returning back to the magic of Havcire. This one's a thunderbird. She's small for her kind, but fast."

"She?"

I watch Phoenix carefully reach his hand out toward the Kaeli's beak. She dips her head so his hand can rest above her beak, on the feathers below her eyes. Her eyes are the only part of her body that isn't the white of the cloud. They perfectly match the blue of the sky, as if they're a mere reflection of it, her usual environment. I half expect Phoenix's hand to pass right through her, but the area solidifies at his touch.

"Her name's Arrow," Phoenix answers.

"Is she yours?"

The second the question leaves my mouth, Arrow's head turns to face me accusingly, her sky blue eyes narrowing.

"Kaelis don't belong to anyone. They're not pets but they do form loyalties to certain people, who they allow to name them. And no, I didn't name Arrow."

"Sorry, Arrow," I tell the bird.

Her eyes soften before turning her neck to face forward again.

Phoenix walks to Arrow's side and easily jumps up onto her back, at least eight feet up in the air. He pats the side of her neck, and she responds immediately. She bends her knees and sits down on the ground, making her look like a huge pile of feathers. Now, she's only about five feet high.

Phoenix holds a hand out to me.

"Come on," he says.

Up close, it's easier to see that Arrow's body shifts between vapor and solid, shimmering like the sunlight reflecting off water as it does. One second a place on her body looks as if my hand could pass right through, like any other cloud. Then, a moment later, white feathers fold over like one of those sequined objects that have two differently colored sides. With a wave of your hand, you can brush the sequins over to their other side, creating a new image; in this case, covering up the translucence of Arrow's coat.

As the area directly in front of me solidifies to reveal the feathers, I draw my hand across it. They feel like ordinary, soft feathers, like those of a hawk. I can feel Arrow's breath expanding in her chest. The area dissolves into vapor, my hand passing right through the surface, exposed to cold air underneath. I pull my hand out and take a step back.

"How are you sitting on her back if she's made of air?" I ask, looking up at Phoenix, whose arm is still expectantly extended out toward me.

"Of air *and* magic. She can control what parts of her are solid. Keeping the majority of herself as a cloud helps her blend in more."

"Impressive. All right," I say, holding my hand out to him.

Phoenix grabs onto my forearm and I his. He effortlessly pulls me up onto Arrow's back behind him.

Phoenix holds his hands out in front of him, palms up. A thin, golden rein appears across his palms and around the neck of Arrow. It looks smooth enough to slip right out of Phoenix's grip but he holds onto it steadily.

Arrow stands back up on her feet, tilting me backwards as she does. I strain to keep myself upright, tightening my legs around her. Then she tilts forward, and I have to work not to fall forward into Phoenix and knock both of us off Arrow's back.

Arrow's wings expand out on either side of us, sweeping above our heads, and with one powerful thrust, she lifts us high into the air, the impact of the quick ascent keeping me squarely on her back.

Before I know it, we're among the clouds, the ground barely visible beneath us.

Startled by the sudden height and a fear of a long fall down, I wrap my arms around Phoenix in front of me. Though I am no stranger to heights or flying, it's a bit different to be surrounded by open air on the back of a creature that is, at best, partially solid.

I feel Phoenix stiffen slightly and go to pull my arms back but he grabs onto my hands, keeping them in place.

"It's a good idea to hang on," he says. "It's going to get a bit more turbulent now. You're not prone to motion sickness, are you?"

"No," I say, "but—"

"Good," Phoenix says, cutting me off, as he lifts the reins higher.

Before I can say anything else, we're off. Arrow responds immediately, moving her wings as fast as a hummingbird but with the strength of an eagle. I question the aerodynamics of it all but understand how she got her name as we shoot forward through the sky like an arrow sprung forth from a bow, the air sliced in two around us. I'm reminded more of a ship in the water than a plane in the sky, as the clouds seem to part for Arrow like water splitting away from the bough.

Although my eyes are tearing from the wind, I fight to keep them open. Arrow's wing cuts through a cloud on our left, and it explodes in a firework of white cotton. Strands of my hair whip behind me.

We dip a bit lower, and I can see the deeper blue of the Atlantic Ocean below, the sunlight reflecting off it, forming what looks like a blue sky full of stars.

It's odd how a lake, as the light reflects off it, looks like a video that's stuck on rewind, repeating, its water trapped between land. But, the ocean is always moving, each wave changing it, the water flowing towards a destination.

When did we move away from land?

Arrow slows, the wind dying down. Her wings stay open, and we glide through the air, propelled forward still by her previous speed.

I unwrap my arms from around Phoenix and reach out my hand to touch a cloud close by, my fingers sliding through. I feel the condensed and slightly wet air, just as I had when Arrow's feathers disappeared from beneath my touch. As my fingers leave the cloud, a small trail of white lies in their wake.

"How do you materialize objects?" I ask Phoenix. "Like are you really materializing objects, creating matter from nothing? Or, are you teleporting an object from somewhere else, or transfiguring another object into the object you want?"

"Now that you mention it, I am hungry. That cloud to your right might make a good sandwich."

Did I hear him right? It's still pretty windy up here and he's facing away from me.

I look back at the cloud we just passed, half expecting it to spontaneously transform into a turkey club, until I realize Phoenix has turned his head to look back at me. It's clear from his facetious smile he's mocking me. Stupid cloud. I shove Phoenix in the back, which only makes him laugh.

Shifting the gold reins from one hand to the other, Phoenix slides around to face me, the reins clasped in his hands behind his back. I look behind me to back up and give him more room, but Arrow appears to be vapor in the space behind me. When I look back to Phoenix, though, he's already scooted further away from me, more towards Arrow's neck.

I stay put. Our knees are still touching, but it's not like that bothers me or affects me in any way. Being only a couple feet away from Phoenix is better than falling through vapor and plummeting to the ground... most likely.

"You've been exposed to too much Harry Potter," Phoenix says.

"No such thing as too much Harry Potter," I tell him indignantly. "But, I get it, you don't use transfiguration."

"It would mean I was *super* powerful if I could just create matter from nothing," Phoenix says, and he says it like that is in fact what he does and he's ultra proud of it, too. "I can't, though."

Bragging about a Power You Don't Even Possess 101 - Class taught by Phoenix.

"So you use teleportation."

"Yes, theory two out of your one hundred."

Sure it's like pulling teeth, but Phoenix is actually answering my questions for once.

"Is teleportation a power only you have?" I ask.

So, I might as well try to get as much out of him as possible while I can. I've asked around during my short trips to Havcire, the trips where I'm forced to meet with the Council in between lives, and I've gotten a good amount of information about Celestials, Incanters, and Havcire in general, considering my limited opportunity. I've gathered what I could, leaving me with bits of information, all random and scrambled.

"Teleportation and illusions are uniquely mine," Phoenix answers. "Celestial magic manifests through innate abilities. Incanter magic, on the other hand, allows them to interact with magic and manipulate it for their use, as if they're connected on some wavelength to all the magic around them. Technically, we have more power than Incanters, as Celestials are the second generation, but the Incanters have more flexibility with their magic."

"Wait. When you teleport stuff to you, like the watch from earlier, are you stealing?"

Phoenix brings a hand to his chest in mock offense.

"Here I am, trying to answer your questions to instill trust, and you immediately accuse me of a crime?"

I smile.

"You gave yourself away. You're only being helpful to trick me into trusting you again."

He drops his hand and the act.

"I said nothing of trickery, and don't you worry. I returned the watch right back to its owner, and he had no idea it was ever missing."

"It's like magical pickpocketing."

"Except, I returned it," Phoenix points out again. "I can also teleport things in from Havcire if I need to, which is stealing from absolutely no one, as there's an unlimited supply of resources."

"Just because it can be replaced, doesn't mean it's not stealing."

"Makes it not morally wrong, though."

"I'm not sure about that."

"Morally gray, then."

Phoenix shifts back around, readjusting the reins so he holds them in front of him and with both hands again.

Arrow begins to pick up speed. As the sun lights on her feathers, a golden glint catches my eye. Each feather is outlined delicately by gold, but it's not just decorative. The ends are sharp, like the edge of a fine blade. I get the feeling they would cut easily with the faintest touch to the point. The feathers are angled inward toward Arrow's body, seemingly to avoid harming anyone, for now.

"Buckle your seatbelt," Phoenix shouts back to me over the crescendo of the wind.

I look down, my hands already in motion. There is no seatbelt. Of course. I am sitting on a huge bird made of cloud. I drop my arms and glare at Phoenix's back. Before I can comment, Arrow's wings push back hard, and I rush to hold onto Phoenix before I fly off her back.

Minerva, as usual, sits with perfect posture on her silk throne, her feet planted solidly on the ground.

Barnabas has a more casual posture, with his left arm leaning on the golden armrest, causing him to lean a little more towards Minerva and away from Lucifer.

Lucifer sits comfortably, with his ankle resting atop the knee of his other leg.

Max attempts to stand tall and still in front of the Council but fidgets against his will from whatever news he has come to discuss. Finally, or at least what seems like forever to Max since entering the room, Barnabas clears his throat to signal his permission that it is time for Max to begin.

"Her points have gone significantly up," Max blurts out and then curses himself in his head. He had prepared. He meant to be clear and concise with this report; but in the end, he's never been great at public speaking, especially with all the pressure involved with speaking in front of the Council.

"Max, could you be more specific?" Barnabas asks, while Lucifer smirks at the Experimenter's discomfort. Max takes notice of Lucifer's mocking expression but forces himself to focus, gathering his thoughts.

"My apologies. Dawn's points have accrued in a way that no one's points have ever in the history of this system. At first, her decrease in sentence was gradual throughout this most recent life so I didn't really take notice of the change. However, today, she gained one hundred points just in the past hour. While the increase in points itself is nothing illegal, it has never happened before, and I thought you would like to be made aware of the situation," Max reports and shows visual relief after having said everything necessary.

Lucifer, while Max was speaking, unfolded his legs, planting his feet on the ground. He leans forward with interest, resting his forearms on his knees. Even Barnabas seems mildly interested but, like Minerva, he stays frozen in position.

"So Dawn might actually be joining us back here permanently in the near future is what you're saying?" Lucifer asks, amused and even seemingly excited at the prospect.

"Well, it no longer seems impossible," Max admits.

"As stated," Barnabas begins, "it is not illegal for a Subject to complete their sentence and become a Citizen. In fact, it is the point of the Subject System for every Subject to have this opportunity. Still, it has never happened and is therefore suspicious that Dawn has made such progress in a single life. We should make sure that everything is right with the system and that there isn't something unusual interfering with Dawn's points. Minerva, can your griffon tell us what he has seen in regard to this situation?"

Minerva nods towards Barnabas and turns to face the griffon perched on her shoulder. Instead of communicating with Minerva as he usually does, the griffon screeches directly into her ear and flies out of the room through one of the windows high up in the wall.

Neither Max nor the other Council members notice Minerva flinch away from the creature that has been by her side for an eternity.

"He's been temperamental recently," Minerva says. "I think Phoenix is rubbing off on him more and more. Regardless, he hasn't shared with me anything unusual about Dawn's most current life. He reported that she has had no friends as planned, and the last update I got was that Phoenix had arrived on time."

"If your griffon has been temperamental of late, then we need an alternate way to keep a closer eye on Dawn to ensure this decrease in sentence is natural," Barnabas says.

"You know who would love the opportunity to do anything that would make her look more responsible?" Lucifer asks the other two Council members, knowing they are both well aware of who exactly he his talking about.

"No," Barnabas responds, putting a quick end to that idea. "We don't need yet another pair of eyes with questionable loyalties."

"Lucifer has a point," Minerva chimes in, causing Lucifer to look genuinely shocked Minerva is agreeing with him. Barnabas immediately reconsiders, for if Minerva believes there to be a point, there must be. "After all, it would get her out of our way for some time, as she would be busy in Vestigium looking after Dawn."

Barnabas lets out a long sigh and turns back to face Max.

"We'll send her to you so you can explain how she can successfully blend into Dawn's environment without ruining the experiment, and then you may send her to Vestigium."

"I'll have her prepared and sent as soon as possible," Max responds, before nodding respectfully to the Council and turning to exit the room.

CHAPTER 13

Turns out the big Halloween party the flier referenced is at my good friend Ryan's house. He's that football player I sang to, without his knowledge, at school. Truthfully, I'm still not positive his name is Ryan but I believe he looks like a Ryan and henceforth shall be named Ryan.

Ryan is dressed as a football player (not very creative considering but we won't judge). He seems perfectly nice, actually standing at the front door and greeting people with a big, white toothed smile as they come in. I, of course, walked right in without being noticed but I'm special.

I get to comfortably sit on the floor and no one looks at me twice. My perch is the perfect place to spot where I'm needed. I'm seated at the edge of the grand balcony that looks out over the first floor of Ryan's house, my legs dangling out between the bars of the railing.

Below, on the first floor, the nice couches that usually, probably are arranged in the center of the room to make for a neat and cozy living room are pushed to the side to create room for dancing in the center.

Music plays. It's actually good, Halloween themed music. Another point there for Ryan. I hear news that a band is supposed to play later, which is supported by the fact that, below my dangling feet, there's a stage set up.

My fellow classmates, some of whom I vaguely recognize, are dancing, or at least they start to when a song to their liking plays. Many are congregated by the kitchen, just past the living room, where the drinks and snacks are located. Most, however, are just standing around talking, both upstairs and downstairs.

So, here's the situation.

I shift slightly to look behind me, to where the two people I've been eavesdropping on for the past few minutes are standing, and I get a face full of fairy wing. I keep forgetting I'm wearing those. And, back to looking down in front of me at the first floor.

As I was trying to explain, this is what's going on. Carly caught her boyfriend kissing Vanessa. Vanessa is Carly's best friend! So, naturally, the assumption was made that the boyfriend was the guilty one and Vanessa, which was verified by Vanessa, was innocent in it all. Not only that, but Vanessa is telling Carly that before Carly's boyfriend planted one on her, he confessed to only having dated Carly in order to get closer to Vanessa. Jerk move, right?

Right. Except... I saw what really happened, which was that Vanessa intentionally kissed Carly's boyfriend just as Carly was walking by, and Carly's boyfriend (sorry I haven't overheard his name yet) actually ended up pushing Vanessa away.

This could all be easily fixed by Carly talking to the guy but, by the time Vanessa is done with her, Carly won't even look at him anymore.

I can't believe no one is dancing to "Thriller."

Well, Fairy Godmother Dawn to the rescue. I will tell Carly the truth. She will forget I exist the second the words are out of my mouth but the message will stay with her. Hopefully, it will be enough to convince her Vanessa is lying or at least enough to convince her to hear her boyfriend's side. Then, I can dance.

Remember the wings, I have to repeatedly remind myself as I get up from the floor. I get up stiffly and without twisting to ensure I don't hit my wings on the railing, which is curved on either side of me.

It was a nice spot, made me feel like I was cut off from everyone else, in my own little cage. Sounds like that wouldn't be a good thing, but I've been stepped on at these things before. The cage seemed like a safe option.

I pivot around, ready to approach Carly and Vanessa.

"Dex," I state stupidly, as I find him standing right behind me.

"Hello," he says, sounding as formal as ever. Per usual, he's wearing a suit. Although, he does look a little fancier than normal, with a bow tie around his neck as well. "I didn't expect you to come to a party like this, seeing as you are essentially invisible."

Over his shoulder, I check on Carly and Vanessa, who are still standing there talking. They're both dressed as... actually I don't know what they're dressed as. They're wearing corsets and short skirts but I'm not sure they're really dressed up as anything.

"First," I tell Dex, "you have no idea just how fun a party can be when you know no one can see you. And, second, these parties are the perfect opportunity to work the system, lots of people in need of help."

Dex reaches out and pokes my fairy wing that peaks over my shoulder.

"Explains your outfit. You're out here helping make wishes come true."

I smile. Dex gets it.

"Exactly. It helps me get in the mood to be wonderful."

I look down at my outfit. I sewed the wings to this plain, blue dress. It's nothing fancy but it fits me well. Though it's strapless, the bodice is tight enough to stay up comfortably, fitting a lot like a corset, and the skirt starts at my hips, loosely falling down to just above my knees. I also wore my black boots that come up to just below my knees. They're my favorite shoes, and there's no one to tell me they don't fit the outfit.

"Plus," I add, "I like dressing up for myself. So, what are you doing here?"

"Spying on you," Dex answers. A moment too long passes before he adds, "Just kidding." He holds out his arms as if to display more clearly what he's wearing. "I'm dressed as James Bond." I feel my eyebrows raise into the air. "He's a spy?"

"Yeah, Dex, I know who James Bond is," I tell him, shaking my head. "It's just that you're dressed the same as I've seen you before."

In fact, I even thought of James Bond when I saw Dex for the first time two days ago. Dex fidgets with his bow tie, straightening it.

"I'm wearing a bow tie. I don't usually wear a bow tie," he says.

I can't help but laugh. "Okay, I'll give you that."

I see that hint of hazel in his dark eyes again, and his lips twitch in the corners, as if he wants to laugh, but the down to business expression returns so quickly I'm not sure anything else was ever really there.

"Thank you. So, who needs help? Teach me your ways."

Alright, I can share.

"Carly," I tell Dex, nodding behind him to where she stands. He looks and then looks back at me, nodding, ready for the details. I really do feel like I'm talking to Bond here. I fill him in.

The good thing with Dex is that he'll have a better chance of getting through to Carly because she'll actually remember him after. She'll know where she got the information from, that it's not just some gut feeling of her own to question Vanessa.

Besides, Carly wouldn't have been the first person I helped out tonight.

There was the punch bowl guy before. He knocked over the punch bowl accidentally. He would've been covered in it if I hadn't stepped in at the right time, which is why the front of my blue dress is currently one big pinkish, red stain. I don't know where everyone thought that punch just disappeared to, but it was me. I was the human punch catcher.

There was also the girl dressed as the devil. Her dress strap broke. Her friends were doing their best to cover it up, huddling around her, but they seemed stuck on the issue that none of them had a sewing kit on hand. I broke her other strap and tied the two together, converting the dress into a halter. I think it looks even better now. She seemed happy with it.

After Dex is briefed, I send him off with well wishes. I intend to oversee his first mission but Phoenix walks up to me, appearing out of a crowd of people.

I wanted to be able to dance crazily in a room full of people tonight, all of whom would be completely oblivious, but Phoenix and Dex are really ruining that plan.

Phoenix, like Dex, looks dressed as he usually is. Unlike Dex, I can't find a single difference in his attire. He wears jeans and a leather jacket over a black t-shirt with a rainbow design in the center.

"Now, why are *you* here?"

"I'm actually spying on you," Phoenix says. He leans against the railing next to me and watches as Dex pulls Carly aside to talk to her without Vanessa.

I'd take his claim as a joke if it weren't for the fact that Phoenix was intentionally using the exact same words Dex did earlier, proving he really was watching and listening. It's beyond me why he would readily admit to such a thing.

"That's creepy." I turn to walk away but he follows and almost bumps into my right wing. I quickly dodge before he can make contact. I worked hard making these wings out of quality hangers and hose. "Whoah, watch the wings if you're gonna come along."

Phoenix holds up his hands in mock surrender. He follows but keeps his distance.

"The wings suit you," he says.

We reach the stairs, which have a smooth, wooden railing. The staircase elegantly curves as it declines into the living room. I look at Phoenix.

"This would be the part of the evening where I try to slide down the railing without any worry that someone might witness my failure."

"Go on," he says, motioning me ahead.

"No, you've ruined it."

"Maybe the momentum will give you enough lift to fly."

I take the stairs, the correct way.

"It was nice of you to help Dex out just now," Phoenix says.

He follows me on the stairs, which is difficult to do. Because he's interacting with me, he's invisible, which means dodging people.

Imagine what it's like when you approach someone walking directly towards you in a crowded hallway. There's that moment when you both see each other and decide who's going to move out of whose way. Except, when the other person can't see you, it becomes your job to always move out of the way. On a staircase full of people, there's the added challenge of being on uneven ground.

Out of the corner of my eye, I see Phoenix jump to the side of me to avoid the person walking down the stairs behind him. He steps down in front of me to let the guy walk by.

"This is ridiculous," Phoenix says, looking around in dismay at the number of people heading up and down the stairs.

I'm not going to lie, it's kind of funny to watch him struggle with something so mundane. Well, mundane for me.

He looks over the railing and, next thing I know, he's jumping up onto it and hopping over the side onto the floor below. The people he lands nearest to look at him startled, but it doesn't take long for them to start commenting on how cool it was that he landed that jump.

So dramatic. I finish my game of dodge the people and make it to the living room, where I drag Phoenix away from his new fan club.

"Speaking of helping Dex out, why are you really interested in fixing the Subject System?" I ask him.

Thankfully, no one is particularly interested in the current song playing, so the majority down here are standing in place talking. Less movement to dodge. I head towards the kitchen.

"You pulled me away from my new friends," Phoenix says, looking back at the group by the stairs.

"They'll still be there after you answer my question."

"You're always interrogating me," he complains. "This is why I have to find new friends."

I give him my most insincere face of pity. He simply grins at me and stops walking.

We're so close to the kitchen, right in the open doorway, and I've been wanting water for the past hour, but I stop walking also because he has that face that says he's actually going to tell me something of substance for once.

"I actually love your interrogations. They're how all my more fun dreams start but you normally have me tied down."

Shameless flirt. I should have gone for the water. I will do that right now because, despite all my efforts to keep the blush from my face, I fear I'm failing.

But Phoenix doesn't let me get far.

"The reason I'm helping out with the Subject System is because it's the best lead I have for figuring out who is manipulating the Council, and I need to stop whomever that is because I have a feeling they won't stop at just manipulating the Council— Did you hear that?" Phoenix says, interrupting himself.

"What? You actually being possibly truthful for once?" I ask, even though I did hear *something*. I thought it was part of the music possibly. It sounded kind of like a large tree branch cracking off.

Phoenix, brow furrowed, leans in close to me. For a second, I think he's going to hug me, which would be weird and random, even for him.

The volume of the music gets significantly lower, and I realize he's leaned toward me to reach the volume dial for the music, which is right behind me. Protests ring out all around me.

"What happened to the music?"

"Who turned down the music?"

"Someone turn it back up!"

Phoenix stays still, listening, waiting. The zipper of his leather jacket brushes against the exposed skin of my collarbone, sending a shiver down my spine. The smell of the leather mixes with his familiar fresh, winter day scent, and I need to snap out of it.

I catch sight of Dex up on the second floor. He's looking down at us, eyebrows raised in question. He's the only one who can really see what's going on, who's turned down the music. I don't have any explanation for him.

"Hey, Phoenix?" I ask. "I know they can't see you and all, thanks to me of course, but you should probably turn the music back up anyways. There might be—"

Thunder. That was definitely thunder, and it sounded like it was right over us, the house shaking from the force of the sound.

A shrill scream echoes around the house, but it's quickly followed by a nervous giggle. I see the girl responsible. She's dressed like Cher from *Clueless*.

"Sorry," she says, sheepishly.

Her friends start to laugh and others join in, including Cher.

"A big thunderstorm on Halloween," Ryan shouts from the second floor. "Party!"

As if on cue, Phoenix turns the music back up, and everything returns to normal, except for Phoenix's expression.

He steps away from me, on high alert. There's no more of his carefree attitude. He stands solely on his own two feet for once instead of casually leaning back against the wall. I've rarely seen him stand up tall. He looks rather imposing.

"How long do you think it'd take to clear everyone out of here?" Phoenix asks me.

He's focused on the large window that takes up most of the far wall of the kitchen. Rain is falling so heavily that it looks like the window has layers of water fighting for dominance over its surface. It's really dark outside, like I swear there were at least street lamps on the road outside when I got here.

"You mean how long would it take to force them out into the pouring rain in the middle of a party for no apparent reason?" I ask.

Phoenix pulls his focus away from the window long enough to look at me.

"Yeah, that's what I thought."

A sword appears in Phoenix's hand. It's fully gold, even the blade. The cross-guard is ornamented to look like a pair of wings that curl back around Phoenix's fingers where he grips the sword. Phoenix catches me staring wide-eyed.

"Don't worry," he tells me. "I didn't steal it. This one's mine."

Right, cause that's what I was worried about. How about the reason why he feels the need to arm himself with a sword right now?

A loud crash of thunder prevents me from asking. This one is even audible over the music, and it causes the partygoers to shout with excitement. Following the thunder, a bolt of lightning cracks, striking the ground right outside the kitchen window.

It may just be me, but I thought the lightning was supposed to come *before* the thunder.

"Out of the kitchen!" Phoenix shouts to the five people currently staring in amazement at where the lightning struck. They don't move. "NOW!" Phoenix orders, and they scramble to obey.

Phoenix and I move out of the doorway and into the kitchen so they can exit. Once the last person exits, a familiar face enters.

"What's going on?" Dex asks, and then his eyes go almost comically wide. "Scratch that, what is *that*?"

The window shatters, glass raining down, as something big crashes through.

CHAPTER 14

Phoenix pushes me and Dex behind him at the last second, blocking us from the stray shards of glass. A roaring shout fills the room accompanied by a loud footstep, which sounds like another rumble of thunder.

"You wanted to know what happens to Subjects not in the Subject System," Phoenix says.

I peer out from behind Phoenix. I feel like I do when I'm watching a horror movie and slap my hand over my eyes to block out the scary bits but spread my fingers so I can still actually see what happens.

"Oh my god," Dex manages. His voice sounds strangled. "That's a Subject?"

That is an Oni.

He stands at ten feet tall, wearing only a loincloth that looks to be made from a tiger's pelt. His skin is blue, and every single muscle on his body is defined and frighteningly large. To say he has fangs would be an extremely understated statement. His top fangs are so long they look like tusks. His bottom fangs are shorter, but they curve up out of his mouth and come to deadly points. On top of his head, poking through his long, black hair are two horns, which point straight up and also end sharply.

He holds no weapon but I'm thinking a weapon might not be a necessity for him. I don't want to be crushed to death by bare hands.

The Oni looks right at me with his inky, blue eyes. I should fight. I should find some type of weapon to defend myself. Or, I should run. I should definitely run. I don't think I'm even breathing.

The Oni looks right past me and to Dex, who is peering out from behind me. In any other situation, I might find our position funny with me peering out from behind Phoenix and Dex peering out from behind me, but I do not right now.

The Oni moves on from Dex, his eyes focusing on Phoenix. He ROARS, causing the whole house to shake again like it had from the thunder.

And yet, I breathe for maybe the first time since the Oni crashed through the window. He couldn't care less about anyone else here. He's here for Phoenix.

The Oni charges forward. I pull Dex to the side, away from Phoenix.

Phoenix meets the Oni halfway, deflecting a blow from the Oni with his sword, which would have sent him flying across the room and probably through a wall. The hit from the sword pushes the Oni's arm away, but it doesn't even leave behind a scratch.

The Oni quickly aims to hit Phoenix again with his other arm. Wow, an ambidextrous Oni. Phoenix dodges, rolling to the side, under the Oni's arm. He comes up on the other side of the Oni and hits him hard in the back of the knees, causing the Oni's legs to collapse.

"Oni are SWORs?" I shout to Phoenix.

He shoots me an incredulous look. What? Like he's busy?

He looks like he's going to reply but he instead turns away just in time to avoid the Oni's attempt to crush him. The Oni still remains on his knees, but he holds up a fist to bring down right onto Phoenix.

"Oni?" Dex asks, his eyes fixed on the Oni and Phoenix.

"They're demons," I tell him, "according to Japanese folklore."

Like I've mentioned, I've done a lot mythology research in this life. Apparently, Oni are real and my personal future if Max ends his experiment. I mean, I knew life as a Subject Without Redemption was not going to be all sunshine and rainbows but I was still ignorantly hopeful.

The Oni's managed to get up from the floor. He aims to kick Phoenix, but Phoenix easily jumps up five feet into the air to land on top of the three feet high kitchen island, which brings him almost face to face with the Oni.

"Go Phoenix!" I hear a girl shout.

The other people at the party have crowded around the entrance of the kitchen to watch the fight. They look on with excitement, cheering when Phoenix lands a blow. I look between them and the fight and realize they must think this is some kind of planned show. Anything, of course, would be more believable than the truth.

"Get him Phoenix!"

When did all these people from my class learn Phoenix's name? He only got here a couple days ago.

The Oni lowers his head and charges, his sharp horns aimed at Phoenix's chest. Phoenix jumps back on top of the island to avoid the Oni, who runs right into the edge of the island. Phoenix's foot lands in a spilled drink on the counter, and he almost slips.

A laugh escapes me. I mean, come on, felled by soda? That's funny. Dex looks at me as if I've lost my mind.

"Shouldn't we do something to help?" he asks.

"He's fine. Look," I point to Phoenix, who's currently flipping backwards on top of the island like it's a balance beam, "he's not even breaking a sweat."

"Do Celestials sweat?" Dex asks.

Huh.

"I actually don't know." I watch Phoenix and try to think about if I've ever seen him sweat. "The thing about an Oni, Dex, is that they only go after evil-doers, so it's only right we let it do its thing."

Phoenix lands a kick to the Oni's chest, pushing him backwards toward the opposite wall, where he leaves a dent and one leg goes right through, momentarily keeping him stuck.

The spectators cheer. None sound too concerned about the damage to the house. I wonder where Ryan is.

Phoenix jumps down from the island and lands directly in front of me. I hear a few people wondering where he disappeared to. He really isn't sweating. Although, he is breathing harder than usual.

"An Oni is extremely biased in favor of whomever hires them," Phoenix tells Dex, but looks pointedly at me. "One's evil-doer may be another's hero."

"So they're like guns for hire?" Dex asks.

The Oni pulls his leg free, further breaking the wall and sending plaster crumbling to the wood floor.

"Your friend is coming back," I tell Phoenix.

The Oni shakes off the hit and heads right back for Phoenix. Phoenix jumps back up onto the kitchen island to better face the approaching Oni. He doesn't just jump, though. He flips up onto it, landing perfectly on his feet. That can't be necessary. Show off.

"Phoenix! He's back!" a girl cheers. It's Vanessa. Of course she made her way to the front of the group.

"They can be," Phoenix answers Dex. "But it's supposed to be illegal—" Phoenix ducks out of the way of a hit aimed at his head, "—to use an Oni in this way."

Phoenix dodges the Oni's following hit by sliding forward on his knees closer to the Oni. He jumps back up in front of the Oni and hits him with his sword across the face. Again, the blade isn't able to break through skin, but it does knock the Oni's head to the side and disorient him.

"Can the thing not die?" Dex asks. "If Phoenix can't even make it bleed, how will this ever end?"

"I don't think an Oni can be killed. I only know it doesn't stop till it succeeds."

"And that doesn't concern you?"

"It's after Phoenix," I say. "I figure he has some kind of plan to deal with it."

The cheers of the crowd drown out even the music. They're so sure Phoenix will win this fight but they also think it's all fake, choreographed. Clearly Phoenix looks like the good guy in this scenario, and the good guy must be scripted to win. Still, I know it's real, and I still assume Phoenix will figure it out and win.

Am I just as clueless as everyone else here? I mean, worst case scenario, Phoenix dies. Is that bad? I wonder if I have time to make a pros and cons list. I guess I kind of need him to figure out what's going on with the Subject System and the Council.

The crowd near the kitchen door is backing away, all except Vanessa, who is staring right at the Oni because he is now focused solely on her, his head having been turned toward that direction when Phoenix last hit him. He moves fully to face Vanessa.

Imagine being so evil you distract an Oni from his hired job.

"Dex, get Vanessa out of here," I tell him.

Dex runs to Vanessa's side. The Oni ROARS, having found his new target.

Vanessa actually laughs, still thinking this is all an act. All the others who had been standing in the kitchen doorway with Vanessa and cheering before have backed away and look like they're having to work harder to convince themselves this is all fake. Yet, Vanessa stands there and laughs off Dex's warning.

The Oni charges. Phoenix looks about ready to teleport right into his path. I scan the multiple bowls of candy sitting on the kitchen counter and pick one up. There's no way this works.

I dump the round gum balls out onto the floor. They roll right into the Oni's path, crushing under his heavy feet. When he goes to take his next step toward Vanessa, his foot is stuck. He tries the other foot. Stuck, too. He pulls harder, and I can see the pink gum stretch up from the floor to the bottom of his foot.

There are some mutterings from the onlookers about how cool the gum trick is and how it seemed so real that the monster was going to hurt Vanessa for a second, and then the Oni pulls free from the gum with a loud, frustrated groan.

Phoenix slides between the Oni's legs and stands up right in front of him, drawing the Oni's attention back to him before he can focus on Vanessa again.

Vanessa, not even phased, continues to cheer for Phoenix. She literally swats Dex aside like an annoying mosquito when he tries to convince her she should still get out of here.

"I could have let her die," I tell myself.

Phoenix, unnaturally fast, runs around and around the Oni's legs. The Oni keeps trying to swipe at him, but he's clearly getting dizzy trying to keep up with where Phoenix is at any given moment.

The Oni stomps, and the floor of the house breaks under the weight of his foot. The wood floor splinters and broken planks lift up like disturbed tectonic plates. Cracks in the wood spider out across the kitchen floor. Phoenix trips against the now uneven floor and barely manages to catch himself before he falls. He's getting tired, and I still don't see any big plan of his playing out.

A Kanabō, almost as long as the Oni is tall, appears in the Oni's hand. It looks like a big wooden bat with sharp, metal spikes sticking out of it.

There are gasps from the crowd. One hit from that weapon and I don't care how durable Phoenix is, he won't be all right. The Oni raises the Kanabō, and I'm surprised it doesn't hit the roof.

Next thing I know, I'm standing in front of Phoenix, staring up at the Oni, the Kanabō about two feet away from our heads.

My body is buzzing like I just sprinted at full speed, and my knees threaten to collapse, but that may have more to do with the fact that I've run directly into life-threatening danger.

The Oni stops, the Kanabō frozen above our heads. I hear and feel Phoenix breathe out very slowly in relief. The Oni looks between me and Phoenix. His eyes are two wells of dark blue ink.

It looks like the color moves around, swirling, as if moving with his thoughts. He lowers the Kanabō to his side.

I don't dare move as he walks around us, through the kitchen, and back out the broken window, where he disappears in the darkness.

I don't know what just happened. The crowd remains outside the kitchen. It's like the kitchen is a taped off crime scene or, depending on one's viewpoint, a stage, and they don't have backstage passes, let alone access to the stage itself. Their commentary is ongoing.

"He's just leaving?" I hear someone question.

What I know is, I knew the Oni wouldn't kill me. He was after Phoenix after all.

"That was kind of anti-climactic," another says.

"Shut up. It was cool."

I would not risk my life for Phoenix. Right? Definitely not. I knew the Oni wouldn't kill me. *Hindsight bias is 20/20,* some other part of me reminds me, but I tell that part that I really did know I'd be fine.

"Why'd the monster just stop, though?"

"That's the point! We're supposed to be left questioning and talking about it."

Dex is walking up to me.

"Dawn?" Dex asks. "You okay?"

I just met Dex the other day. Still, I feel I would have missed him if I'd just died.

There's something strange about him, like the whole suit thing seems like just the tip of the iceberg in the strange department but I like the guy. I think. I'm not dead, though. All is good. Plus, I've died before, not squashed by a Kanabō, but I'm not afraid of dying. Except, I kind of need more time in this life to figure out the whole Subject System thing.

"Yeah," I tell him. "Yes." Dex doesn't look like he believes me.

"Are you always this self-sacrificing?" he asks.

"Thanks, by the way," Phoenix says.

I look behind me to find him by the broken window. His sword is gone, and he's brushing the shattered glass up against the wall with his foot, as if he really cares if some random kid here were to step on the glass and hurt their foot. He stops the clean up job to look at me.

"The only way to get rid of an Oni tasked with killing a supposed evil-doer is for an innocent to put him or herself between the Oni and its target," he explains.

So that's why it just left after I stepped between it and Phoenix. But, "innocent?" As a Subject myself, that's never really been a word used to describe me. The Oni must judge innocence relatively. As in, compared to Phoenix, I looked like an angel.

"You could've mentioned that earlier," I tell him.

"It wouldn't have worked if I told you to do it. You had to do it on your own accord."

"Well, I knew I'd be fine."

"Did you?" he asks, sounding extremely skeptical, not to mention his grin that also indicates he highly doubts it.

"Who do you think sent the Oni after you?" Dex asks.

"Whoever's behind the Subject System and manipulating the Council must be onto the fact that I'm onto them," Phoenix answers. "Here's to hoping they stay ignorant of your involvement."

Apparently the awe has worn off enough that those who were crowded outside the kitchen have gathered the courage to actually enter because they swarm Phoenix, pushing Dex and me aside. I try to find the gaps so I can avoid being completely, blindly run over.

"I didn't know you were an actor!" Vanessa says, touching Phoenix's arm, tagging him as hers. "You look like one, though."

I make it over to the kitchen counter and push myself up onto it to sit. It's as far away from Phoenix and the crowd as I can get without actually leaving the kitchen. I seem to have lost Dex in the bustle. The sea of costumes makes it harder to find someone than usual.

"Where'd you learn to fight like that?" I hear someone ask Phoenix. Wait, that's Ryan. Is he not at all concerned about the state of his house?

"Is it stage fighting?" someone else adds. "Do you have to take actual martial arts lessons for stage fighting?"

"Or maybe," I shout to Phoenix over his fan club, "the Oni was sent by one of the other many people you've pissed off."

Phoenix spots me through the crowd and smiles.

"Is that your way of confessing?" he shouts back.

"I'd rather kill you with my own hands."

"Such sweet words."

Yeah, I guess I don't really believe it either. Phoenix has upset plenty of people over the years but the timing of this would be too coincidental. Someone out there is not happy about Phoenix investigating the Subject System.

Vanessa, confused, looks at Phoenix. "Who are you talking to?"

Phoenix points to his ear, where an air pod is suddenly conveniently visible.

"My agent," he tells her.

CHAPTER 15

I move the mashed potatoes around on my plate, the one food item this cafeteria can't manage to make inedible. I add more salt, enough to keep any ghost away. Ironically, I'm the only thing in here that's been dead. Well, and Dex.

Where is Dex? I could've sworn he was sitting across this lunch table from me only a second ago.

I turn to look around the cafeteria for him but Phoenix, having just walked up, blocks my view. I come face to face with the front of his t-shirt as he sits down on the bench beside me. It says, in black writing, "I'm not arrogant. I'm just awesome."

"I forgot to mention I ran into Eros the other day while you were off causing trouble. I hadn't realized you two had met," Phoenix says.

Wow, is that salty. I swallow down a big spoonful of mashed potatoes. It's good though.

I saw Eros once on my way into a Council meeting. I don't know what he was meeting with them about. I tried to get that information out of him but, unsurprisingly, he was a big flirt and wasn't very informative. He was surprisingly nice and not entirely annoying.

"Yeah, we did."

"He told me to say hi to you."

"Tell him hi," I say, smiling at the memory of the pretty decent conversation Eros and I had a while ago.

"I know it's my job to send messages but that's just a bit dull," Phoenix complains. "You know, he still hasn't gotten over the fact that you didn't swoon at the sight of him. Now, do you have more of a message for me to deliver?"

"No one swoons anymore. Anyway, that can't have been the first time that happened to him. And no, hi will suffice."

"One swoons for the Celestial considered by many as the god of love. You do know he's been considered as the god of love across multiple cultures for a reason, right? So, why weren't you charmed?"

"Charmed?" I repeat, laughing. "Is that what he is? Charming? He is nice enough, considering he's a Celestial. Why do you actually care about this? Is this truly such a concern for Eros?" I ask, and then something slightly horrifying occurs to me. "Oh my. You're not his father or something, right? I can't keep track of how you all are related. Are you personally offended by me turning down your son?"

Phoenix raises his eyebrows, stunned. He lets out a short laugh, which it sounds like he half chokes on.

"That took a turn," he says. "But, no, that wouldn't even be possible, as we're both Celestials. All Celestials are part of the second generation. I also do not have any sons... or children, for that matter."

"Oh, right."

Phoenix grabs the apple off my lunch tray, the only thing other than the mashed potatoes that I had planned on eating and takes a loud, crunchy bite out of it.

"Anyway," he continues, "Eros cares because he's always looking for ways to improve his craft - love and desire, the lust type of desire—"

"Yeah, I got it," I interrupt, when it sounds like Phoenix is gonna go on to further describe the concept.

One might think I wouldn't be a prude after lifetimes of living. One might be wrong.

Thing is, many of the years I lived through, it was common for most people to be prudes, at least to the outside world. Plus, I rarely live past my teen years. I've never been married, and I'm apparently genetically predisposed to keep people at a distance.

Prude might be the wrong word but another blush was definitely on its way if I let Phoenix continue. Not to mention, Phoenix is well aware of all of this and seems to get a certain joy out of getting a reaction out of me. Not appreciated.

"It is practically his job," Phoenix concludes.

"You may tell him," I say, snatching the apple back from out of his hand, "no offense intended, but he's just not my type."

Phoenix looks skeptical. His eyebrow with the scar rises up to a dark piece of hair that falls over his forehead.

"Your type isn't a man who literally magically personifies beauty?"

"I guess not. Maybe he's just too perfect, and looking at perfection can get boring. Boring isn't charming, for me, at least," I answer, and can't help myself from studying Phoenix in comparison. The scar that cuts through his right eyebrow throws off the symmetry of his face.

I wonder what the scar is from and why it never healed in the supernatural way that all his other injuries heal. I mean, at the party, he blocked me and Dex from getting hit with multiple shards of broken glass from that window, and he came out without a scratch.

"I'll let him know," Phoenix says, smiling. "He'll appreciate having this information, I'm sure."

"Was there something else? News about another Subject or something, who sent the Oni?" I ask.

I watch Phoenix watch me deliberately bite out of the apple from the opposite side he had. Do Celestials have normal germs?

"No, just here for the pleasure of your company," he says, making me question even more why he is actually here, with possible scenarios ranging from spy on me for the Council to stealing my apple.

"You ensured that they," I say, pointing around the room in a circular motion, as if the Council members are this omniscient presence, which they are not, at least not anymore with the griffon on Phoenix's side, "couldn't see what's going on so we don't have to pretend to be friends this time."

Phoenix looks for something in my expression. There's that sole attention he's so good at giving. I find myself wishing that whatever he's looking for he finds it.

"You're right," he says. "I'll see you around then."

"Okay," I say, but he's gone before the word's left my mouth.

CHAPTER 16

Two whole weeks later

After hours spent catching up on homework, it's a relief to arrive at the dog shelter for volunteering. Unfortunately, there's little left to do by the time I show up.

Everyone's left for the day. The dogs' empty dinner bowls sit on the floor of the cages waiting to be taken out and cleaned in the morning. I, too, probably should've gotten dinner rather than coming here, but I actually have come to enjoy my time volunteering.

I clear out the bowls so the morning shift will have one less thing to do and take some of the dogs out for an extra walk.

The wind chimes attached to the door ring out, as I walk back in with Frank, a pug named after *the* Frank in *Men in Black.* Lazily, I lean my back against the door to get it open instead of going through the effort of lifting my hand to push it open. I look down at Frank, who sits patiently on the sidewalk outside, as he waits for me to literally put my back into it.

"He told me, 'I'll see you around,'" I tell the dog. "Can you believe that, Frank? It's been weeks."

I give Frank's leash a little tug, and he follows me through the door. Turning around, I almost bump into Dex on his way out.

Dex's suit jacket is carelessly thrown over his shoulder and he's unbuttoned the top buttons of his gray dress shirt. I realize his shoes don't match the rest of his look. Instead of dress shoes, he wears black converse that are dirty from wear. I wonder if I just hadn't realized them before or if he's pulled them out from the back of his closet. His dark hair isn't styled in its usual way, with gel firmly holding it in place. The straight strands now fall messily into his face.

I guess I'm not the only one left at this hour.

"Oh, hey," he says, startled, and then clears his throat, seeming to collect himself. "Hello. I apologize for my appearance. I think I hit myself with the hose water more than the dogs when I was washing them earlier. They kept hitting the hose, which would make me drop it and spray myself in the face with the water."

"It happens," I tell him. "I recommend keeping them on their leash and tying it to something before bathing them next time, keeps them from moving around too much."

"Were you talking to Frank?"

I look down at Frank. He's looking up at me, as if we've both been caught doing something stupid.

"Why do you always wear suits?" I question.

"My parents always say 'dress to impress,'" Dex says, pulling himself up to stand taller.

"How about 'know your audience,' which is a room full of dogs in your case."

"I don't know, I think Frank would approve of my attire."

"Should we ask him?" I say, cracking a smile. "I was just going to bring Frank back in and then head out."

I expect Dex to say bye and leave for the day; but instead, he follows me back into the hallway with the dogs' cages.

Even though we've been spending a considerable amount of time together in school since he came with Phoenix a couple weeks back, I'm still not used to the idea of having someone I could actually call a friend in this life. It's especially odd because he actually knows of and understands my situation. But, I guess that is what he is. A friend.

In school, we've started a sort of friendly competition to see who can do the most good things in the most ridiculous way to help other people out.

The other day, some guy tripped in the hallway and instead of trying to help catch him, Dex just threw himself down on the floor to cushion his fall. The method was effective and extra entertaining to see the surrounding students' reactions. They all stared at Dex.

Even the guy he'd helped just gave him an odd look before walking away, but Dex didn't seem to mind what they thought. He even gave a little speech after to the remaining students about the importance of doing for others, how helping one person can have a domino effect if that person then helps another and so on and so forth.

I haven't seen much of him outside of school, though, despite also volunteering at the same place. As someone who's familiar with keeping others at a safe distance, I can recognize when the same is being done to me. For whatever reason, Dex is determined to keep our time spent together limited. And yet, here he is now.

As I put Frank back in his cage, Dex throws his jacket on the long table across from the cages and sits on top of it. I would think he'd be concerned about wrinkling it but maybe he figures it's too late for that anyways.

"You did tell him to leave you alone."

I hop up onto the table to sit beside him. "Who?" I ask, even though clearly I know who it is he refers to.

"Phoenix. Heard of him?"

"Funny. Yes, but he hasn't talked to me for two weeks, and there are things I need to be kept informed about."

Dex doesn't bother to respond. He just stares at me, an eyebrow raised in challenge.

"Okay," I relent. "I did tell him he could, you know, leave me alone, but I didn't tell him to leave me alone."

"I see. That is a significant difference," Dex says, a small, amused smile revealing itself.

Frank pads across the floor and plops down onto his stomach right behind the door of his cage. He rests his head on his paws and stares inquisitively up at me and Dex, as if he's interested in joining the conversation. I wish he could. Maybe he would support my judgment of Phoenix.

"Serious question," Dex says.

Frank tilts his head to the side. Same, Frank. I don't know where this is going either.

"Shoot," I tell him.

"Okay, if you could choose to be a Celestial, what would be your choice, taking into account their individual abilities and such?" he asks.

"Seriously?"

"Seriously. Why? Do you think I should instead be asking you about more important questions related to our reality, which is already complicated enough?"

"No, why would you do that?"

"I wouldn't. So, what's your answer?" Dex asks.

I look at Dex, attempting to analyze his face. He looks genuinely curious so I give into the conversation.

"I have to think about it," I say.

"You haven't?"

"No, have you?"

"Of course," he says, as if offended I would even consider that he hadn't.

"Well, who?"

"Phoenix, definitely."

"You are clearly not informed enough to make this decision because why in all of Havcire and Vest would you want that?"

I look to Frank as if he'll share my astonishment at Dex's answer but the dog has fallen asleep.

"For one, have you seen the guy?" Dex says, raising his eyebrows. "And, he always seems one step ahead of everyone else. I'm glad I'm on his good side because it seems to me to be the winning side. Plus, he can teleport."

"Dex, he wins because he's always tricking everyone else. Where's the honor in that?"

"What's this you speak of? Honor? He's not some fictional knight, Dawn."

"Actually," I say, "the stories of King Arthur and his knights are another interpretation of the Celestials, supposedly."

"Now I feel like you're helping to prove my point," Dex says, as I narrow my eyes at him. "Anyway, Phoenix has good intentions."

"I have never considered him to be well intentioned."

"Yes, but you don't judge him realistically."

"Why would you say that?"

"You can't see the whole picture with your nose up against the canvas," Dex says.

I openly stare at Dex for a minute. He seems invested in a piece of thread that has come loose from around the button on his sleeve. The way he eyes the loose piece of thread makes me think of the way one might regard a hole in a hazmat suit.

"Tell me, should I know what you mean by that?"

"Have you decided?" Dex asks, having left the thread behind after wrapping it around the button a number of times.

"Yes," I admit on a sigh, "Styx."

"The river in Greek mythology?" he asks, raising a charcoal eyebrow that gets lost beneath the mess of his normally neatly gelled back hair.

"She's actually a Celestial who guards the River Styx in Havcire. It's one of the few portals from Havcire to Vest that still remains open."

"So, why Styx then?"

I push myself further back on the table so I can lean comfortably against the wall behind us. I think back to the one time I saw Styx through a tile in the Ziggurat hallway.

She was sitting on a large rock beside the river, her long, white hair blowing behind her in the wind. She turned in my direction; and although impossible, I could have sworn she looked directly at me through the tile. Not a moment later, the river and she disappeared as the tiles shifted back into their opaque marble, her mercury eyes gone.

Later, I'd forced all the information I could out of Max, refusing to get in the tub until he gave me something.

"I've heard little about Havcire's history over the years, but I have picked up some things."

"Picked up?" Dex asks.

"Sorry, I've forced information out of unsuspecting Havcirians," I clarify with a smile.

"Got it."

"After the separation between Havcire and Vest," I continue, "there was a power struggle of sorts. Styx fought on the side of the Incanters to help ensure that the Celestials wouldn't be given more authority and power merely because they were second generation."

"She turned against her own people?" Dex asks.

"She chose what she thought was the worthy fight and let that define her rather than the blood that ran through her veins."

"Sounds to me like you respect a Celestial. Maybe you don't dislike them as much as you claim," Dex says, smiling as if he knew exactly what my answer would be. Or, maybe he just always intended to find a way to reach that conclusion regardless of my answer.

Again, something about Dex strikes me as unusual. Unusual is quite usual in my life but something doesn't add up about him. And yet, I feel like I should like him, like there's something just good about him. Maybe it's that he reminds me of someone I'm fond of, but I can't think of who that would be.

That came out wrong. There are plenty of people I've liked and cared for in past lives, it's just that none of them remind me specifically of Dex or vice versa.

"It's not about like or dislike. We're both stuck in these lives because of the Celestials and their Subject System," I point out.

"Are we?" he asks. "I mean, the being who really started the Subject System could be something else entirely, not even a Celestial. And, even so, you'll judge all the Celestials based on one's actions?"

"I—" am a horrible, prejudiced person apparently. No, it's not true that I dislike all the Celestials just because of the Subject System, but I am possibly unfairly weary of them. I've always associated them all with the Subject System. "I'm just saying that I admire Styx's actions," I continue. "There's also the whole she can make others invincible thing that is pretty cool."

"All right, keep denying that you are team Celestial," he says, taunting.

"There are no teams," I say, rolling my eyes, "but, if anything, I'm team Vest."

Dex clears his throat. He shifts, scooting back so he can sit up taller. He stretches his neck. These are signs of either someone who's restless or someone who has something they're reluctant to do.

"I really hate to ruin this nice sharing thing we got going here, but I think there's something you'd like to know," he says.

"What is it?"

"I went with Phoenix to see another Subject in Colorado. He was part of an experiment dealing with antisocial personality, and we went to prevent him from being placed with an abusive family in foster care," Dex says, seemingly in one breath.

"I missed a trip to Colorado? I love Colorado," I exclaim, glum, before reminding myself that's not the point. "Sorry, and by that I mean, why didn't he tell me so I could come along?"

"Phoenix told me it would be best if you didn't come."

"Oh, Phoenix said so, did he?" I take a breath, reminding myself that Dex is just the messenger and to save my killing for Phoenix, ironically the official messenger of the Celestials. So, I *can* kill a messenger. "Why?" I ask instead. "What did he claim was the reason for me not coming?"

"I didn't ask him to expand on his reasoning."

"Why not?" I ask, working to keep it together.

"I figured he had a good reason."

"Never figure that."

"Consider it noted."

"Thank you," I say with a smile.

Dex leans against the wall, seemingly relieved to discover he's gotten through his report unscathed.

"Phoenix does often seem sincere, though. Like I said before, good intentions," Dex says, backtracking, and my smile fades.

"This conversation is over," I say, pushing myself up from the table. "You're hopeless."

"Oh, I'm just kidding. Kind of," Dex yells after me, as I walk ahead to the front doors.

Meeting me at the front, he tosses me the keys to lock up behind us.

"Nice mythology knowledge by the way," I say, "knowing about Styx in Greek mythology. Have you been studying?"

"I have actually. Thank you for noticing."

154

CHAPTER 17

Walking onto the school field, I pull my backpack open and retrieve the football I'd found in it after my fourth period class.

I shouldn't be surprised to find Phoenix lying on his back on the bleachers, as I suspected the football was a message to meet him here, but it's been a while since I've seen or heard from him.

He looks comfortable, with one jean covered leg bent at the knee, his foot resting atop the bleacher and the other leg hanging off the edge of the bleacher, his foot brushing against the grass on the ground. His green t-shirt, darker than the green of his eyes, matches the grass almost perfectly. He has one arm stretched back behind his head. It pulls the shirt up at the hem, exposing a bit of his muscled stomach.

I throw the football at him. As it passes right above his face and is about to hit his knee, Phoenix, at an unnatural speed, reaches up with both hands and plucks the football from the air. He tosses it up and catches it again before swinging his legs forward to sit upright.

"Hey," he says, nonchalantly, throwing the football out towards the field with perfect form.

The football blips out of existence and appears back near the locker rooms to drop into the bin that holds the other sports equipment.

"Yeah, hi. What motivated you to come to school today?" I ask.

"Yeah, hi? Is that how you greet everyone these days?" Phoenix asks, ignoring my question.

"Yeah," I say, figuring that if I don't give into a conversation regarding my greeting techniques, he'll give into answering my question so I can ask him what I actually came here to ask him about.

"I'm here," Phoenix says after a few minutes of us both being stubborn and not saying anything, "because I had a feeling you had something you wanted to discuss with me."

"You had a feeling?" I ask. "Is that some Celestial superpower you neglected to tell me about, feelings? Do you get vibes, too?"

"Possibly," Phoenix says, half-smiling, "but it's not exactly a secret. You know I specialize in delivering messages between people and worlds, so I tend to sense whenever there's a message that needs delivering. Otherwise, how would the message get to me that there's a message that needs delivering if I couldn't deliver the message to myself?"

"I guess that technically makes sense," I admit, sitting down on the bleachers next to him. "About that message you're here for. You knew I would want to go help another Subject so why didn't you tell me about it?"

"I didn't involve you for your own benefit—"

My short laugh cuts Phoenix off.

"You're going to have to be more believable than that," I tell him.

I am to remain calm. That was my plan. If I remain calm, I have a better chance of staying focused and getting a real answer out of Phoenix. This is me reminding myself of this.

"I'll do my best," Phoenix says. "What you did for Helen and Melanie must have significantly decreased your sentence. I didn't want the Celestials getting too suspicious with another decrease like that so soon," he explains.

He makes an alright point. I glare at him anyways.

"I really like Colorado," I say, and I feel my traitorous face lose its glare and morph into a pout.

"Well, if I'd known that..."

"Still, then why did you keep it from me?" I ask.

All I get in response is a shrug.

"That's it? You've got nothing?" I ask, incredulously.

"I just didn't think about it. I have a lot going on you know. My only job isn't to go to school, which is good because I would not be doing very well if that were the case."

"Do you think I want my 'job' to be to go to school for the thousandth time and play the role of this isolated teenager?" I ask, standing up from the bleachers, my voice rising along with me.

"Do you think I want to worry every second about if I could be doing more, if I could be doing something that would make me be considered a better person according to some scale I'm not privy to?"

Calm is so overrated.

"You could have fooled me," Phoenix says, making it sound like some sort of challenge.

"What's that supposed to mean?"

Phoenix stands up to face me.

"It seems to me like that *is* what you want. You go right along with Max's experiment, playing the role he's set for you. I gave you all your memories back, and you're still just attempting to beat an unbeatable system."

"Nothing's unbeatable," I insist.

"How admirable that you think that but it is unbeatable when there's someone on the other side cheating, ensuring that no one can in fact beat it."

"So then I'll just cheat also!"

"You'd never, and the fact that you could've done practically whatever you wanted with this life but you remained the dutiful Subject is evidence of exactly that."

Before I process what I'm doing, Phoenix is stumbling backwards, righting himself before he falls.

I pushed him, and I'm not even completely sure why, but I know I don't regret it at the moment. Phoenix looks a little startled, but not surprised. He knew he was bating me. He just didn't expect me to physically push back.

"You wouldn't understand," I say, and contradictorily open my mouth to explain. "The Subject System has trapped me for centuries. This was my chance to really try, to give this life all I had. I didn't know it was rigged."

"Or," Phoenix says, closing the distance between us again, risking another possible explosion from me, "it could have been your chance to let go and enjoy a life, for the most part, under your own control."

"For the most part," I echo. "Is that all I'll ever get?"

I hear how pathetic I sound. I practically sound like I'm begging for pity. It's not pity or sympathy that heats up Phoenix's eyes, though. I'm not sure what it is but it may be the first real emotion I've seen from him in all my lifetimes.

The icy eye thing he had going on is gone. The color now reminds me of that chemistry lab, where the flame changes color depending on what substance is burning. Copper made the flame green. I'm almost tempted to fan him down. Of course, if he's a living flame, that would only make him burn more.

"What makes you think that anyone has complete control?" he asks. "We're all forced to react to what we can't see coming."

I know he has a point.

"But, we don't all get treated like lab rats," I counter.

Subjects are the ones forced to become an Experimenter's lab rat but maybe I really do deserve all of this, and there's the pity again. Actually, my experience is more comparable to a guinea pig on one of those wheels, going around and around. Do rats also use those wheels?

Phoenix looks about to say more but something catches his eye across the field.

A girl walks toward us from across the field. It's still lunch time so no one should be out here.

Phoenix looks hastily back at me.

"Forget everything I just said," he says, urgently. "Be a good Subject, and act like Haley Dawson."

All traces of our conversation disappear from Phoenix's expression. Goodbye fiery eyes, and hello nonchalant smile. Sure, we were just having a normal, friendly conversation. I force myself to look convincingly upbeat like Phoenix, as the girl approaches.

It is clear she is a Celestial. Something about her just screams Celestial, or maybe everything about her.

To start, her hair not only looks golden like a ray of sun but it actually seems to shine like each strand is a piece of light. It makes my past concerns about my light brown hair, with its sparse golden highlights, drawing attention seem even more ridiculous. Her long and elegant face allows her to pull off the fringe bangs that fall just above her slightly darker eyebrows and onto her ivory skin.

We wait for her to say something. She is the one who walked up to us, but she stands there staring at us expectantly with narrow, almond-shaped brown eyes.

"Hi," I say, breaking the silence, "I'm Haley. Are you new at the school?" I am horrified to hear my anxious, random British accent come out on its own accord, as my voice rises naturally to pose the question.

I hear Phoenix stifle a laugh at my side. This Celestial is going to think me completely bonkers.

"Fairly new, yes," she responds, managing to ignore me even though I asked the question. Instead, she looks only at Phoenix. Typical.

"Principle Abernathy said you could show me around the school. It's Phoenix, right?" she continues, with a smile that doesn't quite reach her eyes.

I get the feeling that her eyes aren't much accustomed to showing a wide range of emotion.

"Right. And, of course, I'll show you around," Phoenix replies, before turning to me. "I'll see you after school."

"Bye," I say, good-naturedly. I even continue smiling as they walk away.

East Olympic High does not give welcome tours administered by students. Even if they did, the principal would not assign the new student to Phoenix of all people, who may or may not attend school enough to know one building from another.

I watch them walk into the boys' locker room off to the side of the football field, as if that would be a part of the tour. However, it is somewhere that would surely be empty right now. I watch the door shut behind them. And then, I follow.

CHAPTER 18

Phoenix made the decision on his own that it wasn't necessary to inform me about the Subjects. Who's to say he won't think it necessary to tell me about whatever is about to be discussed? Naturally, the only solution is to eavesdrop on their conversation and find out for myself.

I make sure to close the door quietly behind me as I enter the locker room.

Their voices drift towards me, originating from behind the second set of lockers to my left. I stand up against the lockers on the opposite side from where they talk. Grimacing from the everlasting smell of sweaty gym clothes, I focus on what they're saying.

"What are you doing here, Lada?" Phoenix asks.

I've heard mention of Lada before. Finally meeting her in person, I can see how her name, taken from the Slavic goddess of beauty, is perfectly fitting. I'd say she has ample proof to believe she is the Celestial from which the myth of Lada originated.

"I'm here to assist Havcire and do my job, as I should," Lada says, coming off sounding a bit self-righteous.

"Do your job?" Phoenix asks, skeptical. "You don't have a job. You've always made sure of that. What is it you always say? 'We separated from Vest for a reason—'"

"'And we should honor that decision,'" she says, finishing Phoenix's quoting of herself. "I am aware of my own words, thank you. But, you know I have turned over a new leaf, and now I'm working to prove myself useful to the Council so that I might be given more responsibility and have more of a say," Lada responds, indignantly.

"Well, that seems likely, darling," Phoenix says, sarcastically, in a purely British accent, much more accurate than my nervous habit.

All those native to Havcire, Celestials and Incanters, have accents that sound unlike any particular Vestigium accent. I've heard Phoenix speak fluently in multiple languages throughout my lives. Then again, so have I, depending on where Max placed me to grow up for each particular life. But, Phoenix has always spoken as if he never became linguistically dominant in any one language but, instead, simultaneously proficient in all. Although, in this life, so far, he has pulled off an American accent, with only hints of others sneaking in periodically.

"So then," Phoenix is saying, "what exactly is the job you were sent down here to do?"

"Keep an eye on you, of course. And Dawn. Her points have seemingly unnaturally gone up recently. You wouldn't have any idea what that's about, would you?"

"Other than the fact that in this life she's irritatingly a goody two-shoes, which makes it really difficult to pretend to be her friend? No. She's real into volunteering, helping people, saving the world, and all that jazz. Perhaps the loneliness really brings out her Mother Teresa," Phoenix responds, sounding convincingly irritated with my supposed saint-like qualities.

"All that jazz?" Lada asks. "You know I don't know all these Vest references. Most Celestials don't spend the majority of their time here like you do."

"Oh, come on. And all... that... jazz..." Phoenix says, singing the lyrics. I might acknowledge that he sounds pretty damn good, his voice low and—

"Anyways," Lada goes on, "I'm here to make sure there's nothing suspicious about how she's gaining points. And, to make sure you're not up to anything. I know Max actually sent you down this time but I know you, and I know you can't be trusted when it comes to Dawn."

Wow, people know of me. Lada knows of me.

Wait. What's that supposed to mean? I almost move out from behind the lockers to ask Lada that very question but I force myself to stay still and quiet.

"What?" Phoenix scoffs. "I stopped having anything to do with Dawn a long time ago, and I'm only here now because Max sent me down, like you said. Plus, you know the only reason I even dealt with Dawn to begin with was to mess with Max and the experiment."

"Yeah, sure," Lada says, dropping the air of formality. "That's why you chose to stay for years with her and went through the effort of getting the griffon to lie for you so no one would find out. At least, until we did and Max was forced to officially make you a variable to fix your mess. Barnabas had to literally drag you away from Vest."

What?

"Believe what you want, but that was the most successful sabotage of an experiment I've ever done; and frankly, I'm proud of the work I did," Phoenix responds smugly, despite Lada's goading.

Phoenix wasn't working with Max during my twentieth life like everyone led me to believe.

If I could find any air in my lungs at the moment, an involuntary gasp would surely escape. Thankfully, I can't because the smallest sound would surely give me away.

But, why would they lie to me about it? It's not like knowing the truth would have affected any of my other lives. I wouldn't have remembered it anyway. Why would *he* have kept the truth from me? Why—?

The school bell trills, saving me from further spiraling. Lada, very un-Celestial like, curses, at which I can't help but smile.

"We have to finish talking later."

"Sure," Phoenix says, begrudgingly.

"You should know, I'll be watching both you and Dawn," Lada says.

"Thanks for the heads up."

Someone should tell her that it's most effective to spy on people if you don't first inform them about the fact that you intend to do so.

My breath, having found it again, catches as I realize the direction from which Lada's footfalls are sounding. Also, not great to get caught eavesdropping.

Quickly, and as quietly as I can, I step into one of the lockers. As my weight shifts onto the flimsy metal floor, I make sure not to lift my foot again and cause the echoing sound of the metal popping back up. I close the door just in time to avoid them spotting me.

Through the slits, I can see Lada and then Phoenix round the corner. They both walk out the door that leads back out to the field without taking notice of me. When the door closes behind them, I let out a breath I hadn't realized I'd been holding in. I push on the locker door but it doesn't budge.

Oh no.

The boys' locker rooms have the type of lockers that lock automatically when you close them, the ones that need to be opened with the combination from the outside. Of course, what would be the point of being able to open a locker from the inside? Unless, like an idiot, you happened to lock yourself inside of one.

I take a calming breath, attempting to search for where the locker latches closed. Maybe I can find a way to break the lock from inside. It's too tight inside for me to bend my neck to look down so I have to try to feel around with the little space I have.

I'm not exactly claustrophobic but I also don't care for being trapped, especially within small spaces. The only source of light is through the slits in the door.

1941

I wish I could see less. The slits in the flimsy closet door are big enough to let in enough light so that I can see my own body in the dark closet. The yellow star pinned on my shirt is too bright, and I wish I could melt into the shadows, blending in with the grayness of the world around me.

If I can see myself, then they can find me. They can find us.

I shift to look behind me, careful that even the small movement doesn't rustle the clothes in here. I can hear that no one's in the house, at least not right now, but I still feel the need to do everything quietly. I breathe softer and blink slower.

Behind the clothes, Sam is hidden, crouched down. Thank god for the long dresses my mother once forced me to wear, that now serve as another layer to shield my brother from sight, myself being the first line of defense if it came to that.

I had questioned what role appearance played when selling bread at our family bakery. The people came to eat, not to look at me from across the counter. They didn't care what I looked like. If they ever did, they for sure couldn't care less now. Unless, of course, they were scouting for certain traits that have nothing to do with attire.

I guess I was wrong after all. Appearance turned out to matter more than I could have ever imagined and carried consequences far beyond being good or bad for business.

We no longer have our bakery, and food is a very well hidden treasure.

"The deportations are over!" a man's voice shouts from outside. "Those left may come out for food!"

Sam gasps and bumps into my leg, eager to get out and get food, but I bend down more to face him better before he can reach past me for the closet doors. I flinch at the sound my shoes make against the wood floor of the closet but it's nothing in comparison to what would happen if I let him run out of here.

I place a hand flat against his chest, which feels awfully too bony, to hold him back. My other hand I rest against the side of his face, a technique that always works to calm him, as if it reminds him to use his head and think first.

"You cannot go," I whisper. "They know how hungry we all are. It is a trick. We must hold out here for a bit longer."

Sam deflates. There will be no food out that door, only a one-way ticket to a foreign place that will offer no reprieve. At eight, he shouldn't have to understand all of this but, at the same time, I'm also thankful he does understand exactly what I mean.

He nods his head slowly and quietly leans back against the wall, pulling his knees to his chest.

The front door bangs open, cracking against the wall. The sound is startling but what's worse are the heavy footsteps that follow.

I close my eyes, ironically wishing they were brown so they wouldn't draw any attention in the dark room. Even closed, I can see in my mind the black, shiny boots of the soldier.

He walks around the room, throwing our belongings on the floor as he searches. The cacophony he causes helps mask the thundering of my heart. I take advantage of the chaos, leaning in closer to Sam.

"No matter what, stay hidden and stay quiet. Always," I tell him.

"Evie," Sam pleads.

There is no other option.

I kiss Sam on the forehead and turn back to face the front of the closet doors, keeping my head lowered, focused on the floor outside the closet. As the soldier steps near, I no longer hear anything. It's as if I've submerged under water, only a slight ringing through my ears. I watch him reach out to open the doors. Before he can, I push them open, hitting him hard with the doors as they fly open.

With the soldier distracted, looking the other way, attempting to stop his bleeding nose, I step out of the closet and close the doors behind me, Sam safe inside. The soldier turns back to me, his face red with anger and his own blood, but he's completely and only focused on me.

The locker door swings open, unlocked. I swipe an escaped tear from my face and waste no more time getting out of that locker and out of the locker room. Phoenix is waiting outside for me.

CHAPTER 19

It had actually slipped my mind that my spying on him and Lada was the reason I was stuck in that locker to begin with.

I have yet to lose my mind in a past life, but having all these memories finally back in my head might be enough to do the trick.

I attempt to ignore Phoenix, walking around him. Rather than listen to any lies that could confuse everything even more, I think I'd have better luck figuring things out with a few silent moments alone. Still, when he loudly clears his throat from behind me, I stop and turn back to talk.

"Yes?" I ask, noticeably peeved.

"I assume you heard everything Lada and I discussed," he says, pausing for a second for me to contradict him if I hadn't. When I don't say anything, he continues. "So, you know I was never working with Max."

"All is well then, right?" I ask, sarcastically. "Should we also address the fact that you still lied me about that life even if it wasn't in the way I'd previously thought? Or, what about the most recent omission about visiting the Subject, which you didn't actually explain? And, let's not forget about your belief that I've wasted away this life of mine so far."

"I didn't realize you kept such close track of these things. Did you make an official list of grievances?"

"No need. My mind is extremely organized when it comes to remembering your misdeeds."

"Fine. Maybe we can come to an agreement then. If you agree to help me fool Lada, and thereby the rest of the Council, that all is well and we are good friends, as Max intended, then I promise to honestly inform you about every little thing from now on, which would include any Subject news."

"Is that a vow?" I ask, skeptical.

"It's a vow."

It is a vow.

A formal agreement made with a Celestial is no small thing. The stories of faeries' inability to lie stems from Celestial agreements. Once one is made, the Celestial and whoever else is part of the agreement is bound to uphold the promises within.

I promise to honestly inform you about every little thing from now on.

Phoenix noticeably makes no specification about when he is required to keep me informed. The promise is open enough that he could get away with merely intending to eventually inform me about every little thing. However, if I directly ask a question, he would be required to answer honestly. Of course he has to find some way to avoid agreeing to complete, one hundred percent honesty with me.

A clap of thunder explodes overhead, and I look up to see how dark the sky's become. I can't help but foolishly feel that the gathering clouds, threatening to pour on us any second now, are a bad omen for agreeing to anything with Phoenix.

"But," Phoenix says, "here's a free truth before the vow is even in effect: As for my beliefs regarding how you live your life, if you were satisfied with your decisions, then me sharing my opposing views wouldn't bother you."

"It doesn't bother me," I lie.

"Great. Is it a deal then?" he asks, reaching out a hand to shake on it, only to almost immediately pull it back away. "Oops, there is something I should probably tell you if I'm agreeing to be honest."

"What?"

"I think Lada is under the same mind control as the Council. She never before showed such interest in the Subject System and the Council," Phoenix explains. "The good news is that once we meet with the Incanter I contacted, we'll have someone nearby who we can test for mind control."

"Is that all?" I ask.

"Yes."

Phoenix is watching me, trying to gather what my response will be to what he's told me.

To be honest, there's no saying no to this deal. I need to figure out who truly is behind the Subject System. I need Lada to believe nothing unusual is going on just as much as Phoenix does. Plus, the deal gets him to agree to be relatively honest. It's something. If I know the right questions to ask, it's significant.

A raindrop falls, hitting my fingers that fidget at my side.

"Deal," I agree, holding out my hand, mirroring his actions from moments before.

He holds his hand back out with a smile and we shake, making the plan to tolerate each other and work together official.

"There is one more thing," I say, *after* the deal is struck. "Why didn't you tell me yourself about not working for Max?"

"You really don't let anything go, do you? I got busy looking into the Subject System," Phoenix says.

"That's all? You didn't want to take the time to make yourself seem like the good guy again?"

"Does it really matter?"

"Only if I'm actually going to trust you. Now, what is the whole reason why you didn't tell me you weren't working for Max?" I respond, trapping him in the terms of the deal we just made.

Phoenix's green eyes bore into me, holding resentment, forcing me to remember that he is a powerful and ancient Celestial.

If he didn't want to be forced into telling the truth, then he shouldn't have willingly entered into this agreement. But, maybe he didn't expect me to actually compel him to uphold his end of the deal. I wonder if there's any chance Lada might come back right now so he can once again put on the jolly act and stop looking at me like I'm torturing him just by getting him to speak the truth.

"I *was* busy investigating the Subject System and how it came to be," Phoenix answers, "but I also was forbidden from visiting you in your lives after what I did in the twentieth. I couldn't risk drawing more attention to myself and the digging I was doing so, for once, I obeyed the Council. I figured it'd be easier for you to view me as another Celestial you disliked if I wasn't going to be around anymore. Anyway," he says, brushing off the subject quickly, having said all he was required to, "I'll see you tomorrow. You better get off to volunteering. And remember, we're best friends now," he ends flatly, rather than with his usual frivolous air, before turning his back on me to walk away.

He's right. It sure is easier to hate someone than miss them.

I'd like to tell myself that I wouldn't have spent much time missing Phoenix, but the fact that I didn't just dislike him but hated him for betraying me is evidence enough that I would have. You can only hate someone if you care enough about what it is they do or don't do, and I hate the fact that I seriously care about what Phoenix does.

The reality of his answer speaks louder than his negative reaction to having to provide it, which is why, despite his evident need to vacate the premises because of my prodding, I silence the voice that warns me against saying anything further.

"Careful," I yell after him. Squinting through the quickening rain, I see him pause, though he doesn't turn back around. "I might think you actually care."

After a moment, Phoenix throws something up in the air above him. It disappears but, before I can wonder what it was, a stray piece of white notebook paper drifts down from the air above me.

I snatch it before it can get too wet from the rain, shielding it to examine. On it, Phoenix has written, "I do care about you, bestie."

Laughing softly, I look back up from the note but Phoenix has left.

CHAPTER 20

The thing about living only one life is that there's this sense that the years you lived weren't only good but better than the years you didn't. A generational pride.

"This new stuff isn't real music," or "Kids used to play outside back in my day." Whatever the statement, the implication is always that it was better when we were younger, during our prime time.

When you've lived multiple lives, however, you come to realize that it's best to view life as a whole, as continuous, building on itself. Why listen only to 1920's jazz when you can have 1950's rock cued up to play right after? It keeps life more interesting.

Dex convinced me to stay after school with him today to work on homework together, instead of going home and working alone like I do every day. I can't imagine I'll actually get much work done with Dex.

When we first met, I thought his steady stream of chatter was from nerves over meeting someone new. Now, I realize that's just Dex. Normally, I might find such constant talking tiring but the nice thing about Dex is that he doesn't even need me to respond half the time. He always leaves room for me to interject, though. He's talented like that.

It's nice to have someone to talk to that I don't have to hide anything from. I made sure to inform Dex about everything Phoenix told me yesterday. Like the previous information dump, he took the news swimmingly, as though he was prepared to find out about the presence of yet another Celestial in our lives.

I balance my pen between my fingers, hitting it against my Biology textbook to the beat of the pop song playing through my earphones. I can at least study while I wait.

I check the clock on the wall behind me. It's fifteen minutes past the end of school. He's probably just getting his books out of his locker. More reading about enzymes it is.

"Oh shit."

The words escape my mouth on their own accord before I can even think to stop them. Even through my music, I can hear the voice that reminds me of one of the reasons I usually rush off to the Dawsons' immediately after school.

"That shirt does not help your situation," I hear Vanessa say. Just her voice makes me cringe. "I mean, it would look good on me but you should really wear clothes that do more to cover up this."

It's ridiculous that I feel the need to avoid this teenage girl. It's not her specifically that's so frightening but the unexpectedness of her. She's like a horror movie jump scare.

Did I mention that Max, for some reason, gave Vanessa a horrible, torturous superpower? Her superpower is being the only one in this school that can take notice of me, merely to insult me. It's not a consistent thing. After all, even a bully's constant attention can make someone feel, at the very least, not invisible and I am supposed to feel, above all, invisible.

One second I'll be invisible to her like I am to the general high school population and then suddenly BAM! she sees me.

I follow her voice over to where she sits behind a computer in the media center. Thank whatever greater force there is in this world that I can't actually see her face from behind the screen. If I can't see her, she can't see me. However, I do catch her manicured hands disapprovingly gesture to her friend sitting next to her.

Part of me is tempted to get up and defend her so-called friend but that isn't something Haley Dawson would do.

Haley Dawson has spent her life being ignored and would expect nothing to come of standing up to a bully. She would just be ignored once again. Haley waits to approach the bullied and plant some safe rebellion against Vanessa in their head, behind the scenes, like Haley planned to do at the Halloween party.

Then again... Max himself said that my environment rarely has much effect on how I behave.

So, since Haley Dawson *is* me, who's to say that Haley Dawson would let a history of being invisible stop her from trying once again to be seen? I don't think it would.

Or, am I letting Phoenix and his judgment get in my head? Claiming I try to be the perfect little Subject. Shame on him. I simply try to be a good person... for the sake of my Subject System points. Only for the sake of my Subject System points? Is that true? Do I need to have an existential crisis right now?

I look around the media center. I don't see anyone among the bookshelves, and no one sits at the surrounding tables and couches. Other than Vanessa and her victim, the room appears empty. Here I am, with no one watching me from either Vest or Havcire, and I'm still thinking about how I should act to keep up appearances.

It's been a while since I've done anything without thinking about how it would affect the Subject System, my points, and Max's data. Except, I didn't think about any of that before I rushed onto the ice to help Helen and Melanie, and I for sure didn't think at all when I put myself between Phoenix and the Oni.

Phoenix is definitely messing with my head.

I set my textbook aside and stand up, determined. I can act however I see fit. I'm going to confront Vanessa and hope this is one of those moments she can actually notice me.

The media center doors open, and Dex is there holding the door open for Lada. In one not so fluid motion, I sit back down and quickly place the textbook back on my lap, forcing myself to focus on the words in front of me.

That's right. There is someone in this world still keeping an eye on me.

"Haley," Dex greets me, as he makes his way over.

I see a flash of Vanessa's strawberry blonde hair from behind the computers and silently curse Dex for announcing my presence to the room. Looking up from my textbook, I act as though I only just noticed him and Lada.

"Hi," I say, smiling.

Unlike Phoenix, Lada sticks to the all white wardrobe characteristic of Celestials in Havcire.

She wears a casual halter dress that flows loosely around her, ending a couple inches above her knees. Except for the matching white color of her shoes, the combat boots on her feet seem to contrast with the rest of her delicate look. However, they do help her blend in a little more convincingly as a high schooler. Maybe that was her intent.

The two of them approach my table, but Lada makes no move to sit so I stand up to greet them. I can tell from Lada's expression that she didn't expect to come across me here, which means she wasn't with Dex just to find me and, therefore, doesn't know he's a Subject.

She looks about to say something but I speak up before she gets the chance.

"You're Phoenix's friend, right?" I ask, hoping to signal to Dex that this is Lada, despite whoever she's claimed to be. I don't risk glancing over at Dex to make sure he understood my meaning.

"Yes. Are you two friends?" she ask, indicating Dex and I.

"No," I answer. Dex quickly shuts his mouth. "We're just working on a school project together."

To say yes would be providing evidence that this life is not as Max designed. I should have no friends, Phoenix being the only exception at this point.

"We better get to work if we're going to get it all done today. It was nice to meet you, Alana," Dex says.

Lada takes that as her cue to walk away but I don't miss her lingering gaze on me. She blindly grabs a book off the shelves and sits down on a couch, her long legs stretched out in front of her. Thankfully, she's too far away to eavesdrop.

Between her and Vanessa, it feels as though I'm surrounded, and I'm not positive who is worse. I almost wish Phoenix were here. While I may be invisible to Vanessa the majority of the time, she certainly has noticed Phoenix's presence at this school. He would be a good distraction for both of them, keep the sharks at bay.

Dex pulls his own textbook out from his bag and sets it on the table.

"Alana is not Alana. Alana is Lada?"

"Yeah."

"This makes sense," he says, looking over his shoulder at her. "A lot of sense," he repeats, still staring and sounding very close to awe.

"Hey there," I say, waving my hand in front of his face to get his attention back. "I know she's beautiful but she's on the wrong side of things. The dark side to our light side. Don't go to that side."

Dex faces me, smiling.

"Lada pretty but bad. Got it," he says, facetiously. I continue to stare him down. "Seriously, I get it. I'm not one to be fooled, even by a gorgeous, otherworldly face."

I give in, returning his smile. I can sense his sincerity, despite his jokes.

"Shall we learn now?" I ask.

"Oh definitely. Enzymes, and catalysts, and activation energy oh my."

I laugh at his forced enthusiasm and then notice Lada looking suspiciously up from her book and try covering up my laughter with a cough. It must already be suspicious enough that Max somehow allowed me to be partnered up with another student for a project. Hopefully she doesn't look too much into that.

"Speaking of catalysts and things that go boom—"

"I don't think that's exactly what they do," I interject.

"How's your relationship with Phoenix? Have you see him today?" Dex continues, ignoring me.

My relationship with Phoenix. Our day old, fake best friendship is going smoothly so far.

"Phoenix?" Vanessa says, and I nearly fall out of my chair.

I turn around. She's standing directly behind me.

"Sorry?" I ask, looking up at her.

"Do you know where Phoenix is?"

"No," I answer, perplexed.

I don't know exactly when she became capable of being summoned like a demon from hell by the mere mention of Phoenix.

"Ugh," she exclaims, as if I've just wasted her precious time. "If you see him, tell him to call me."

"Will do."

I don't mention the fact that the stupid Celestial charged with being *the* messenger for Havcire doesn't own a cellphone.

She looks at me, as if searching for something else to say. Or, maybe she's hoping Phoenix will magically appear at my side. Honestly, if that were the case, she wouldn't be too crazy for expecting something like that to occur.

"Thanks," she settles on, sounding like the word had to fight against gravity the whole way up and out of her throat. Maybe she really did have to struggle against whatever magic Max has working on her to ensure she doesn't say anything remotely nice to me.

I watch her leave the room and then turn to face Dex, amused.

"I think that is the most civilized conversation Vanessa Harding has ever had," I tell him, to which he rolls his eyes.

The doors barely close behind her before Phoenix strides through.

Without a word, he sits himself down at the empty seat at our table. Making himself comfortable, he leans back in the chair and crosses his legs at the ankle atop the table between our two textbooks.

"What a shame," I say. "You just missed Vanessa, practically by a second."

Phoenix lets out a dramatized sigh of distress.

"Quite the shame. That girl is surprisingly omnipresent for a human," he says, sounding actually distressed.

"Did you come to study with us?" Dex asks, smiling.

Phoenix shifts his eyes over to where Lada still reclines on the couch with her book.

"I've come to make sure a specific someone doesn't get suspicious about my best friend hanging out without me, especially since I'm supposed to be her only friend."

"I knew it would come to this," I say to Phoenix. "You're jealous of the friendship that has quickly formed between me and Dex."

"It's okay, Phoenix," Dex says, sounding extremely sincere. "Dawn and I have a special bond but you can be our friend, too."

"You see right through me, the both of you."

Dex had asked about how it was going with Phoenix. Here's the thing, it's hard to fake a friendship with someone you want to ensure does not become your friend again. It takes constant reminding that the friendship is, in fact, fake. It's only been a day we've been pretending, and I already feel like I'm in need of a break.

"I'm going to get something to drink from the vending machine. Anyone want anything?" I ask, getting up.

Dex pulls his textbook closer to him, as if he intends to actually read it, while Phoenix glides a coin that wasn't there a second ago between his fingers. Both shake their heads at me in answer. Okay.

The vending machine is against the wall right outside the media center's glass doors. I'm debating about whether to get a soda or be healthy and just get a water bottle. It seems a waste to get water from a vending machine when I could just drink from a water fountain. Plus, it's not like bad physical health is something I'm concerned about bringing on the death of me.

I've settled on the soda by the time I open the doors and find the school's courtyard gone.

CHAPTER 21

Mid-step, my right foot is yanked back against my control to clap against my other foot, my ankles painfully banging against each other in the process. At the same time, my hands are whipped behind my back and tied together against a wall that wasn't there a moment before. I struggle automatically against the restraints but, except for a little leeway I'm afforded, there's no getting loose.

The platform on which I stand is raised about three feet off the ground. Light comes in from the arched entrance to the cave. From this angle, all I can make out from outside the cave is a grassy ground.

The platform shifts. Fragments of rock break off the side of the platform and then, with a groan, it bursts up higher in the air at a speed worthy of a theme park death drop.

Reflexively, I reach out to grab onto anything for support and find a hand near my own. Squeezing tight, I hold back a scream, as the quick ascent leaves me fearing an equally fast descent.

The platform comes to an abrupt stop and, thankfully, stays in place. I peer over the edge to find I'm at least fifty feet above the rest of the ground now and quickly press my back against the wall behind me to keep the drop hidden from my sight.

"What the hell?" That's Dex.

I look around the corner of the wall I'm tied to and find Dex standing there in the same position that I'm in, hands tied behind his back to what I now see is a triangular pillar that extends out from the base of the platform.

"Dex?" I ask, alerting him to my presence.

"Oh, hello," he says, looking pleased to see me despite the situation and definitely relieved. "How are you?"

"Peachy," I tell him.

I realize I'm still gripping another hand when I feel fingers lightly squeeze my own.

I turn to my right to look around the other edge of the pillar, where I find Phoenix tied in place like Dex and me. I quickly release his hand, traitorous heat rising to my cheeks.

He takes his time letting go, his fingers brushing against my palm as he pulls away.

Besties, I remind myself. *Fake* besties.

"Welcome," a deep voice says, echoing throughout the cave. "I am Gatlin, your host for the upcoming trials.

"The Incanter," Phoenix informs, quietly, as if he's concerned about interrupting.

"We are here to test if you are worthy of my assistance. The pillar you stand on will rise with every wrong answer. You will notice the ceiling high above you. It will squash you in the end, like a bug, if you should fail. All you must do is answer truthfully and your answer will be correct," Gatlin continues.

"Great," I say. "We're going to die if we have to rely on Phoenix being honest."

Barely a second after the words have left my mouth, the platform is rising in the air again. This time, a small scream does escape me before we've come to a stop.

"That's sweet. I knew you didn't actually believe that about me," Phoenix says, and the platform once again rises.

I squint against the gust of wind and sigh, relieved, when there's no more movement.

"If you two don't shut up I'm going to—" Dex exclaims, stopping abruptly, "well, to be honest, I wouldn't actually do anything but I will be extremely angry if you get us killed before any questions are even asked."

That's fair.

"Lovely demonstration of how this works," Gatlin says, sounding drowsy. Actually, he sounds oddly familiar.

"Why does he sound like the caterpillar from *Alice in Wonderland*?" I ask, whispering to Dex and Phoenix.

"Absolem," Dex says.

I turn to Dex, puzzled, and see Phoenix do the same.

"The caterpillar's name," Dex explains, with a shrug of his shoulders.

"Right," Phoenix says. "Gatlin likes playing at different roles."

"Now," Gatlin continues, "shall we begin?"

I hold on tighter to the ropes that keep me restrained, as if they could offer protection from the impending ceiling.

"Please state your names for the records," Gatlin says.

"Gatlin, you know who I am. We're..." Phoenix says, pausing, and I realize he's searching for something that will pass for the truth, "friendly acquaintances," he settles on.

I'm surprised to feel no movement.

"Names," Gatlin says. "And, don't bother lying. I already know who you all are."

"Phoenix."

"Dex."

"Dawn."

I say my name, still not exactly sure of the point.

"Very good," Gatlin says. "Phoenix, do phoenixes exist?"

"No," he answers.

Really? I guess so, as we're not moving up closer to the ceiling.

"Follow up question for Phoenix. Phoenix, then why the name?" Gatlin asks.

I feel more than see Phoenix shift uncomfortably against the ropes keeping us in place. I've always thought he'd be comfortable even on a bed of nails, or at least put in the effort to make it appear that way.

"I didn't want to take a name after a Vestigium mythological hero or god based loosely on who I was eons ago. I wanted to be able to aspire to something. A fictional bird created purely from imagination to symbolize hope and perseverance seemed like a fair option," he answers, sounding bored with the personal topic.

"Interesting," Gatlin says. "I'll admit, I've always simply been curious about that. Thank you for your honesty. Granted, anything else would have taken you a step closer to your death, but still."

Yeah, Gatlin, I'd agree that's interesting, as well. Not to mention, unexpected.

I can't believe I never questioned Phoenix's name before. I've known for a long time that most Celestials derive their names from the myths written about them after Havcire's split from Vestigium. I think it's their way of showing their appreciation of the stories that have kept their memory alive on Vest even when their true existence has been forgotten. And yet, I never questioned Phoenix's decision not to choose his name in the same way.

Then again, there would have been no guarantee he'd tell me the truth, at least not before our deal.

Even when he's honest, deciphering his meaning can be like trying to uncover which of two glasses is poisoned. Is it the one closest to me because my opponent wants to keep the poison furthest from himself? Or, is it the one further from me because he believes I'd automatically assume the former?

"Dawn," Gatlin says, pulling me away from my thoughts, "what is it you most desire?"

"To be free of the Subject System."

The platform sharply rises into the air again, fast enough that I only have the chance to sharply gasp in surprise. I jerk forward from the lack of motion when we stop and am glad that I'm securely tied to the pillar behind me.

Oh my god. I'm gonna be the one to get us killed.

"Dawn, what is it you desire most?" Gatlin asks again.

"I don't know. I thought that was the truth," I admit and flinch in apprehension, but the platform doesn't move.

"Dex," Gatlin says, moving on, "with whom does your loyalty lie?"

"With those who prove they are worthy of my loyalty," he responds.

The platform stays still. Maybe vague answers are the key. If that's the case, then it doesn't seem like a very good test of honesty.

"A simple moral dilemma, then, for those who were unable to answer truthfully in the first round," Gatlin says.

I feel called out.

"The trolley problem, Dawn. You stand by a railroad where one track diverges into two. A train is coming. It heads for a group of five people on the track. There is one man on the other, safe track. None of them can move. A lever appears before you to direct the train. What do you do?"

"I direct the train towards the one person, saving the five, and push the man alone on the tracks off them so he is safe," I answer.

I have honestly always hated these scenarios.

Gatlin lets out a slow laugh, sounding more like Absolem than he had ever before in this conversation but the platform doesn't rise any higher.

"It appears you truly believe you could manage that," he says. "Shall we test it?"

I blink, and I'm no longer in the cave.

I look at my free hands in front of me, no longer tied up. I stand in front of a lever as Gatlin described, with the train tracks before me. Instead of the strangers he described, Phoenix is on the tracks closest to me and on the other is a dog, a little beagle. Pathetically, I stare at the innocent dog as the train's whistle blares.

"Before you ask," Phoenix says, "I don't seem to be able to move, let alone teleport."

"Great."

I move the lever so the tracks shift to direct the oncoming train towards Phoenix, just as the train is about to pass through, and then dive for Phoenix.

Clapping echoes throughout the cave, as I find I'm back on the platform, tied to the pillar.

"It's cheating not to choose," Gatlin says.

"You changed the conditions," I argue.

"What happened?" Dex asks.

"She chose a dog over me," Phoenix tells him.

"Only temporarily. I saved them both," I say, defensively.

"That you did," Gatlin says, "as you claimed you would, so I'll let the cheating pass for the truth it revealed. One last question for all of you."

The rope disappears, and my hands are freed once again, but Dex and Phoenix are gone from the platform.

In fact, no longer is the pillar of rock rising up from the center. Instead, the glass doors to the media center are back. Through them, I can see a familiar Incanter town, one I've seen many times through the portal in the Ziggurat hallway. It's the tile I often focus on, wishing I could escape. I could go through those doors now and live my life as a Citizen, as I've always wanted. No one would know who I was in the town, and no one who did know me would know where I'd went.

"Choose," Gatlin's voice whispers in my head.

Heat rises up to me, much hotter than it'd been in the cave before. Where's the choice?

I look around, wondering what he could mean. Lava covers the ground below me, bubbling and rising slowly. There are other small islands of land, around which the lava flows. Atop the one closest to me, I notice two bodies lying there unconscious.

Phoenix and Dex. The island they're on is slightly wider than my own, but not by much, and it's much lower, much closer to being submerged.

I don't waste any more time. Getting down on my hands and knees, I look over the edge and down the side of the platform. It's rough, with ridges that could function as footholds and handholds.

Once I get low enough, I can jump to their island and hopefully have some success waking them up. Otherwise, I'm not sure how I'll manage getting them both back up to safety. One problem at a time.

I precariously lower myself down the side, reaching for the first foothold.

The doors leading to the Incanter town disappear, replaced by a regular cave opening. I look away and focus on the climb down. I made my choice.

My foot slips. I go to catch myself but there's no need.

Ow.

I bring my hand to the side of my head, where a bump seems to have already formed.

I'm lying on the cement floor back outside of the media center, as if I just collapsed onto the ground after coming through the doors. Actually, I realize that is exactly what happened. I get up, feeling a little dizzy, and go back inside.

Dex and Phoenix are lifting their heads up from the table when I join them, seeming to have just regained consciousness, as well. At least they were sitting when it happened.

Lada is still on her stakeout. Of course, taking what appears to be a spontaneous communal nap is not a crime but it's also not exactly normal. Fortunately, she's not in a position to have seen me collapse on the ground outside.

"What was that?" I ask Phoenix, gingerly sliding back into my seat at the table.

"All part of Gatlin's test. He must have spelled us, made it seem real but it was really more of a lucid dream. Except, not completely lucid because we didn't know it wasn't real," he says, looking disoriented.

"What?" I ask, confused.

Dex just stares at Phoenix, looking slightly concerned for his well-being.

"I don't think I'm fully awake yet," Phoenix says.

"At least you were sitting when it happened. Did we pass?" I ask, eagerly.

A page of Dex's textbook transforms into an elegantly handwritten note, the shiny and sticky page of the textbook becoming a fine piece of parchment rimmed in onyx with a border around the message made of emerald leaves and silver branches.

Dex leans forward to more closely inspect the page.

"'It has been long since my help has been given without first tests of loyalty and integrity,'" Dex reads. "'You three have passed, despite some cheating.'"

At this, Dex looks up at me accusingly.

"Is no one else caught up on the fact that Phoenix passed a test for *integrity*?" I ask, diverting attention away from myself.

"Surprised?" Phoenix asks, eyebrows raised.

"Beyond."

"There's more," Dex says, before continuing to read. "'I will meet you by the Celestial tree in the Graveyard at first light...' That's all. The Graveyard doesn't sound so good."

"It's not great," I tell him.

"In Havcire," Phoenix explains, "the Graveyard is a place for wayward immortals."

I look back to the message from Gatlin but it's disappeared, replaced by the textbook page that previously occupied the space.

CHAPTER 22

I feel tiny again, spinning through space.

This time, though, it feels like we're experiencing turbulence as Phoenix teleports Dex and me. Rather than a continuous forward movement, there's resistance, something on the other side pushing back against us.

My body vibrates. My head, I think that's my head, feels like it's shimmying its way off my shoulders.

I stabilize. It seems like the individual atoms that make up my body miraculously find their way back to their rightful places, and I breathe.

My feet find solid ground, which is a relief, but the resistance I'd felt as we teleported remains, pressing in, as if the air around me is unsure of where I came from, keeping me in place until it can decide whether I belong here or not.

All I can see are colorful streaks of light in the darkness. There are greens, oranges, and purples, like shards of stained glass.

I tell myself to just keep breathing even though it's hard through the pressure. Where are Dex and Phoenix? They could be right beside me for all I know. They probably are. The pressure will pass. I, at least, think Phoenix wouldn't lead us to our deaths.

My vision clears, and the greens become dominant. The air itself appears green. I look up and need to reach out a hand to steady myself.

The sky isn't visible. There's a ceiling of leaves through which the sunlight shines, casting the green light on everything below. There's not one sliver of yellow light that seeps through the dense canopy above. The trees are so close together, there isn't any place in my near surroundings where I could spread my arms fully without hitting bark. I wonder how the roots have enough room to anchor down in the crowded soil, whether the trees perform an ongoing battle for sustenance.

I hold onto the trunk of the tree closest to me. It feels normal enough but the bark is odd. It stretches over the trunk, not fully covering the surface. My breath hitches, and I yank my hand away.

Where the trunk is exposed, the tree breathes, the second layer of wood beneath expanding out to meet the outer layer of bark. The inner layer's texture is different from the outer bark. It's smoother, more like skin. While the bark is an ashy brown, the wood beneath is richer, with hints of mahogany. More vibrant shades of red line the mahogany skin, giving it the appearance of veins flowing with blood rather than sap. I don't rule out that possibility.

Looking around, I realize the other trees are structurally the same. On the surface, however, each trunk is unique, the bark spiraling and stretching in different ways to form various patterns.

The one I'd leaned on depicts three separate symbols, but I'm unable to interpret their meaning or even identify the language in which they're written.

On the tree directly behind me, not more than three feet from the other, the trunk depicts gears. I circle the trunk to find that there are four in total, so detailed I can almost hear them clink and grind together, as if powering the tree to life.

"Sheesh," Dex says on an exhale, and I look over to find him hanging his head down, his hands on his knees.

His dark hair sweeps down in front of his face, but I can see his pale skin is significantly more pale than usual. Phoenix, looking unaffected, places a hand on Dex's back.

I walk to Dex and press my thumbs to the insides of his wrists.

After a moment, Dex looks up, taking more steady and slow breaths.

"Thanks," he says, offering me a weak smile as he straightens out.

"Pressure points," I say, answering his unasked question.

"Good?" Phoenix asks, to which Dex nods. "Great," Phoenix continues, "welcome to the Graveyard. The Incanter—"

"What was that?" I ask Phoenix, cutting him off.

"If you mean our trip here," he says, "that was hard work. The Graveyard doesn't much care for visitors. It's not easy to teleport here."

It couldn't have been too hard. Phoenix looks perfectly fine, annoyingly perfectly fine.

"So, the Incanter said he'd meet us at the Celestial tree. It's not far from here. Look for the one with a design of wings," Phoenix says.

I walk around the tree with the gears. On its other side is a tree with its bark twisted to form the shape of a key. The tree in front of the key tree has an infinity sign. Phoenix traces the infinity sign with his hand.

"Do all the designs have meaning?" I ask.

"We think so," he answers, moving along to the next tree. "There have been theories that say the trees represent certain souls, both those on Vest and Havcire, but there is no proof of that. We've named some of the trees in order to navigate in here." He passes a tree with a bark that twists and curves to depict gusts of wind, and I'm reminded of the Kaeli.

"But the Celestial tree, according to that theory, couldn't be an accurate name for it," Dex says from a few trees over. "It would have to represent a specific Celestial, not Celestials as a whole."

There's no wind in here, not even a little breeze. The trees probably block any breeze that exists outside of the forest but the leaves above move against each other, causing a rustling. On the ground, there is further evidence of outside elements.

Leaves fallen lay in piles atop the dirt. Oddly, it seems as though someone came through with a rake and organized the fallen leaves. Rather than being randomly scattered across the ground, there are neat piles at the base of each tree, wrapped around the trunks like a scarf. Some of the leaves on the ground are brown, while others look as though they've just fallen and are as green as the ones that remain on the branches above.

"That's true," Phoenix agrees with Dex, "but the names are just for convenience."

"Then Celestials must have wings for the tree's name to make sense. Do they?" Dex asks.

I look to Phoenix. He opens his mouth to answer.

"Hey!" Dex says, interrupting what would have been the answer to his own question, but apparently we have a dog with a squirrel situation here. "This remind you of anything?"

Dex is pointing to the tree he's stopped by. Its bark forms what looks to be a snowflake, which reminds me simply of... snow, but it doesn't matter because Dex is clearly asking Phoenix, not me.

"Elsa, of course," Phoenix responds, sounding very serious, as if the mere implication that he wouldn't know what Dex was referring to would be an insult.

I look at the tree in question more closely. And, you know, I do see what they're talking about now. The snowflake does bear a strong resemblance to the animated one from the movie. Interesting.

"Very nice," Dex tells Phoenix. "The knowledge you have gained is more than I could have ever hoped for. Our Disney princess movie marathon was a success."

"I'm sorry, your what?"

Dex and Phoenix have continued walking on, examining the other trees, so I can't catch their expressions. They have to be messing with me.

Except, Dex isn't really the mess with you type. They turn to answer me, and neither looks like they're joking, which is saying a lot since Phoenix's resting face is practically a smug, "I'm not serious" face.

"We had a Disney princess movie marathon," Dex states.

"They start off a little rough but they get so much better," Phoenix says. "Like in *Sleeping Beauty*, she really does just sleep the whole time. Not very exciting. Then, though, you get to a movie like *Mulan*, and it doesn't get much better than that."

I'm not sure I've ever seen Phoenix talk about anything this genuinely, and I'm trying really hard not to laugh because he's not wrong; Sleeping Beauty is pretty lame.

"Phoenix is in love with Mulan."

"I won't deny it."

"I'm a Rapunzel fan."

"When did this happen?" I ask, unable to hold back anymore.

"We watched last night, after our trials with Gatlin revealed that Phoenix had never seen *Alice in Wonderland* or any of the other Disney princess movies," Dex explains.

"Right, because that was the most important take-away from those trials. Alice isn't even a Disney princess," I say, but honestly...

I cannot believe I wasn't invited. If anything, it would have been interesting to see Phoenix when he's not busy scheming and instead apparently enjoying himself. Unless, somehow, he gained evil inspiration from the Disney villains.

At a crinkling sound, I look over my shoulder.

"I'm sure I could find some way to pass Alice off as a princess," Phoenix is saying. "She is essentially Wonderland royalty."

Dex and Phoenix walk on ahead. They don't show any indication that they heard the noise, as they continue to debate Alice's Disney princess status.

I catch some of the leaves in a pile beneath a tree, with its bark shaped like music notes, settle back down on the ground, recently disturbed. Slowly, I back up.

From the leaves, something pops up like a jack in the box.

Instead of a spring propelling it up, I see thin legs, like those of a seagull. Its body, however, is that of a turtle. It precariously walks out of the pile of leaves, wobbling on its legs like a kid in heels. Once on the solid dirt again, it goes to walk further but falls down, rolling onto the back of its shell, its legs sticking up in the air.

I've heard stories about the Graveyard that warn you to be wary of the creatures you come across here. They are cursed beings or immortals who have suffered through violence, past the point of recovery. It is those who are not cursed that are the most dangerous. They are the ones that cannot leave the violence behind. They are stuck reliving it and are blind to the world around them. They are referred to as the Entrapped.

I hear Dex and Phoenix still talking but they're too far away now for me to make out what they're saying.

Despite the warnings, I take a step in the direction of the turtle seagull creature, the tugull, I decide. It can't get back up onto its feet.

"Dawn, it's over here," Dex shouts from up ahead.

"Coming," I shout back, but hastily jog over to the tugull.

Reaching it, I gingerly grab onto either side of its shell and pick it up. I turn it around so its legs are back on the ground and let go.

It's head, peeking out from its shell, looks up at me kneeling next to it. It excitedly jumps up as if to say thank you.

"You're welcome," I say.

A moment later, it can no longer support its weight and falls again, its stick-thin legs collapsing out from under it, leaving the tugull this time flat on the stomach of its shell.

Huh.

"I hope you don't mind." I grab the tugull by its shell again.

I carry it with me to join Dex and Phoenix over at the tree that I now see clearly has two extended wings depicted on its trunk.

It *is* odd to name the tree with wings after the Celestials when I've never seen a single Celestial with wings. But, why should anything start making sense now?

The tugull doesn't seem to mind being kidnapped by me. It stays still and content in my hands. Phoenix, however, looks at me with exasperation when he notices but makes no comment.

"The Incanter should be here in a minute," he says.

"What is that?" Dex asks, indicating the tugull.

Before I can respond, a man appears before us.

I had half-expected Gatlin to show up as a blue caterpillar with a hookah after hearing him during the trials. He looks fairly normal, though, and un-bug like.

He leans against the Celestial tree, I'm certain having not been anywhere in sight a second ago. It would be hard to miss him if he had been there this whole time. It's not so much that he's dressed extravagantly, rather that he looks out of time and place. He would be properly dressed if he were to be teleported back in time to Victorian England.

He holds a black top hat in his hands, spinning it idly between two long fingers. Atop a white button down shirt, he wears a black vest and a long burgundy coat of velvet material that clasps closed with three copper buttons. The coat is long enough to cover his lanky body down to the backs of his knees. Around the collar of his shirt, is a neatly tied, matching burgundy cravat. His high waisted, tan pants are tucked into the tops of his black boots.

With the hat off, his gray hair falls around his face in smooth strands, reaching his pointed chin. Despite the color of his hair, he looks to be only thirty but his navy eyes speak of more years.

"Hi. Nice to meet you three officially," Gatlin says in a pretty strong New York accent, which contrasts with his style.

"You know me," Phoenix says. "In fact, you owe me a favor, which I thought would have made the whole pre-trial a non-issue."

"I do owe you a favor, which I intend to make good on today. I still think it's necessary to know with whom I'm dealing," Gatlin says.

"Nice to meet you," I say. "Now that we have passed the tests, would you be so kind to do me a favor?"

Something about Gatlin has me speaking in a more formal manner. Phoenix had said that Gatlin likes playing at different roles, and I get the feeling he appreciates others playing along. It's not too hard to do, considering that I did live at one point during Queen Victoria's reign. Two can play at being posh.

"You mean other than the one we've met here for? I *have* been known for my generosity," Gatlin says, in such a way that suggests he is known for quite the opposite. "Okay, what's this other favor?"

I smile kindly, holding the tugull out towards Gatlin in answer. Its thin legs wiggle in the air, and it peers out of its shell curiously at him. It looks pretty adorable. Good job, really milk it, buddy.

I place him down on the ground and don't have to wait long for Gatlin to see the issue when the tugull almost immediately collapses.

Gatlin frowns sympathetically. He gives his hat one last spin before placing it atop his head.

He quits leaning on the tree and makes to move closer to the tugull but stumbles, tripping over his own feet. He quickly rights himself again, standing up straighter than before as if overcorrecting his error.

"Are you sober?" Phoenix asks Gatlin.

"Yes."

Gatlin turns his attention to the tugull, kneeling down on the ground. With a finger, he traces a square in the dirt around the tugull with four perpendicular lines through the center of each side of the square.

"If I held up my fingers, could you tell me how many I was holding up?" Phoenix questions.

Gatlin looks up at Phoenix, whose hands remain at his sides, and squints.

"Are you holding them up?"

"Oh wow," Dex says.

"He is not," I whisper to Gatlin conspiratorially.

"No, you are not," Gatlin says.

"No," Phoenix confirms for Gatlin, but he looks at me as he does, clearly having heard my whisper, which admittedly came out more as a stage whisper. He rolls his eyes at me.

Sure, I'm being a bit of a suck-up but ridiculousness can get one far when looking for help from unusual sources, and Gatlin sure is unusual. So, I respond with a smile to Phoenix's eye roll, throwing some of his usual smugness back at him.

Unbothered, Gatlin focuses back on the tugull and dusts the dirt off his hands.

Holding up both hands in front of him, out towards the tugull, he begins speaking words in a language I don't recognize but they have a certain rhythm to them. Extending his fingers, he pushes his wrists forward, and silver smoke engulfs the tugull. As it clears, merely disappearing rather than dispersing, Gatlin's incantation ceases.

The tugull stands up on its legs independently, no longer struggling to remain upright, and runs swiftly, weaving between the trunks of the trees. I smile and wave goodbye to the creature, as it disappears deeper into the forest.

"Thank you," I tell Gatlin, as he stands back up. "How did you do that?"

"I made his shell lighter so it will help pull him up rather than down," he says.

"Like a balloon?"

"Magic instead of helium, but yes," Gatlin answers.

"What does she owe you in return?" Phoenix asks, before I can ask a stupid follow-up question like, "Will he float away?"

"She owes me nothing. She didn't ask that for herself, but for another. I won't have her pay for a selfless request."

It may be foolish but I had believed Gatlin wouldn't ask for something in return for helping the tugull. Still, I do feel some relief hearing as much confirmed.

"Except for the fact that you have a reputation of always collecting," Phoenix says, still skeptical.

"Then we'll ensure that my reputation remains intact. As your friend, I know you have a talent for secrets so that shouldn't be an issue," Gatlin says.

"That he does," I say, eagerly agreeing.

"Dawn and I don't exactly run in the same social circles as you two," Dex chimes in, "so your secret benevolence is perfectly safe with us, as well."

"I like them," Gatlin tells Phoenix, indicating Dex and me.

"Great," Phoenix says, dryly.

"Now," Gatlin says, as if he's a showman announcing his greatest act, "for the information you came here for. I found a spell that can reveal brain waves. Theoretically, if someone were using mind control, the spell could allow you to see the foreign thoughts in their brain."

"Could it help us trace the foreign thoughts back to the person sending them?" Phoenix asks.

"Theoretically," Gatlin answers.

"Theoretically?" Dex asks.

"Yes. It's all theoretical because the spell hasn't ever been used for this purpose before. I manipulated a spell for telepathy to work to identify mind control. I don't know anyone that can actually use mind control to test it on so I can't provide any assurances. However, I am fairly confident that it should work. Brain waves are unique, like fingerprints, and the spell will make them visible to the eye."

Gatlin reaches into his pant's pocket and pulls out a vial filled with clear liquid. The liquid gives off an eerie glow that betrays it as something other than just water.

"I have already cast the spell so when it comes time to use it, you need only to drink a small amount for it to work."

Dex reaches out for the vial, for Gatlin to hand it to him. Gatlin raises a skeptical eyebrow and looks between Dex and Phoenix. It's clear Gatlin expects Phoenix to be the one to handle the vial.

Dex pulls his hand back, unsure now, but Gatlin reaches out and places the vial in his hand, apparently having made up his own mind.

Phoenix watches the transaction with amusement but doesn't show any indication that he minds Dex holding onto the vial.

"So to reveal the person using mind control, we would at least have to be in the same room as the victim of the mind control in order to trace the foreign brain waves back to their source, like following breadcrumbs," I say.

"It's good we know of a victim nearby then," Phoenix says.

"Here," Dex says, handing the vial to Phoenix, where it almost immediately disappears from his hand.

"Thanks," Phoenix says. "It's somewhere secure."

I look down at Phoenix's pants pockets before realizing he clearly teleported it somewhere else entirely. It could be literally anywhere.

"There's no room for it there, Dawn."

I look back up at Phoenix's face, only to realize I was looking further down on his body for a significant amount of time, and Phoenix's expression suggests I was focused on something else, not the vial.

My eyes drift back down on their own accord at the sexual innuendo. As if I need to fact check Phoenix's statement, prove to myself that there would, in fact, not be enough room down there for a small vial of magical potion. Someone kill me.

Dex snorts, as he tries to hold back a laugh. The guy's a traitor. The two of them with their movie nights and now this? He's not allowed to laugh at my social awkwardness.

"Well, sounds like you have yourself a plan," Gatlin says, saving me from scrambling to find some response to Phoenix. "It's been great. Bye."

Gatlin turns with a flourish, his burgundy coat sweeping the ground, stirring leaves into the air in one dramatic farewell. There goes the neat little piles surrounding the trees.

And then, he's back, not a second later. He's facing, specifically, me.

He stands directly in front of me, his head inclined forward, inspecting my face.

I take a reflexive step back to create some distance but he reaches out and grabs my chin, holding me in place.

Out of the corner of my eye, I see Phoenix take a protective step closer, ready to intervene, but I don't pull myself out of Gatlin's grasp, and Phoenix hesitates, waiting for me to make the first move, to signal that I actually need help.

I stay still, returning Gatlin's inquisitive stare. Despite the abruptness of the action, I don't sense any real threat. Gatlin's fingers framing my chin aren't holding on tight. I could easily slip away with one step backwards.

"I wondered what was so familiar..." he says, trailing off in thought. "It's the eyes I've seen before. They were different the time before. Well, the same, but very much different."

Gatlin speaks as though to himself, and I struggle to understand whatever it is he seems to be unfurling in his own mind.

As if doused with a bucket of ice water, he backs away and tightens his already perfectly tied cravat. He pulls on the bottom of his coat's sleeves, erasing the creases, and smooths the front of his vest with the flat of his palm.

"Good luck." He smiles. "Feel free to call on me again, only if dying or on the verge of dying," Gatlin says, along with one more word in an unrecognizable language, before disappearing. This time, for real.

"Okay?" Dex says, the word drawn out, which mirrors my own thoughts pretty perfectly.

One doesn't make such odd remarks without any attempt at an explanation and then just abruptly leave. Apparently, Gatlin does do that. I turn to Phoenix and do what always makes sense to do.

"I thought you said you were the only one who could teleport," I say, accusingly.

"You're choosing to fact check me now?"

I nod. It's always reasonable to question Phoenix's lies. When in doubt and all.

"I will have you know, there are other ways to disappear from the human eye besides teleportation. Is it really necessary to question everything I have ever told you?"

"Isn't it?"

A loud screech fills the air.

The leaves above us rustle loudly, the fallen ones lifting briefly off the ground as though there were geysers of air below them. The whole forest seems to move with the sudden activity from above. Even the trees are more alert, the smoother layer beneath the bark thrumming to a faster beat.

I look up to find the source. Through the thick canopy, all I can see are shadows of what appear to be birds with large, bat-like wings and long, sharp beaks. I hear the wings flapping like a kite pulled taught by the breeze.

"What are those?" I ask Phoenix.

"Pterodactyls, but what's more important is why they're in a rush to get far from here," Phoenix says.

"The extinct kind?" Dex asks, having to speak more loudly over the commotion above but then the pterodactyls are gone, and the forest goes still again.

"Apparently not," I say.

If it weren't for the trees still pulsing at a fast beat, I would have thought the pterodactyls were a simulation, smoke and mirrors. It's almost too quiet, and I find my own heartbeat matching that of the trees.

Phoenix grabs onto my arm and Dex's. I feel the ground begin to slip away, as he prepares to teleport us out but something slams into me, yanking my arm out of his grip.

CHAPTER 23

My back hits the very present ground, knocking the air out of me and killing the scream that was building in the back of my throat.

A person kneels on top of me, preventing me from escaping. I smell his breath, dirt and mold. He's so close to me. His eyes are bloodshot to the point that I can't even begin to guess what color they might have once been. They are permanently widened in fear and anger; and yet, they appear blind to their surroundings.

The man looks like he's survived a bomb, shards of glass sticking out from his skin like piercings. Staring right through me, he lifts a fist to my face.

I hold my arms up to block the punch and then quickly pull back my right arm. My fist connects with the side of his face, and I flinch when my knuckles not only hit his cheek but also the shard of glass sticking out from that side.

Despite the impact of the punch, which forces his head back, he doesn't appear to register any pain. But, it's enough of a distraction for me to free a leg and knee him in the stomach, pushing him away and onto the ground beside me.

Ignoring my own pain, I jump up from the ground and prepare to face him again but he remains where he is.

Slowly, like a zombie, he gets back onto his feet. Rather than turning to attack me, however, he continues walking forward, seemingly unaware of my presence.

A couple trees down to my right, two more run at Dex, but Phoenix teleports into their path. He punches the one in the face, who appears to be female, her long hair matted with blood. Phoenix kicks the other one in the stomach, directly at the axe that is already lodged there so that it's forced in even further.

"Dex," he shouts, "head to a tree and climb up."

Dex follows his orders and, a moment after Dex moves out of the path of the two zombies, Phoenix teleports away, landing beside me. The two he left behind, the ones who were after Dex, continue on. They don't change direction to go after Dex, nor Phoenix. The one that had attacked me is now a good distance away.

These are the Entrapped, stuck in their own minds and always carrying with them the violence of what would have been their deaths if only they were mortal.

They only attack what is directly in their path, unable to see clearly through the hallucinations that plague them.

I hear muted footsteps; I'd guess at least five more are headed our way. Dex has made it about halfway up a tree, using the oddly shaped bark to find footholds.

"Come on, I'll teleport us back to Vest," Phoenix says, reaching for my arm, but I pull away.

"Not without Dex."

"I will come back for Dex. He'll be safe in the tree, out of the way, but we won't be. The Entrapped usually travel in groups, and it will be harder to avoid so many of them," he says.

"We leave together," I tell him, and I hear him mumble something incoherently.

I don't think he's too happy with me. Regardless, he grunts in agreement. How hard could it be to play a game of dodge the Entrapped? It's not like they can aim for us. We just have to stay out of their way.

Ten more Entrapped appear among the trees, looking like the risen dead. Unfortunately, they are not slow like in many Vest stories but some do stop to attack the trees before realizing that they don't fight back and moving on.

I might find the whole tree attacking thing comical if it weren't for the extreme brutality of the attacks. They hit with the force of their whole bodies, nothing holding them back. They have nothing to lose, only horrors to dispel.

Phoenix grabs onto my arm, and I let him pull me along toward the tree Dex climbs because I'm not positive my legs are working very well on their own right now.

They're closing in quickly, and ten is enough to almost completely cover the space we need to cross to get from where we are to Dex. We're bound to come across at least one Entrapped and, unlike with the Oni, these guys are not at all picky about their target.

One of the Entrapped makes his way to us quickly, having avoided many of the trees along the way. This one has an arrow going straight through his head, looking much more like a Halloween prank than something that actually exists and is alive and running. I end up directly in his path, and he reaches out to grab me around the waist and tackle me down.

There's no time to move out of the way so I duck to avoid his arms. I throw my arms up above my head to protect myself and wait to be plowed into.

Phoenix kicks a leg out in front of me.

The Entrapped trips over his leg only inches away from my face, just as Phoenix holds his arm out in front of the Entrapped's chest and simultaneously grabs the Entrapped's arm with his other hand. Taking advantage of the Entrapped's sudden instability, he flips the Entrapped head over heals right above and over me.

I straighten back up, my breathing ragged, and continue running toward the tree.

We're so close, when two more Entrapped run at us, on a path that will surely intercept our own.

I could simply stop running now and avoid both of them but Phoenix wouldn't be so lucky. If he stops, he'll be in the path of the Entrapped closer to me, an Entrapped who is blindly charging with a sword pointed out in front of him.

I am not waiting around to be attacked this time.

"Duck!" I yell at Phoenix. Hopefully he listens.

I jump back, out of the way, as the Entrapped approach and kick out at the sword wielding arm of the Entrapped.

The force of my kick sends the Entrapped's arm, along with the sword he still holds, swinging over a now crouching Phoenix and around to the other Entrapped at his side, where the sword slices right through him and— blech! That was more effective than I imagined it would be. I look away before I gag.

Phoenix is already standing again.

"And if I hadn't ducked?" Phoenix asks.

"I might have felt a little guilty," I tell him, before taking off for the tree.

We arrive, no more Entrapped encounters. Phoenix gives me a boost up to the first foothold.

The design on this tree is that of a double helix, which happens to make for a fairly good ladder. As I reach for the bark to pull myself up, I realize my hands are shaking. I take a deep breath, focus on the task at hand, and hold on tight to the bark, only letting my hands relax for seconds at a time as I reach for the next handhold in order to keep them steady enough to function.

The tree shakes, an Entrapped plowing into the trunk below.

My foot slips, and my breath catches in my throat but something stops my foot from falling further, and I'm able to readjust so my other foot is more steadily on the bark.

I glance down to find Phoenix's hand still holding me up, his sarcastic expression telling me to take my time. I shift as quickly as possible so I can get both of my feet securely back in a foothold.

As I reach the top of the dense canopy, Dex holds out a hand through the thick branches of the tree, and I accept the help.

A second later, Phoenix pulls himself up beside us. He braces himself against the branch above me, his arm an inch above my head.

Sure, Phoenix, why don't you just make yourself comfortable in these tight quarters? I stare accusingly up at his arm. It is a very muscular arm that did catch me only a moment before, for which I admit I am grateful, especially since a moment before that I almost was to blame for getting him decapitated by sword.

Why is it still dark? We should be able to see the sun more clearly from up here. There are leaves still blocking the view of the sky but it's more than that. Above this tree, there seems to be a whole other, separate canopy.

I test the branch out beneath me, shifting my weight, checking its strength. When it doesn't budge, I decide it's safe enough.

I push Phoenix's arm out of the way, earning a small sound of protest from him, and stand up to push the branches aside. I can see it now.

There are two layers, one belonging to the tree we are in and the other belonging to another tree, whose trunk spreads out into the sky above, as if the two trees are resting on each other's backs.

Unlike the tree we're in, the trunk of this other tree looks normal, just a plain, solid brown tree trunk. At its bottom, or top from this perspective, the trunk branches out in four separate directions like thick roots feeding off the sunlight above.

Phoenix clears his throat, having stood up beside me on his own branch.

"What is this?" I ask him.

"It's the tree. They're all like this in the Graveyard."

I lift up onto my toes, balancing on the branch below to try and better see the surrounding trees, but I'm still not tall enough and roll back down to the souls of my feet, disappointed. Maybe Arrow would give me a ride some time to see the Graveyard from the sky.

I mentally scoff at the thought, as if I'd ever get the chance to do some sightseeing, especially in Havcire.

I could pencil it in between restoring power back to the Council and earning my place as a Citizen. Except, I would probably have to become a Citizen before I was allowed to go Sightseeing in Havcire, so I'd have to rearrange that plan of course. And, since I'll probably never become a Citizen even if we do somehow manage to make the Subject System fair, I won't be getting to that sightseeing.

Now is so not the time for a pity party, though.

We got the potion from Gatlin so the plan is coming along. I just have to keep going and not get the voice of Dory stuck in my head singing, "Just keep swimming." Sure, I haven't had it exactly easy, and I've been trying for centuries to become a Citizen but life would be so boring if it was easy, right? What's a story without a little conflict, after all?

Now is the time to look at these unique Graveyard trees, which I can't actually get a good look at because I'm too damn short. I mean, would it kill Max to tweak my DNA just a little one of these times to make me just a bit taller?

"You need a boost? Want to sit on my shoulders?" Phoenix asks, seeing my short person struggle.

I try really hard not to roll my eyes at him and fail. And then he leans in closer, close enough that my eyelashes brush across his chest, the fabric of his t-shirt doing little to prevent my mind from thinking about what it'd feel like if there was no t-shirt there.

"I wouldn't mind your thighs around my neck, or your—"

I push him away, forgetting, yes, that we're in a frickin tree.

Phoenix loses his balance, and I reflexively reach out to hold onto him and pull him back before he can fall, leaving me with my arms tightly around his hips and his around my waist and absolutely no space between our bodies.

His chest is shaking, and I realize he's laughing. Because...

"I would've teleported before I found myself falling out of a tree."

Of course.

Irritated, I go to pull away but he's still holding onto me. His hand comes up to my face, his thumb gliding over my cheekbone, making me squirm, which only makes me more aware of where our bodies are touching. I force myself to freeze so I don't do anything stupid. Or worse, humiliating.

"But I appreciate your concern." The smile he looks down at me with doesn't feel smug now, but sincere, even a little vulnerable, and I want to—

"Should we get out of here before something else tries to kill us?"

Dex's voice has me pulling back.

His head appears through the canopy of the tree below, eyebrows raised expectantly, waiting for an answer.

"Yes." My throat needs clearing. "For sure."

This time, when Phoenix teleports us, it's less disorienting, maybe just because I know what to expect, or maybe it's because the Graveyard is better with letting people go than it is with letting them in.

There's the usual shrinking feeling, the death drop, heart in throat sensation, and then the spinning return to normal. It's not relaxing but it's also not as discombobulating this time, and the landing is without turbulence.

There's no resistance as my feet find solid ground again and chilled, soft air caresses my hair.

"Perfect timing," Phoenix says.

I expect him to be looking at another stolen watch on his wrist; but instead, I find him looking out at the school's field through the slits in the bleachers, where students have started gathering.

I guess Dex was right. People do hang out under bleachers.

Dex looks to have taken the teleportation better than when we had arrived in the Graveyard, already standing up straight and steadily. The sun is especially blinding after having spent time looking through green-tinted, diffused light.

"How so?" Dex asks.

"We have Gym with Lada now. Let's play."

Phoenix winks, actually winks, as he holds up the vial from Gatlin.

CHAPTER 24

"**O**w," I exclaim, rubbing my abused face.

"You're supposed to hit the ball with your head, not your face," Phoenix says, picking up the assaulting soccer ball.

"I'm going to pretend that wasn't intentional because we're friends," I say, sending a pointed look over in Lada's direction.

Friends. Not even. *Fake* friends, I have to keep reminding myself. But then, what was that in the graveyard?

He started it.

Yeah, even I know that sounds lame. What am I? Five years old? Plus, Phoenix is a flirt. I know this, which means it's my own fault if I feel anything at all. I'm just falling for the same BS all over again, maybe because my favorite pastime is lying to myself when it comes to Phoenix.

We were never anything more than friends in past lives. Still, that doesn't mean he didn't have me thinking about the prospect of being more in those past lives. He just never felt that way about me. Which. Is. Fine.

Convincing.

I'm too logical to think that could happen. I'm a Subject. He's a Celestial. This isn't some star-crossed thing.

I'm just saying, Celestials are practically gods. While I know, *oh I know*, one hundred percent know, Phoenix is totally completely flawed, for me to think I could be with him, even as a friend, is crazy. Flawed or not, he is still as close to a god as you can get, and I am not the type of person to think that I could or should possibly be with someone like that. That'd be crazy.

Speaking of Celestials...

Lada's currently surrounded by the majority of the boys in our gym class. The only reason it's not the entirety of the boys is because some are still in the locker room changing into their gym clothes.

From the surrounding huddle, all I can see of Lada is the top of her golden-haired head. As the boys shift around her, though, I catch a clearer view of her. Every smile and turn of her head seems posed, perfected as though the eyes of those around her are cameras, with every blink a beautiful picture taken.

I'd expect the other girls in our class to be looking on with jealousy or at least irritation over all the attention Lada is getting. Instead, they stare with admiration and some with equally as much interest as the boys.

"What's wrong with the girls?" I ask Phoenix.

"Lada's charm isn't restricted to just the male species," Phoenix says, dribbling the soccer ball between his feet, a small smile lifting the corners of his mouth. "Plus, you do know that there are some girls who *like* like other girls, right?" he adds, with a raised brow.

"You do know that sometimes I *hate* hate you, right?"

I'm not lying. It just doesn't happen to be the case at this particular moment.

Phoenix laughs. "Is that like a two negatives makes a positive thing?"

"Exactly, I positively hate you," I tell him with a saccharine smile.

Phoenix returns my smile but his looks much more genuine than I imagine mine does, which makes me automatically suspicious. How is he taking this conversation seriously, while simultaneously taking my words in jest?

He stills the soccer ball under his foot.

"I positively *hate* you, too," Phoenix says, except he says it like we're both declaring the opposite.

"Don't say it like that," I protest before I can think better of it because of course I know how he'll respond, with the innocent question of...

"Like what?"

Phoenix is staring at me, and I've walked right into a trap, one which has led me dangerously close to the sun.

I can't do this as seamlessly as he does because we both know this is just how he is, what he always does with everyone. I, on the other hand, if I play along, it might be construed as real and not play, and he can't think it's real for me. But, if I don't play along, I've already lost.

"Like you feel the opposite of hate. You're not allowed to lie to me anymore."

"Dex!" Lada yells, saving me from his answer, from delving deeper into that.

I take a step back from Phoenix.

Lada's stopped shifting her gaze, seemingly no longer concerned about keeping all those huddled around her feeling like they each have her full attention. Her act dropped, she's focused solely on Dex, who's just now walking onto the field. She leaves the group behind to jog up to him.

Somehow, her jog makes it look like she's gliding over dirt and grass, a gazelle in gym clothes.

Dex greets her with a smile, which she genuinely returns. I can't hear what they say from here, but I can see Lada's face. Her smile is small, unlike before. Her hands fidget at her sides, playing with the bottom of her gym shorts that fall mid-thigh.

Something's different. Maybe she's not using her charm, as Phoenix put it, with Dex. She seems almost... nice.

"I think the Goddess of Love fancies Dex," I say, surprising myself with the fact that I actually might believe it to be true.

"Fancies? What century are you from?" Phoenix asks, and I pull my attention back away from Dex and Lada.

"Many, okay? I get confused, but that's not the point."

Phoenix chuckles, lightly kicking the soccer ball over to me.

"Okay. And yes, she does. Are you just now realizing?"

I kick the ball back, slightly rougher than he'd passed it to me, and look back over at Dex and Lada. I've been a bit preoccupied to notice, but it makes sense. Dex is the type of person that encourages sincerity. I look at him now, as in really look.

It's the first time I've seen him not in his usual suit, but in the flattering gym clothes we all have to wear. It's just a crappy gray t-shirt and shorts, but they show off the fact that he's not as scrawny as I would have guessed. Even from a distance, I can see the lean muscles on his legs and arms. Together, he and Lada do look nice, like partners in a ballet.

Phoenix nudges me.

"Yeah?" I ask, wondering what Phoenix wants.

Was I considering my current foe as a good match for my one and only friend? I should not take up matchmaking. Also, must I call myself out on the fact that now I'm apparently supporting a Celestial/Subject couple?

"What? Do I need to have an agenda in order to get your attention? We could just talk you know," Phoenix says, defensively.

I stare at him, fully attentive, waiting for the talking just to talk conversation to begin.

He rubs the scar that crosses through his eyebrow with the hand that isn't holding the soccer ball. It looks like the type of action one would do if the injury was still healing, applying pressure to numb any lasting pain. With a shrug, he drops his hand back to his side.

"I was just going to say now would be a good time to take the potion."

I sigh.

A loud whistle pierces the air.

Coach Jennings stands in the center of the field. She heads over to the group of boys still talking in a huddle after Lada's departure and divides them into two, sending half over to the goal we stand by and half to the other side. She does the same to the girls and then breaks up Lada and Dex, sending Dex to our side and Lada to the other.

Yay! Dex is on our side. Coach Jennings coming through. Even she knows Dex and Lada should not be together. It was only me who had the momentary lapse of judgment.

Except, it probably would make things easier if Lada were assigned to the same team as us, leaving her on the same side of the field as us. Oh well, it couldn't be too bad.

Coach Jennings begins assigning positions, and I watch Lada fall in with the other students.

Dex walks up, leaning against one of the goal posts, and Phoenix takes the vial out. Although it appears in his hand spontaneously, he does make it seem as though he pulls it out of his short's pocket. Turning away from the rest of the field, he lifts the vial to his mouth.

"Poindexter and Haley will be center backs," Coach Jennings shouts.

"Remember," Phoenix says, holding out the vial to me and Dex, "just a little each should work."

I let Dex take the clear, oddly glowing, liquid first. From his expression and Phoenix's, I'd guess it doesn't taste anything like water. I can't help wanting to put it off. I used to be the worst at drinking those disgusting liquid medicines. It would take multiple countdowns for me to finally force myself to drink them. And, by the way, no spoonful of sugar would have helped the situation.

"And Phoenix, you'll be the goalie," Coach Jennings continues.

Blech. Yeah, it tastes like coconut water if coconut water could go horribly bad. Can coconut water spoil?

I hand the vial back to Phoenix. There's still plenty of the potion left. Everyone gets into position on the field, Lada taking her place in the opposite goal. With all the other players in front and around her, it seems almost as if she's the one being guarded rather than the goal.

I was wrong. This is pretty bad. The other team blocks her from our view. Worse, nothing looks unusual. Maybe we didn't take enough of the potion for it to work.

"Phoenix," I say, turning around to face him, "I don't think—"

Around his head, waves of teal blue ripple, weaving in and out of his brown hair like a crown. They flow smoothly, at a constant frequency, as he stares back at me.

"It's working," he says.

I look at Dex, who stares out at the rest of the field with wide brown eyes. He has his own crown of waves like Phoenix, but his are less calm. As the waves go up, they rise taller and faster than when they descend below the midline. They also differ in color, coming across as a dark orange, vibrant against his black hair.

Looking around the field, I understand Dex's expression.

The colorful brain waves flow around everyone's head. From a distance, especially those on the opposite side of the field, the waves and colors seem to blend together, creating an array of colors. The waves blur like the lights of the aurora borealis, and it's hard to distinguish one person's from another.

It's pretty, and I would appreciate that fact more if it didn't mean Lada's brain waves were lost in the beautiful disarray.

CHAPTER 25

Coach Jennings blows her whistle again, signaling the start of the game. Everyone's brain waves seem to jump, startled by the noise, even Coach Jennings'.

"We need to get closer to Lada," Dex says.

"It needs to seem natural. Lada can't figure out what we're up to, especially if we prove today she is being mind controlled," Phoenix says.

"Goalies can't leave their goal," I say.

The ball is kicked over in my direction, a lame attempt to score, and I lazily kick it back out to my left.

"So it will have to be one of us, then," Dex says.

I look back over my shoulder to Phoenix, who's looking at me seemingly deep in thought, having observed my half-assed involvement in the game.

"Dawn can do it," he says, confidently.

"Cause she's such a great soccer player?" Dex asks, sarcastically, as he watches me kick the soccer ball away again with what is most likely bad form.

Despite Dex's valid interpretation of my lack of soccer abilities, he still gives me an apologetic look for his reasonably sarcastic dig. Shaking my head, I make it clear there's no need to feel bad about it. I, too, have no idea where Phoenix thinks he's going with this.

"No, because I taught her how to fence."

Is he serious? Does he have a mental hat from which he randomly selects responses from on a frequent basis because I cannot see the relevance of fencing to our current...

1627

The light of the full moon glints off our blades in the otherwise dark garrison. I have my hair tied back out of the way but a few ringlets have fallen loose as the night has worn on and my breath has sped from exertion.

We train in the dark, an hour past midnight, so no one will see, but I still try to cover up in case the darkness doesn't offer enough of a disguise to hide the fact that I am neither a man nor a musketeer.

"En-garde," Armando says, backing away and getting in position.

I do the same, bending my knees and distributing my weight, as I raise my right arm holding the rapier and my left arm behind me.

"Pret," Armando warns. "Allez!"

I watch his movements, and I listen for the shuffle of his feet, for his front foot to move, signaling an attack. We circle each other, alert, but neither making an approach. Through the darkness, I see his light green eyes shift.

He lunges, but I block and quickly attempt a counterattack. Before I can make contact, in one seemingly inhumanly fast motion, his blade hits my own aside, and he twists his wrist, sending his blade back around towards my chest. He stops short before the blade can cause any real damage.

I sigh, backing up. I have improved with the instruction of the King's Musketeer over the past fortnight, but there has not been once that I have come even close to getting the upper hand. Despite this, he gives me a slight nod of approval.

"Your moves are predictable," he says.

"All I know is what you have taught me," I respond, twirling the rapier in my hand. "How am I to make my actions unpredictable for you?"

"You know how to fight. You can diverge from the set methods. There is also a reason I insisted you learn not to depend on one side, that they be of equal strength."

I stop twirling the rapier and tighten my grip on the hilt.

"En-garde," I say. Armando prepares for another round. "Pret. Allez!"

This time, I lunge first, and Armando quickly blocks. I shuffle backwards and to the side before he can counterattack. As he turns to face me, I toss my rapier from my right to my left hand.

Expecting to hit the inside of my blade, parrying an attack from my right hand, he doesn't have enough time to switch the direction by which he thrusts his blade. It doesn't take a lot of strength to knock his blade aside, as he was prepared to meet resistance from the opposite direction.

The tip of my blade comes to a stop in front of his chest. Keeping it in place, I straighten up out of my lunge with a smile. At a slight pressure against my abdomen, I look down. Armando holds a dagger there in his other hand. I feel my proud smile fade into a frown.

"Does that count as a draw?" I ask.

He flips the dagger around in his hand, so the point no longer faces in my direction, and places it back in the holster around his hips.

"Well done, Mademoiselle."

...Oh. Yet another lagging memory.

"Le bien, Armando de' Phoenix," I say, in the best French accent I can muster after centuries of nonuse. "I'll need some time to make it work."

We'd be in much better shape here if any of us really played soccer but I guess fencing lessons will have to do.

"I feel like I'm missing something here," Dex says, "but I'm okay with that. I'll just enjoy the pretty light show."

I look back out at the field. Again, no significant amount of time seems to have passed while I was experiencing my deja vu. My other classmates continue to play, their colorful waves of thought dancing around their heads.

"Dawn will take care of it," Phoenix tells Dex. "Make sure you let her get the ball as often as possible when it comes in our direction."

Dex gives us both a thumbs up, no further questions asked.

I turn my attention back to the game. I kind of do still have to pay attention. Not many of my classmates come even close to qualifying as pros, but I'm even worse. I have to make sure I can get the ball enough for this to work.

Haley Dawson, soccer champion. I imagine the voice of a sport's commentator announcing in my head. The youngest, most promising athlete on the field, known for her skill playing Center Back, always putting as little effort as possible into her returns.

I kick the soccer ball again, having to move a little into Dex's territory to reach it this time, but he easily moves out of the way for me. Once again, I kick the ball with my right foot off to my left, and I notice everyone starts moving over about a second before I even kick it this time. I really prepare for it, too, dramatically shifting my weight over to my left leg before. I, perhaps even too obviously, stare off to my left side as I prepare to kick, spotting the exact place I intend for the ball to go.

My inner sport's commentator personality continues.

The ball goes off, a player from the opposing team receiving the ball. Quite unusual for one of Haley's shots to be intercepted. She must have done it intentionally, for some strategic reason that is far above our abilities to understand.

"Do you ever stop thinking?" Phoenix asks from behind me. "Your brain waves constantly look like an erratic EKG reading."

"Let me think about that and get back to you, thought perv," I tell him.

The ball comes to me. This time, once all the other players notice it heading in my direction, they automatically begin shifting to my left, leaving the right side of the field open, a straight shot to the opposite goal and Lada.

"Coach Jennings is not going to be happy with me. She doesn't like it when Center Backs get too far from the goal," I say, half to myself.

I shift my weight quickly away from my left leg and onto my right leg and kick the ball hard off to my right, and I run.

The field is empty in front of me so I sprint freely after the ball. By the time I've caught up to the ball, everyone has registered the fact that I didn't kick it where they'd expected. However, the realization hasn't yet spurred action, as no one is close enough to attempt to steal it away.

I don't bother dribbling the ball between my feet to keep it guarded. Instead, I kick it far ahead again, while I still have the time, past the halfway line.

Now others are running up beside me, gaining on me, as I approach the ball again.

My breath is quickening from the sprint across the field, but I have one focus. I'm close enough now to try and kick the ball into the goal.

Lada leans against the goal post, seemingly uninterested in the game. When she sees me approaching, though, she straightens up and goes to the center to guard. Making the goal is not the point, though. I kick the ball hard towards the goal, hoping it at least offers enough of a challenge in order to distract Lada. I ignore its trajectory, turning my attention fully to Lada.

The lavender crown of waves surrounding Lada's head is thankfully easily visible now without others surrounding her. A spike appears in the waves as she reaches to block the ball. Other than the abnormal spike in attention, the pattern of waves reminds me of a drawing of ocean waves, with curved points at the crests. There's nothing unusual about them, no tainted hint of color and no dual pattern that could hint at some foreign form of mind control.

She's clear.

"Nicely done, Haley," Coach Jennings shouts, and I turn away from Lada before she can notice my staring.

Oh! Look at that. The soccer ball is in the goal.

"Whoo!" I cheer, throwing my arms up, partly out of actual excitement and partly to keep up the facade of caring about this game as opposed to Lada's mental state.

"You shouldn't be going past the halfway line as Center Back, though," Coach Jennings continues.

I nod towards her, feeling stupidly shameful for having broken a rule, one of which I was well aware, as if such a thing is really important.

Damn my need to please, honestly. It's not like I did anything actually bad. I didn't cheat. Phoenix would do something way worse, has done much worse, and not spare a second feeling bad about it because he'd believe there was nothing bad about what he did. He wouldn't let someone else's casual reproach affect how he felt. With such a ridiculous little thing such as this, I wish I could share his perspective more, but I can't help the small sinking feeling in my chest as a result of Coach Jennings' reprimand. Again, I know how stupid that is, especially considering the grander scheme of things.

Then again, maybe a little guilt even over something so small is healthy. Maybe it helps keep my morality in check. After all these lifetimes, that's important. Plus, it's not a good idea to start viewing Phoenix as any sort of role model for how I should think. That would be a very bad idea. Very, very bad.

This would all just be much easier if I was invisible to the faculty here as well as my fellow classmates. Okay... that's a horrible thought, so very cowardly of me.

Oh my god. Maybe Phoenix is right, and I have rolled over and given up, just going along with everything Max intended for me in this life. I've become way too comfortable with my invisibility, taken it as an easy way out, used it to avoid confronting anyone and anything. I shouldn't be wishing for my invisibility to extend to others just for things to be easier. Life isn't supposed to be easy. Why do I feel like I have to keep reminding myself of that?

I bet there's a little section of my brain labeled, "Topics in need of constant reminding." Number one: Life isn't supposed to be easy. Number Two: Do not trust Phoenix. Number Three: Phoenix is your *fake* friend.

"Don't worry," Phoenix says, pulling me out of my thoughts, also making me realize I've made it back to our side of the field. "That's not a real rule."

"What?" I ask, before realizing he's referring to Coach Jennings Center Back comment. "Whatever, it's fine."

He could tell it'd bothered me?

I'd completely forgotten that was how my internal tangent began. How's that for helping myself get over my little upset? I am so self-sufficient. I mean, forgetting about it involved upsetting myself over something much larger than just a teacher's stupid reprimand but you win some you lose some, right?

"Lada's not mind controlled, I think," I report, moving on.

"What do you mean, you think?" Dex asks, as Phoenix looks at me skeptically, probably questioning his decision to send me as the one to get this done. Well, too late.

The soccer ball rolls past me and Dex and right into the goal, Phoenix making no attempt to stop it. I hear a few groans of protest from the other students.

"Sorry," Phoenix tells them, "slow reflexes."

He picks up the ball and throws it back out onto the field.

"I mean," I continue, when the ball is back in play, "I didn't get any clear instructions on what to look for, but it seemed like her brain waves were clear, uncontrolled. They were all one color like everyone else and had a distinct pattern."

The bell rings from inside the school, loud enough to hear from out here. But, in case we hadn't, Coach Jennings blows her whistle again.

We'd been in the midst of a game but everyone immediately stops playing, leaving the ball to go change and head to their next class. We're not a very sport enthusiastic school.

We can't stay around here together, at least not with Dex, or Lada could see. Or, do we care if Lada knows anymore what's going on if she's not under mind control? She still could choose to report back to the Council about anything out of the ordinary with me. She had insisted to Phoenix that she was set on proving herself useful to the Council. She— is not out here anymore, I realize, looking across the field to where I had last seen her.

"So then we need another plan to locate the mind controller," Dex says.

"I could help with that," a familiar, disembodied voice says.

CHAPTER 26

Lada appears in front of us, translucent, the sunlight shining through her. Actually, it's not that the light is shining through her, but that it is emanating from her, bending around and reflecting off her. Her skin, hair, and eyes are alight.

The light dims, and Lada appears more like her usual self, including her still radiant hair.

"What?" Dex asks, sounding exaggeratedly shocked, as he stares at Lada.

"It's a little late for that, Dex," Phoenix says.

Dex lets his mock surprise drop and smiles at Lada.

"Hi, Lada," he says, doing a full 180 and not even bothering to use her pseudonym. She returns his smile, with surprising sincerity, considering she's just revealed herself to have been spying on us. "I don't know about Dawn, but I feel the need to be better informed about Celestial powers. You each seem to have a new one pop up on a daily basis."

"Welcome to my world," I tell him.

"I can control light, of course," Lada says. "How else do you think I manage to look like this all the time? I mean, naturally, I'm gifted but it does help."

I'm going to be missing another class.

"What exactly can you help with?" Phoenix asks Lada.

"Probably everything, but why don't we first start with what you three have really been up to?"

Is there really any point to denying anything anymore? Clearly I'm not the Haley Dawson I'm meant to be. We've confirmed Lada is at least not under another's control. So, we might as well make our case for her joining whatever it is we have here before she decides to run back to the Council and reveal what she already knows, which is enough to bring an end to this life of mine.

Even Phoenix seems to have accepted that Lada is now a part of this. He looks to Dex. Makes sense. Dex is the only one of us that Lada seems to genuinely like.

"We couldn't trust you..." Dex begins.

Not the best way to start off this discussion, but Lada stays silent, listening attentively as he goes on. The only indication of comprehension is her barely perceptible head tilt, which shifts her fringe bangs. She doesn't show it on her face but the minuscule action is a tell. When she does it, she's puzzling through new information.

Dex explains how we suspected her of being mind controlled, by who we still don't know, but are trying to figure out with the use of Gatlin's potion. He details our suspicion of the Council's non-involvement in the Subject System and our few little field trips to see other Subjects. I'm not sure all the details are completely necessary to share with her but I don't interrupt either.

"I *can* help," Lada says, once Dex has finished, haughtiness at full power. She even stands up straighter, which I didn't think was possible. She's already quite tall. "Firstly, I wasn't mind controlled. While you may be right about the Council being under mind control, I was possessed."

Possession sounds much worse but either it wasn't as bad as it sounds or Lada's had enough time to somehow come to terms with it. Or, she's simply good at hiding what I would expect was a traumatic experience.

"It's the reason I continued to work closely with the Council after I was… myself again. I wanted to find a way to expose the person who possessed me. So, I guess we really are on the same side. Go team," Lada exclaims, and I'm not quite sure whether she meant for that to sound sarcastic or not.

"How does this make you any help to us?" Phoenix asks.

Lada holds up a finger, reprimanding Phoenix for cutting in. I have to suppress a smile at the interaction.

"Because… secondly," she says, with a tight-lipped smile, "I know who possessed me. She's a Protogenoi. How? I don't know. I had thought they were destroyed in the Firstlast War, as well. You know Shiva, Hindu Goddess?"

"Yes," Phoenix and I quickly respond, as Dex admits, "No."

I'm trying to understand how Lada's claiming a Protogenoi is still alive. I don't know much about them, except that they were the rulers of Havcire before the Council. No one liked them, and they all died. But, apparently not.

"Well," Lada goes on, explaining for Dex's benefit, "myth says she was the ultimate destroyer, believing change could only be brought about with destruction. Having experienced her firsthand, I'd say Shiva was based off this Protogenoi. Regardless, she's chosen to go by Chaos. I would have chosen Shiva but that's just..."

Lada's voice trails away, even though I know she is still saying something.

I've heard of Chaos before in this life but also somewhere else, some other time.

Lada, Phoenix, and Dex disappear. The field disappears. Everything around me disappears until there is nothing left.

It's dark. There are voices but they're muffled. The more I try to make them out, the more unclear they become. I think I feel air leave my own throat. Maybe I'm talking but I don't hear that either. The darkness starts to suffocate, filling my silenced mouth.

The air is back, and I gasp for it.

"Is that normal?" I hear Lada ask.

My vision is spotty. It's a good thing the soccer goal was close because I'm pretty sure I would have fallen over without the post to lean on. I don't actually remember reaching out, but I feel the cool metal against my palm, the edges digging into my fingers.

A hand touches my back. It's comforting, reminding me I'm solidly here.

"No," Phoenix says, his voice tight.

He's moved closer to my side. It's his hand on my back. I realize what's happened.

A memory was triggered but there was no memory there to be revealed. I'm like a malfunctioning computer, with data still missing, despite my programmed belief that I had all my past returned to me. There are still parts missing, and I didn't even know.

Did Phoenix know?

I pull away from his hand, my vision cleared, and back away from the goal, standing on my own. Dex watches me carefully. Even Lada looks somewhat concerned, her narrow eyes scanning me.

"I'm good," I reassure them. "Thank you for the information, Lada. I have to go."

I walk away, not bothering to come up with an explanation for my leaving. I know we still need to discuss our plans for what's next. I know that but also, what's wrong with me?

I lived twenty-six lives before this one, all of which I now remember. The only one I still have no memory of is my very first life but no Subject remembers their first life. Which means, whatever fragment I just couldn't recall has to be from that first life, and why would something from my first life be triggered by the mention of a mythological, supposedly extinct, being?

Most people face problems they know exist. I can't help but feel like my real problem, what I should be confronting head on, is a secret buried along with whatever it is that I still don't know about myself. And, if that's the case, how am I ever to overcome it?

I'm standing in the woods outside the school, having blindly walked off the field, through the parking lot, and out here.

Footsteps hit the pavement of the parking lot behind me. Phoenix followed me but I don't want to see him right now, let alone talk to him. He represents everything hidden from me, even if it's not him holding the curtain closed. So, I do the only thing that comes to mind. I run.

CHAPTER 27

Small twigs on the ground crunch beneath my feet, the soft dirt cushioning my steps. The trees offer relief from the direct sunlight, with only streaks of light seeping in from between the leaves, the light dancing off of me as my legs pull me deeper into the woods.

I've been keeping my promise to myself to run almost every morning, so the movement comes more easily, offering serenity.

I can hear Phoenix behind me, intentionally keeping his distance. He could run much faster than me if he wanted.

I don't care that he's there. I just need to keep running. I let my feet hit the ground hard, expending more energy, each step a stronger blow landed. Every time I connect with the dirt, I focus on something else.

First, the Council. I thought they'd trapped me in the Subject System, a prison disguised as opportunity, but now I know they've been blind to it all.

Second, Max, my puppeteer. He's manipulated all my lives but he is only just a tool in the larger system.

Lastly, Chaos, the one who's been behind the Subject System and its corrupt creation this entire time. She's the real reason I'm never completely whole, with my own life kept secret from me. With her probably lies the explanation for why I still don't remember it all. Chaos is the problem. She's *my* problem.

I stop running, forcing Phoenix to come to an abrupt stop behind me. He wasn't as far behind as I'd thought and now, when I turn around, there's hardly any space left between us.

His arms reach out to close the distance that remains, his hands holding onto my waist firmly. I'm not sure if he holds on in order to steady me or to prevent himself from running into me. I'm out of breath, having put all my energy into that sprint.

In the chilly air, his warm hands on my waist feel shocking. The sensation travels through the rest of me like an electric current, heating my center. I lean into his touch. I'm not just a little unsteady now.

My chest betrays me as I gasp for air, coming within a hair's breadth of his with each inhale, while Phoenix remains unnaturally still, to the point that I can't tell if he's breathing at all anymore. I can clearly see the definition of his muscular chest and arms through his shirt, which I'm surprised to see is slightly dampened from sweat. I guess I wasn't going so slow, after all.

I look up and, this close, my eyes are right in line with his mouth. It'd be easy to reach his lips right now. After all these years, I got used to seeing them lift into a smirk, often at my expense. I've never felt exactly like this before because all I want is for those lips to move closer to mine. It's the only thought, the only need I have.

I can feel the air between us to the point that it seems as though I can see every particle that separates us, and the distance is closing ever so slowly as Phoenix finally moves, leaning closer. His hands on my waist tighten, as they pull me closer. One more step and I'd be flush against him. I want to take that one step. It'd be so easy, his hands already pulling me toward him, along with what feels like every other force. I take it.

Phoenix is gone, suddenly standing feet away from me. It feels like my breath's been ripped out of me. Something clenches painfully in my chest.

"Do you need to rest?" he asks, completely unaffected.

Was that all in my head? Maybe that run took more out of me than I thought. I was simply off balance, and he was making sure I didn't pass out, and that's all it was. I do feel a bit light headed. I'm definitely not thinking straight.

But, wasn't he sweating a moment ago? Did I imagine that, too? I mean, seriously, he looks even more put together than usual. His hair isn't normally that controlled. Normally there's a stray wave falling over his forehead but there's none of that right now. He's making our crappy gym clothes look like athleisure wear. It's that that does it. All my irritation comes rushing back.

Phoenix wasn't a focus of my inner rant, a definite oversight on my part. I lost sight of his role in everything, maybe fooling myself,

right along with Lada, into believing that we were real friends…
again. So much for my "Topics in need of constant reminding"
brain section.

"You," I say, pushing Phoenix away and pointing accusingly at
him. He looks taken aback. Good. "Remember your assurance
that I would remember everything this time around? Surprise! It
turns out I am still missing parts of my life, since I just managed
to have a memory attack with no memory there to see. And,
apparently, it has something to do with Chaos, which would be
helpful to know about right now, don't you think? For some
reason, though, I get the feeling that you know more than you're
letting on. Why would that be? Maybe because that's always the
case?"

"Okay," Phoenix says. "You're angry."

"Rightfully so."

"Not at me. Though, you are. Always. You go out of your way
not to show it but it's there, and it's blinding you," Phoenix says,
irritatingly calm.

At least if he spoke in a patronizing manner I could decide not
to listen to him but he's annoyingly empathetic, speaking to me
like he truly understands where it is that I'm coming from and he
simply wants to help me realize it, too. It's still annoying but it has
me giving in, albeit still angrily.

"What is it I'm not seeing then?"

He's deflecting, avoiding my accusations and questions regarding himself. And yet, I still wait to hear what he has to say.

"Who's on your side. And you. Do you know why you couldn't answer Gatlin's question about what you want?"

"Really? You're bringing that up now?"

"It's because you're so busy blaming everyone else for what your life is and has been that you don't even know what it is you want your life to be. But, what is the point of fighting if you don't know what you're fighting for in the end?"

I narrow my eyes at Phoenix, hoping I look like I feel.

Despite his even tone, he doesn't look as convincingly unaffected as it would suggest. The scar on his eyebrow betrays him, standing out white against his dark brow when he hardens his expression in an attempt to keep it stoic. That won't do. If he's expecting me to open up about something that may or may not be true, then he doesn't get to stand there acting like nothing at all affects him.

I bend down, grab a handful of dirt, and foolishly throw it at his chest. Some sticks to his t-shirt, while the rest falls limply back down to the ground. He doesn't look away from me even when the dirt hits him but his light green eyes widen. His fists clench at his sides. He's losing it, and I have to hold back a smile at my success. All it took was a little dirt.

"You're insane. You do realize that, right?" Phoenix asks, not bothering to wipe the rest of the dirt off.

"Insane?" I repeat, sounding insane. "Yes, I realize! But, you are just as crazy if you think that your psychoanalysis of me can distract me from getting answers. Tell me, Phoenix, did you know that I was still missing memories?"

"Yes! Okay?" Phoenix admits, throwing his arms up in exasperation. I asked him directly. The vow.

"You did?"

"You're surprised?"

"No."

"Dawn," Phoenix says, his voice now soft. There's more? Whatever it is, he's not required to tell me because of the vow. I haven't asked anything else. Alarm bells ring in my head.

"You were a Citizen."

Everything quiets, even the breeze silencing to still the previously swaying tree branches. I watch Phoenix and expect him to correct what he said or look like he's made a mistake, but he continues to unflinchingly hold my gaze, showing no intent to take anything back.

"A Citizen?" I ask, barely above a whisper.

"I found out after your twentieth life," Phoenix says. "You were a Citizen. You became suspicious of the Subject System and began to ask questions about it, about if anyone had ever successfully completed their sentence. Soon after, you disappeared from Havcire and became a Subject yourself. When I found out about it from talking to other Citizens, I went to the Council to discuss it, but none of them even recalled you being a Citizen."

Phoenix pauses, stalling to finally look down and brush the remaining dirt off his shirt.

"That's how I first suspected that there was someone else behind the Subject System, someone controlling the Council, because of you," Phoenix explains, looking at me in a way that I know, for the first time, everything he has said has been the truth. It's the effort he puts into each word that makes as much clear. It's easier, natural even, for him to lie.

I'm numb, my thoughts on autopilot.

"Why?" I manage, without clarifying, but it's the same general question I normally pose for him. Why didn't he tell me the truth?

"I had to continue looking into what you had started, and I knew that if I kept interacting with you against the Council's orders, those behind sending you back to Vestigium would have more reason to suspect me. Now, I realize it was Chaos. It was easier to look for answers under Chaos's radar. I told you why I allowed you to believe I worked with Max at your expense. This was why it was so important that I stay away from you after. That's all of it. The truth."

"I was a Citizen," I repeat.

"There was nothing you could have done with that information. It wouldn't have helped you to know, not then."

I look down at the ground, no longer able to meet Phoenix's green eyes, shining with sincerity for once.

"I deserved to know."

I say the words as much to myself as to Phoenix. I can't look at him, not yet. I don't want to cry in front of him. I don't know if I meet his gaze again if the tears will come or not, if I'll feel tempted to seek comfort from the one person I definitely should not.

I focus on a spider crawling across a leaf by my foot. It's only slightly larger than an ant. I wonder if it knows another world exists other than this one, or if it would care to know.

I watch my feet as I force myself to move. Passing Phoenix, I do look up, above all, to prove to myself that I can.

"Maybe I could have done *something*. You don't know what I'm capable of," I tell him, without any anger, before walking away and out of the woods.

Phoenix wanted to say more, to tell Dawn he didn't doubt she was capable of even more than he realized. He wasn't going to apologize for something he didn't regret doing, though. Or, at least, for something he was mostly in the right for doing.

He didn't know much about Dawn's life as a Citizen. In fact, he knew nothing other than the fact that she had a life as a Citizen. How could he have told Dawn she was a Citizen before without any other information to offer her? For sure she would've had many more follow-up questions for which he would have had no answers to provide.

And yet, was it truly his call to make not to tell her the little he knew the moment he found out? It *was* he who had the information. So... it was technically his call to make. He who holds the cards and all but that's classic Phoenix reasoning, and what's objectively true does not always point to what's right.

And, this involved Dawn.

Phoenix admitted to himself a long time ago something he'd of course never admit to anyone else. Dawn's involvement always meant shuffling his hand of cards and throwing them up in the air. In other words, what usually would be a complicated, yet perfectly laid out plan of his would devolve into chaos. As much as Phoenix loved to create the illusion of mayhem, he wasn't fond of experiencing the real thing himself. Dawn had a way of messing with his reasoning, which he had to think was surely a sign of just how capable she is.

Whether or not Phoenix would have found something more to say to Dawn, or whether he would have decided to say anything at all didn't matter because the Council called.

Phoenix couldn't afford to ignore the Council at this point, as he couldn't risk them becoming suspicious of him, at least not any more than usual.

He also couldn't miss an opportunity to see what they were up to and if anything else seemed out of the ordinary, such as the griffon being nowhere in sight when he teleported into the Council Chamber.

"You couldn't have used the door like everyone else, Phoenix?"

Phoenix looks up to address Lucifer, who looks indifferent despite his statement.

Lucifer likes to act prickly, like with one wrong word he'd be happy to brutally murder you, but it's an act. He's really very good at putting on the act but he's actually the most understanding of the three Council members, something very few catch onto. Dawn seems to be one of the few, based on the offhand way she speaks to Lucifer. That, or she simply doesn't fear what he could do to her, which wouldn't surprise Phoenix.

"Why waste time? I assume you have something important to discuss with me," Phoenix replies, leaving out the fact that if he dropped in, there was a better chance he might catch something being discussed that he wasn't supposed to hear. However, when he had entered, it was silent.

"Inform us, how is Dawn's life proceeding?" Barnabas asks, wasting no time.

Phoenix takes a moment to consider the question, seemingly reflecting on what has happened and how to report the events in the most effective manner.

"Normal," he finally says, with a nonchalant shrug, "That is, until Lada became one of her classmates. Did no one think it a good idea to inform me about her being sent down? Above all, who thought that would be a good idea?"

At this, Barnabas and Lucifer turn to look at Minerva, who Phoenix had almost forgotten was there. Normally, he would sense her immediately, addressing her before anyone else. But today, Minerva doesn't seem like herself, and Phoenix wonders if the other Council members can sense it, too.

"That would be me," Minerva responds. "Dawn needed looking after, and Lada was eager to prove herself to us so it dealt with two issues at once. Like that expression the Vests are so fond of, hit two birds with one stone."

"Kill," Phoenix corrects, automatically.

"Excuse me?" Minerva replies, seemingly offended.

"Kill," Phoenix repeats, more loudly this time. He looks Minerva squarely in the eye. "The expression is to kill two birds with one stone."

"Right," Minerva says, with a laugh. "My mistake. Either way, we didn't want anything to interfere with the experiment so we sent down Lada to keep a low profile and merely observe Dawn."

Lada and low profile don't fit together but Phoenix lets it drop.

"I understand. Is there anything else you need from me?" Phoenix asks, directing the question at all the Council members.

"No," Barnabas says, speaking up. "We just wanted to know if you had noticed anything odd about Dawn's behavior, anything to explain her sudden increase in points."

"I told Lada, I haven't noticed anything out of the ordinary. For some reason, Dawn seems nicer than usual, more patient with people," Phoenix reports, having to hold back a bitter laugh over the fact that she didn't seem so nice or patient when she was yelling at him only moments before. "It's possible that's why her points have increased."

Barnabas and Lucifer look skeptical, while Minerva looks as if she's been exposed to Medusa's snakes and frozen with a face of ambiguity. However, none of them say another word, and Barnabas gives a nod of dismissal.

Phoenix doesn't wait for anything else to be said and takes the dismissal as soon as it's given, teleporting out of the room, again not using the door.

CHAPTER 28

I was a Citizen.

I've been acknowledging that fact for over two hours now. I left school, the day being nearly over anyway, and headed to the dog shelter. There was no way I could focus on homework. Besides, I didn't know if I had homework for that day, as I hadn't exactly been present in class.

I wave absently to the woman at the front desk, who offers up a smile that tells me I look as wrecked as I feel. It also makes me notice the dried blood covering my knuckles from where I hit the shard of glass lodged in the Entrapped's face.

You're so busy blaming everyone else.

I had a whole life I didn't know existed, as a Citizen in Havcire. Who else am I to blame? I don't know enough about myself to blame me for my situation. I do know, now, that I don't have to take the blame for becoming a Subject, as I wasn't one to begin with. I never lived an original life worthy of becoming a Subject. I was a Citizen.

And, there it is again, that fact that I can't wrap my brain around.

The dogs start barking as I enter the hallway lined with their cages. The sight of a person gives them hope for getting out. They calm down when they see me pull out the big bag of food from the storage closet, quieting as if in reverence for the food.

I wash my injured hand and wrap gauze around it.

You don't even know what it is you want your life to be.

I want my life to be in my control. Except, I guess it is. I just feel clueless as to what that truth means for me. What *do* I want, because I'm not so sure anymore that it is to be a Citizen of Havcire if it turns out I once tried and failed at that. Phoenix is right, and I'm not sure if that or everything else going on upsets me more. At least I know the dogs want food and walkies. I can manage that.

It seems especially futile to continue to play along with Max's experiment, since I know I didn't become a Subject because of anything I did in my original life. Still, I've come to enjoy volunteering. I even enjoy being overly nice to my fellow classmates, whom fail to notice I exist. It makes the nonexistence more bearable, helping me pretend there's some camaraderie there.

By the time I've locked up at the dog shelter and made my way home, I've reached a sort of nirvana, accepting my hidden past as a Citizen.

That's a lie. But, I do relax, convincing myself to at least take a break and deal with the fallout further tomorrow.

I hear that plan crash and burn, as I open the door to my bedroom to find Lada lounging on my bed.

"Oh good," she says, dropping her legs over the side of the bed to sit upright.

She gives me a once over. I never changed out of my gym clothes. Although she saw me in them earlier, the way she looks at me now, I feel shameful for daring to show up in my own room looking like this. It also doesn't help that Lada is dressed up to the nines.

She wears a slim, silky white dress that falls down to her ankles. Although it isn't tight, it is shaped narrowly, showing off her long, elegant body. There's a slit in the center of the skirt that begins halfway down her thigh, exposing her legs and the lacy white heels she wears. The neckline is high, coming up just below her neck. It's sleeveless, with two-inch wide straps. Minuscule diamonds are threaded throughout the fabric to form designs of flowers and leaves. She wears no jewelry, but her hair has matching diamonds weaved through the intricately braided crown.

"We have a lot of work to do if you're going to pass as an Incanter."

"What?" I ask, stupidly.

"You missed the rest of the planning," Lada says, leading me over to my own desk. She sits me down in the chair, facing the mirror. "Happy news, we're going to a party! The Havcire Assembly, where all the Celestials meet annually, the perfect place for us to seek out who is under Chaos's control."

"I guess that explains your attire," I say, sounding grumpy compared to Lada's obvious excitement.

"Nothing could explain *your* current state," Lada says, now I'm sure looking at me disapprovingly.

"It's been a rough day," I say, defensively. "Wait, did you say I have to pass as an Incanter?"

"Well you can't be recognized by the Council as yourself," she says, beginning to tug at my hair. "With a little real work from me and some illusion work from Phoenix, we can manage it."

I flinch at the mention of Phoenix, and I think Lada notices. She doesn't comment, though, and I'm grateful for it.

With my hair pulled down from the ponytail it's been in for the duration of the day, its curls are free to rise up around my face in a tangled mess. Lada picks up my brush sitting on top of the desk and raises her hand to pull it through my hair.

I reach up and grab her arm before she can make the terrible mistake. She looks back at me in the mirror, stunned, as if she didn't expect me to touch her even though she planned to do a full makeover on me.

"That's going to be painful for all involved," I tell her with a smile. "Also, don't you think I should shower before you begin?"

Lada scrunches up her perfect nose, setting the brush down in surrender.

"Yes, you do smell. I forgot humans had to shower."

"Celestials sweat, too," I say, before even realizing I know this for a fact now. I push the memory of said sweat far, far away. "Don't you have to shower?"

I push back from the desk to stand.

"We do sweat," Lada says, looking devastated at this fact, "but, in Havcire, it evaporates almost immediately, and the air is a natural cleanser—Oh!" Lada exclaims, noticing the time.

She holds out her hands, palms open in front of her, and a folded-up dress appears there. I was about to grab clothes out of my closet to bring into the bathroom with me to change into after but Lada walks up and shuts the closet door, handing me the dress. It feels silky, like Lada's, or at least the skirt does. The bodice is a different, harder material.

"Phoenix sent it," she explains. "I borrowed the shoes from an Incanter friend of mine, so I will be needing those back."

"You have an Incanter friend?" I ask, surprised.

"Yes, I have friends," Lada says, defensively.

She sits back onto my bed; and although she has to look up at me to reach my eyes, she still manages to look intimidating.

"I didn't question that," I tell her.

"Maybe not explicitly," she says, raising a brown eyebrow up into the light fringe of her hair.

"It's just, I know you've avoided getting involved with the Council before, and I just assumed that meant you didn't interact much with others in Havcire," I say, attempting to explain, and truly hoping I'm not sticking my foot further into my mouth.

"There is more to Havcire than the Council. I didn't involve myself with the Council because I didn't agree with their decision to start the Subject System. We had vowed a long time ago to leave Vest on its own, and the Subject System broke that vow," Lada says.

"I understand that. Actually, it's pretty honorable to value an agreement as you did," I say, thinking back to my conversation with Dex about how I held the Celestials to too high a standard, comparing them to the noble knights of the round table.

"I wouldn't go that far," Lada says, easing up and offering me a smile. "You are right, though, that it doesn't make me extremely popular among the Celestials to disagree with the Council. Hence, my Incanter friend. Now, go ahead."

Lada gives me a delicate shove towards the bathroom, and I comply. Closing the door, I look at the dress in my hands.

It's sleeveless, the bodice form-fitting and made of brown leather. The leather ends at the waist and gives way to a flowing, silky skirt that is designed to crease like a folded paper fan. It's ombre, transitioning from a vibrant orange to a deep red at the bottom, the colors looking like they were brushed onto the silk with watercolors.

I know Incanters don't stick to the all-white fashion that Celestials do; but still, this dress seems like a bit too much for a group of people attempting an undercover operation of sorts.

Then again, I don't think Phoenix has ever done anything without calling attention to himself and those around him.

Although the skirt will cover the length of my legs, with no slit like the one in Lada's dress, I still take the time to shave my legs smooth in the shower. It seems like a crime to wear such a dress any other way. And, while Lada did give me the impression that we weren't to dawdle, I can't help but enjoy the extra time the shower gives me to gather myself. I would look forward to experiencing a party in Havcire if it didn't mean facing Phoenix so soon.

By the time I shut off the calming, warm water, I've decided I will make the best of this. It is an opportunity to uncover Chaos, and we finally know our target. It's also bound to be somewhat enjoyable, and Dex will be there. Lada will be there, too, which is oddly a… comfort?

I can get through the night barely acknowledging Phoenix. Sure, it's an immature tactic, but it's the best solution I can manage at least for this one night.

"I have to go as what?" I ask Lada, shifting in the desk chair to glance back at her.

She forces my head back toward the mirror so she can continue her work on my hair. I blow dried it mostly straight, the ends stubbornly already beginning to curl, so it'd be more manageable for her to style. Thankfully, she's pulling most of it out of my face with a braided headband made of my own hair, but she's left a couple tendrils loose around my face.

"Phoenix and I can go as ourselves. Since every Celestial knows of every Celestial, and Incanters can only come to the Havcire Assembly if escorted by a Celestial, you two have to come as our dates," she explains, finishing up my hair, with a prideful smile.

"I don't suppose I could go as your date instead?" I ask, with a small smile of my own.

"Sorry, you're not my type," Lada says with a shrug.

"I know that," I tell her, absentmindedly brushing back a piece of my hair she'd strategically just placed more directly in my face. "I'm not male but—"

"It's not that," she says, putting the piece of hair back in place. "I love all. You're just too short for me. We wouldn't look good together."

"Huh," I exclaim, glancing at the insulting piece of hair in my face and then back at Lada through the mirror. "I feel oddly offended. Oh, I know. I could wear heels!"

Laughing, Lada turns away from me and walks to the opposite side of my bedroom, towards my bedside table.

"You say that as if it's a novel idea."

Lada grabs something off the floor and brings it over. She holds up a pair of heels for me to see, presenting them with both hands. They look about four inches high and are made of a brown leather that nicely matches the dress.

"Of course you will be wearing heels."

CHAPTER 29

Phoenix teleports us into a hallway that leads to the Ziggurat ballroom. I can hear the symphony of voices and clamoring of movement coming from the end. Here, however, the hall is empty except for us for the time being.

The mirrored walls are only wide enough to allow one of us at a time to walk through, and I catch my first glimpse of myself since Phoenix set the illusion on my appearance.

It's startling to look in the mirror and see someone else, like a scene in a horror film, where the character looks in the mirror to find their reflection moving without them. Except, my reflection isn't frightening. The girl's expression still matches my own, moving when I do. Her face is longer than my own, more square-shaped face, giving her what I think of as a more sophisticated appearance. What's most shocking is the bright, orange hair on my head. It almost perfectly matches the shade at the top of my dress's skirt.

I realize why I had thought earlier I was experiencing some unusual aftereffects of Phoenix's teleportation. I'd seen flashes of orange in my periphery, but it was just my own strands of hair hanging down near my face. Of course, my eyes are no longer their unusual shade of amber, but a relatively mundane brown.

Dex, who walks in front of me, looks like an inverted image of his usual self. His normally black hair is a light blonde. When he glances back at me to offer a reassuring smile, even though I feel I should be the one to offer him such assurance, I see his normally brown eyes are sky blue. His skin is tanned, and his face is rounded in all the places it's normally sharpened.

Phoenix did a good job of ensuring no one would recognize the two of us.

We reach the end of the hallway and funnel out. From behind me, Phoenix grabs my arm and pulls me next to him, while Dex waits for Lada to come stand beside him at the entrance.

I take my arm out of Phoenix's light grasp but remain in my place.

A man in white, a Celestial, stands before us on door duty. He has stubble on his dark, olive skin that lines his strong chin and defined jaw. His black hair is neatly styled, swept up from his forehead and shaved on the sides. Standing out against his white wardrobe, is the golden belt looped through his pants. He looks to be in his thirties.

I don't know who they expect to be crashing the Havcire Assembly but the Celestial holds a clipboard full of names worthy of admittance. Granted, Dex and I are illegally attending but to keep an actual list seems like more of a formality. After all, the Celestials all know each other and could recognize outsiders easily.

"Phoenix," the man says. Case in point. "It's good to see you."

Is it? Phoenix offers him a friendly smile in return.

"And you, as well, Amun," Phoenix says. "I recall hosting this shindig once."

"Yes," Amun says, with a deep laugh, "I think we all recall that."

"Hello, Amun," Lada cuts in.

Light shines off her hair, as she tilts her head in greeting. Her arm is looped through Dex's. Amun turns his attention to her, notices Dex, and then glances briefly at me.

"Lada," Amun says, with noticeably less warmth than he directed towards Phoenix. Although, I wouldn't go so far as to say Amun was acting unkind towards her, either. "I see you have come with an Incanter as usual. And you, too, Phoenix?"

At this, Amun looks back at me, inquisitively. I'm guessing it's not as normal for Phoenix to show up to a party like this, especially with an Incanter, as it is for Lada.

I muster the most relaxed smile I can manage, hoping to seem natural and at ease. Phoenix holds out his arm, and I play along, linking my own arm with his, my hand resting against the inside of his upper arm. His shirt is smooth, made of thin material. His bicep tenses at my touch but he doesn't show any other sign that he's bothered.

Amun looks satisfied, smiling kindly at all of us again.

"Enjoy the Assembly," he says, gesturing to the rest of the room. "The show will begin soon."

I didn't realize there'd be a show. Then again, all of this is new to me.

I look around the room buzzing with conversation. Most of the people have found their seats already so it's not too hectic. There are more Incanters than I would have expected, all of them standing out in their brightly colored outfits. They must make up at least a quarter of the attendees.

As we walk down the wide center aisle, many of the Celestials break their conversations to greet Phoenix as congenially as Amun had at the door. Some even spare me a kind glance, which I do my best to return, while trying not to openly gawk at everything else.

"A real celebrity in our midst," I hear Lada jive quietly from behind us.

"Lada, shut up," Phoenix tells her under his breath, at which she laughs.

The room is set up like a classic auditorium. Rows of red, velvet seats fill the whole room, ending only to allow room for a dark mahogany stage that rises three feet up from the floor. Every part of the room is presented like a stage, as velvet curtains swoop down from the ceiling. They're pulled back, cinched against the wall by a thick golden rope. Being among the rows of seats feels less like sitting in the audience and more like sitting in the wings of the stage.

I let Phoenix lead me down to the fifth row back from the stage, Dex and Lada following. When he motions for me to sit, though, I wait for Dex to go in first and then Lada, separating me from Phoenix.

The seats are comfortable, nicely cushioned, and we are a good distance from the stage to be able to see well. I focus on my skirt to avoid any reaction from Phoenix regarding my avoidance. The silk feels nice against my fingers.

My one hand is still bandaged. I can feel the gauze wrapped around my sore knuckles, but I can no longer see it. Phoenix and Lada thought an injury would be too suspicious. Incanters don't walk around with cuts and bruises, let alone attend parties with them. They heal themselves using magic.

"We'll use the potion after the show," Lada leans in to tell me, "when we can move around better to observe everyone."

I nod my head and am about to ask about the show, when the lights in the chandeliers above flicker and then go out completely. Spotlights from somewhere behind me illuminate the stage so it is the only thing visible in the entire room.

There's an explosion, and I jump in my seat, unable to control my reaction. Yet, there's no heat and no impact.

Up on the stage, floating in the center, a tapestry has appeared, showing a moving picture. It depicts a world enflamed. Its particles vibrate with remaining energy from the explosion, unable to settle. The world spins in a blur of every color imaginable, gaining in speed, until it stops. It no longer vibrates, but holds a steady shape, looking much more like Earth if it still weren't for the odd coloring. The world disappears and the tapestry splits into five pieces, spreading out across the stage to display all five.

The one farthest to the left shows a new image, a volcanic eruption. From the lava rises a giant figure.

The tapestry to its right shows an ocean, each wave an individual tsunami. I can hear the crashing of the water and smell salt. From inside one of the massive waves, a shadowed figure appears.

The crashing silences as I look to the next tapestry, which now depicts a forest wild with trees. I breathe in and can smell the woods. My breath hitches as a loud crack sounds, and the ground opens up, a large hand reaching up from the chasm. A leaf breaks off a tree from the third tapestry and blows away, appearing again on the fourth tapestry, where a cyclone forms.

A hand reaches out from within the cyclone and crunches the leaf. I wait for the last, fifth tapestry to come alive, but it remains a black void. Until, a foot steps out from the tapestry and onto the stage.

The body from the black void is female, long hair flowing behind her from a wind I can't feel. But, no other features are identifiable. She is a shadow, as if come to life from the spotlights. If the darkness drained from the room, the chandeliers lighting once again, she would disappear.

The other four figures, three male and one more female, step out from their tapestries, also appearing like shadows. Giant, frightening shadows.

"What is this?" I ask Lada, expecting my voice to fail me, but it comes out thankfully quiet but enough for her to notice.

"The beginning," she whispers back. "They're the Protogenoi. Reminders to remember the danger of too much power."

The five figures vanish, only to appear again on one side of the stage, facing off against a group of others. The tapestries recombine to form a backdrop for the scene, a desolate field. As weapons appear in the hands of the figures, I realize it's a battlefield.

This is the Firstlast War. The two sides charge at each other, the sounds of metal clashing ringing out across the room. One shadowed figure from the Celestial side sprouts wings and flies toward the other side, sword in hand.

Again, the figures vanish but the tapestry does, also. Out of gray smoke, a wooden table appears atop the stage, along with four of the shadowed figures. The whole thing looks to be made from smoke and mirrors, but I don't doubt the smoke is made from real magic, along with everything else being shown.

On the table is a piece of parchment. The four figures are separated, two on each side of the table. They pass the paper between them, signing it, and then part, looking about to walk off the stage on opposite sides. However, before either group of two can enter into the wings, they puff away, as if blown apart by a breeze.

The parchment on the table floats into the air and rolls itself up into a scroll. As a thin thread of gold appears to fasten the scroll closed, the tapestry drops back down behind it.

The world from the beginning reappears, now completely stable, and obviously the Earth that I know, a green and blue marble. As the thread of gold knots, pulling tight, the tapestry harshly rips right down the middle, splitting the world in two, Vestigium and Havcire.

I know the depiction of the separation of Vest and Havcire is lacking in accuracy but it sure gets points for dramatization. Earth did not split down its center, right through the core, which would have been catastrophic. Really, Havcire is more like a wide ring surrounding Vest.

Music fills the room, a full orchestra, and a woman walks onto the stage. She's a Celestial, a real one, no longer just a shadow of a person created by magic. She begins to sing in a language I don't recognize, her voice sounding effortless despite the range the song demands.

I look to Lada, wanting an interpretation, and find Dex also looking expectantly at her. She directs him to Phoenix, unable to whisper to the both of us. I expect Lada to be at least somewhat irritated to explain the song to me but, if she is, she shows no sign of such irritation. She slides down in her seat a little to better speak to me.

"This second part," she explains, indicating the singer, "tells the story of the first Vest civilization after the split, where no hint of magic was left."

As the song continues, the tapestry grows to cover the entire stage, the singer standing in front of it, off to the side, like a narrator. It now shows a large temple and an ancient city surrounding it, lush with plants. Just outside the temple is a market full of people, but one man stands out among them. He wears a crown fit for a king and appears to be bidding the people farewell from a dais in the center of the market.

"You may have heard of the *Epic of Gilgamesh* before?" Lada asks, and I nod, still staring at the stage.

"Gilgamesh's quest for immortality was a result of him and his people's desire for the magic they lost by splitting with Havcire. With the loss of magic, they also lost their immortality. At the time of the split, after the war, the Celestials and Incanters that left to form Vest intended to one day lose their magic. It was the whole point of the separation, so the magic would never again corrupt like it had with the Protogenoi. But, when the magic actually began to fade and disappear, they longed for it to be returned. This story tells of the hero Gilgamesh who found the strength to let go of that desire and led his people on, despite the threat of mortal death."

The story continues to play out on the tapestry.

Gilgamesh leaves his city with another man. Trees sprout from the ground around them, as they journey further from the city, until they are surrounded by a full forest. In the forest, they battle a large animal, and Gilgamesh's friend dies.

Distressed, Gilgamesh sets off again. The trees on the tapestry collapse, leaving Gilgamesh to face treacherous terrains on his quest.

Eventually, he returns to the city empty-handed, and the story ends where it began, with Gilgamesh standing in front of his people. But, he speaks to them with a new confidence. His words are without sound, as the Celestial's song fills the entire room.

"We must face death, for it proves our courage, and that is where true strength lies," Lada whispers, interpreting. "We live because we one day will no longer."

The people bow to their king, and the tapestry disappears, as the song's final note sounds.

There's a breath of silence before the room fills with applause. The chandeliers burn back to life, and I raise my hands to applaud along with everyone else.

Without any warning that I recognize, everyone stands up from their seats. Lada pulls me up from my own, despite my body's reluctance from having sat in the comfortable seat for quite some time. I realize just how long this day has been, and it's not even over.

The seats move, sliding to the edges of the room, and leaving the wooden floor open. Surrounding the room's perimeter are Incanters, their mouths moving in a silent chant.

Their arms gesture around the room, conducting the redesign. In a unified downward swooping movement, the Incanters bring the thick, velvet curtains swinging down. They fall from the canopy they once formed and hover in the air about five feet above our heads. They rise back up, looking like they're being blown from below, the fabric ballooning upwards. They form new walls of red velvet, behind which they hide the clutter of seats that were cleared from the rest of the room.

I guess the next part of the evening won't involve any sitting.

The whole room now appears like a large dance floor. The Incanters in charge of the redecoration return to the throng of people and music begins.

With all the distraction, I hadn't noticed a group of four walk onto the stage, two Celestials and two Incanters that form the string quartet. The music is beautiful and somehow fills the entire room even though there's no sign of any amplification.

The guests at the Havcire Assembly are already dancing, as if scripted. Although, after who knows how many Havcire Assemblies have taken place over so many years, I would expect such an event to be nothing less than perfectly planned and rehearsed. I, on the other hand, along with Phoenix, Dex, and

Lada, stand out like the suspicious attendees we are by standing immobile in the middle of the room among the dancers.

CHAPTER 30

Dex takes Lada's hand to lead her in a dance. Phoenix slyly hands Dex the vial with Gatlin's potion inside before the two of them separate from us.

Phoenix takes my hand, and I hesitantly place my other hand atop his shoulder, as we join in with the other dancers. He holds me around my waist but apart from him at a respectable distance.

Despite the fatigue that was beginning to set in and the slightly panicked desire to leave here immediately and be back in my bed after the day I've had, I'm reluctant to admit that being in Phoenix's arms now makes me fully leave that desire behind.

I hate that I feel content and even rejuvenated. The one who's lied to me the most, who I've known for the longest, yet can't say I know at all, should not be the one who brings me the most comfort.

But, I'll take the second wind it's afforded me and not deal with the rest of all of that right now.

"Don't we need the potion, also?" I ask, focusing.

He lets go of my waist and lifts our arms up to twirl me around. I glimpse Dex and Lada a couple dancers away from us.

"I separated it into two containers for backup," Phoenix answers.

He pulls me closer and holds up the other vial between us, using our bodies to shield it from anyone else's view. He brings it to his lips and drinks, before pulling me into a dip to tilt the vial into my own mouth. The potion drips into my mouth, and I swallow quickly before I can choke on the liquid. Rising back up from the dip, I glare at Phoenix.

"What?" he asks, innocently. "We have to look natural."

He slips the vial back into his pant's pocket. I hadn't noticed before, maybe because I was working hard not to notice anything about Phoenix, but he's not wearing all white like the other Celestials. He's also not dressed in more vibrant colors like an Incanter either. Instead, he wears what a human would wear to a formal event, or at least a human that wanted to dress down a bit to a formal event.

His shirt is a plain, white button-down. A thin, black tie is neatly tied around his neck. It's actually the most decorative piece of clothing on him, with its subtle design of constellations made against the glossy material in a black suede. His pants are normal, black dress pants. And, now he has his crown of teal blue brain waves adorning his head, his light green eyes making the waves appear more green than blue.

He looks a lot like I'd imagine a fictional faerie prince masquerading as a human to look like, wildness barely concealed behind the guise of humanity.

"Lead us around the room more," I say.

He spins me out to better see the rest of the dance floor.

There are so many colors, seemingly all mixed together as the people dance near each other. It looks as though the differently colored waves weave in and out of each other, intertwining, as dance partners turn around and pass by other partners. The waves create a dance of their own, separate from the physical bodies to which they belong.

I turn back into Phoenix, hand resting back on his shoulder.

"You could lead," he suggests, and it is tempting, especially coming from him at this time. But, it's just a dance.

"No," I tell him, "that's not how this works."

I almost grimace at my own words. When did I become so accustomed to and accepting of the way things just are?

What is the point of fighting if you don't know what you're fighting for in the end?

Maybe I've finally given up the meaningless fight.

I feel Phoenix shrug beneath my hand, and he begins to lead us throughout the room, giving both of us a better view of the dancing Celestials.

As we dance by the individual couples, it's easier to make out their unique brain waves. The colors range from red to violet across the rainbow and every shade in between. What's interesting is that some of the couples' brain waves, even up close, seem to blend together, as if they're on the same level of thought. None, however, reveal any sign of possession or mind control.

The song ends, and the string quartet starts another, transitioning effortlessly into the next. It's slower and more haunting than the last, and it is very familiar.

1816

I look to my mother, who stands off to the side of the dance floor. She watches us dance with a content air, nodding encouragingly to me even as my dance partner steps directly onto my foot.

The song is slow; and yet, the Duke is rushed, much as he seems to be with everything. My mother is overjoyed by the apparent interest he has taken in me and his eagerness to ask for my hand. But, despite his congenial manner, I feel off-put by him. Perhaps it has something to do with the tightness with which he grasps my hand or the way he speaks up whenever my head even tilts in a direction where his face is not the focal point.

The song ends, and I curtsey. I'm about to excuse myself, but the Duke reaches out for my hand again.

"May I?" a voice cuts in from behind me.

I turn to find a man standing there with his hand outstretched toward me.

I've never seen eyes such a light green, the darkness of his hair making them stand out even more. Above all, and much more importantly, however, is the opportunity for escape at least temporarily.

I smile politely even though the Duke still holds my hand in his own, now for certain much too tightly.

"You may," I respond, and place my other hand in his open palm.

The man smiles crookedly, in a charming way. Still, the Duke doesn't let go of my other hand, so I squeeze my trapped hand within his even harder than he does mine.

Letting out a low hiss, he retracts his hand. I'll deal with the consequences of that action later. He nods his head politely toward the other man before leaving. The music starts up again, the song faster paced.

"Insufferable," I say, allowing the music to drown out my words, as I watch the Duke grab onto a new dance partner.

"Pardon?" the man with the green eyes asks, amusement in his voice.

I turn back to him. He couldn't have heard what I said.

"I am Margaret Adley," I say, hoping to move on from whatever he may or may not have heard.

He smiles, unbothered by the sudden introduction. We turn around each other, my hand resting in his hand.

"Pleasure to meet you, Ms. Adley. You may call me Phoenix," he says.

His hand shifts beneath mine, and I turn my hand into his. His fingers lightly drag along my palm before holding onto my hand, pulling our arms up so I may turn underneath.

We continue the dance, stepping out to each side before coming back in, my palm resting atop his shoulder and his other hand against my back. There, his fingers lightly touch my bare skin where the fabric of my dress ends at the top, sending a jolt that travels through my entire body, but he slowly moves his hand down so the fabric is between us again.

"I've never made your acquaintance before."

"And that is why we introduced ourselves," Phoenix says, offering no further information about himself.

"Yes, but I have never seen you around."

He twirls me twice, as we move across the dance floor.

"Do you know everyone there is to know around here?" he asks.

"Evidently not," I reply.

He lowers me into a dip, holding my gaze as he does. As I face him again, he lowers his head down slightly toward me.

"I am merely a friend offering you a reprieve," he says quietly, as if together we share a secret and are not two strangers. "A reprieve from the insufferable."

My hand has moved around to Phoenix's back, and I am closer to him than I remember being before the onslaught of memory. For the first time, I notice my own crown of waves above my head, as they extend further out from me toward Phoenix's, which appear to intertwine with my own. One sharp, golden wave of my own transitions into the smooth, teal of Phoenix's brain waves.

I create more distance between us, sliding my hand back to his shoulder, and evict the past memory from my mind. My thoughts appear to separate, disappearing from my sight, as they retreat back over my head and my head alone.

Phoenix stops moving and drops his arms to his side. I stop with him. He's focused on something or someone over my shoulder. With his eyes still directed elsewhere, he tucks the two strands of hair Lada intentionally styled to hang in front of my face back behind my ears. One hand lingers on my face, his thumb brushing gently along my cheekbone.

"What do you think you're doing?"

Phoenix, distracted, pulls his gaze away from whatever grabbed his attention behind me and looks back at me. Seeming to only just realize the location of his hand, he lowers it quickly back to his side and clears his throat.

"You don't like your hair to be in your face. Now, come on. I have an idea," he says, and begins to make his way through the dancing crowd.

My dress flows around me in a sunset of colors, the silk caressing my legs, as I follow Phoenix. I stay directly behind him in order to draw the least attention to myself.

I guess where it is that we're heading when I find that not everyone in the room has taken up dancing. Against one of the walls of velvet curtain stands Barnabas and Lucifer.

"If we can't find who Chaos has currently taken up residence within, then we'll have to give her a reason to use her mind control," Phoenix says.

"Draw her out?"

"Exactly," he says, a moment before we reach Barnabas and Lucifer.

CHAPTER 31

The two Council members look at me inquisitively, and I have to remind myself that I no longer look like myself. I self-consciously pull the strand of orange hair back out from behind my ear to confirm this fact, only to almost immediately tuck it back behind my ear and out of my face.

"Phoenix, you've brought a date?" Barnabas asks, sounding like a judgmental parental figure, so much so that I have to restrain a laugh.

"Finally found someone that is better company than yourself?" Lucifer asks. "She is at least prettier than you are."

I do my best not to let my surprise show.

It's not just that Phoenix has never brought an Incanter as a date to the Havcire Assembly, but he's never brought anyone. And, technically, he's only brought me as a fake date. My fake friend taking me on a fake date with an illusion placed on me to give me a fake identity. I'm beginning to think I shouldn't even try to puzzle this one out, and I definitely should stop caring about puzzling Phoenix out.

Sure, Phoenix flirts with every person he comes across but I don't even know if he's ever had a single, genuine relationship. After all, why would I know? The majority of the time I've spent with him has been time he's needed to pretend to be someone else. All I know is that apparently he's never taken anyone to the Havcire Assembly, and that's honestly most likely because he's evidently very popular amongst the Celestials here. It's not like he's in need of any particular person to keep him company.

Even about that I was wrong. I had assumed because he gave the Council such a hard time that all Celestials would have some issue with him.

Best not to assume I know anything about Phoenix.

Lucifer pricks his finger on the sharp edge of his jacket, which is made of needles painted white. With intense interest, he watches the blood pool on his finger from the pinprick and then reabsorb into his body, his skin stitching itself closed. A drop of his blood remains on the tip of the needle.

I guess he does that little habit even when not seated on his pointy throne. I wonder if I could go so far as to call it a nervous habit. Does a leader of Celestials have nervous habits? It would be so human of him.

"Tough call, Luce. We'd have to consult the magic mirror," Phoenix retorts. "This is Bell. Bell, Lucifer and Barnabas. Although, I'm sure you already know of them."

"Yes," I force out, "nice to meet you both."

I'm glad to hear my voice come out normal, with no sign of nerves. Except, will they recognize my voice? No, they don't know me *that* well. I feel a small smile spread on my face, as if taking on a life of its own, my body knowing I need to make them believe I'm an innocent Incanter.

"I actually have some questions, for which I am curious about the answers. Phoenix thought you might be able to help," I continue, relaxing.

"Yes," Phoenix says, "as you two are always so helpful."

Phoenix sounds sarcastic, prompting doubtful expressions, but I laugh airily and smile lightheartedly at Phoenix and the two Council members. The tension eases.

"It's my first time attending a Havcire Assembly, you see," I begin, "and I greatly enjoyed the show. With our history displayed like that, it reminded me of our promise long ago to stay separate from Vest. My question is, how did the Subject System play into that later? How did it manage not to break our agreement to stay divided?"

Barnabas rolls his shoulders back, readjusting his posture, although he already stood up straight. The drop of blood that clung onto Lucifer's jacket's needle falls to the dark, mahogany floor.

Despite the continued dancing throughout the rest of the room and the music that moves through the room, a stillness and silence settles over Barnabas and Lucifer. I imagine I can hear the blood droplet hit the floor with a small splash. Neither reply, appearing stumped, and their eyes show no indication of comprehension.

They really do have no clue about the Subject System, nor any ability to address its origins. They're practically frozen, as if waiting for an order.

I realize exactly what it is they are waiting for, when a scarlet wave attaches itself like a cable to their brain waves.

"The Subject System gives Subjects the opportunity to become Citizens, and it allows those on Vest to benefit from findings achieved in Havcire," Barnabas says, seemingly back to his usual, authoritative self.

I glance at Phoenix and see he, too, has noticed the scarlet wave. It trails off across the dance floor to somewhere out of sight.

"Thank you, and it was a pleasure," I tell Barnabas and Lucifer, with a smile.

We turn away to follow the scarlet brain wave before it can disappear. A glance back in their direction reveals that neither Barnabas nor Lucifer seems to have minded our sudden departure. Already, the foreign brain wave has begun to leave their heads, retracting like a piece of yarn trailing after a cat with the full ball of yarn in its mouth.

I pull Phoenix along faster, before the wave can slither away fully back to its source.

As we almost walk directly into a dancing couple, I switch my attention to ensuring we don't bump into anyone, while Phoenix keeps his eyes on the scarlet brain wave. We can't risk walking around the throng of dancers and losing the trail, so we have to make our way through the sidestepping and turning Celestials and Incanters.

Trying to navigate through everyone reminds me of an obstacle course, the billowing skirts as much one of the obstacles as the arms and legs that shift in the dance.

Dex and Lada make their way to our side, sliding between a narrow space on the dance floor between two couples.

"We saw the stray wave," Dex says, his eyes up on said wave.

"We brought up the Subject System to Barnabas and Lucifer, and her mind control began, the wave showing up with it," I tell them.

We come to the opposite side of the room, where the dancers finally thin out again.

"I knew there was something off," Phoenix says.

I follow the wave to its source. The trail leads back to Minerva, where the wave ends and wraps fully back around her head to complete the crown.

There are two crowns. They are of two separate colors, one the scarlet and the other a gray, silver color. The scarlet crown wraps around the gray one, as if caging it in.

"Dawn," Phoenix warns, but I'm already walking towards her, any calm I'd achieved since my conversation with Phoenix in the woods chipping away to make way for the anger and resentment.

She still looks just like Minerva, the Council member I most liked, but I only see the intrusive red above her head.

"Why did you create the Subject System?" I ask, to which Minerva merely looks puzzled.

"Excuse me?" she asks.

"I know who you really are so don't bother."

Her facade of bewilderment drops to be replaced with curiosity, as she examines me.

Minerva's dark eyes, which normally give off warmth, widen in understanding. Before I can stop her, she lifts up a strand of my orange hair. At her touch, the orange fades and its true color shines through the illusion Phoenix carefully crafted.

I pull back, the hair limply dropping from her hand, and the brown disappears once again into the orange.

"And, I know who you really are," she says, with a smile that makes Minerva's face look cruel. "I thought you were dead, Dawn." When she says my name, she whispers it, throwing the fact that she knows my secret back in my face. "You were supposed to be, but that I can rectify."

The meaning of her words hit me too late.

A bolt of red energy releases from the palm of her hand. I'm too close to her to do much of anything except throw my arms up in a useless attempt to shield myself.

The energy strikes my arms, and the feeling of an electric shock awakens me. Like a mirror reflecting light, the red energy bounces off me, finding Dex who'd come to my side in my defense.

Dex falls to his knees, hands covering his abdomen where he was hit. Already, blood is seeping through his fingers. He looks up, surprised.

That wasn't meant for him. He wasn't even in the original course of the shot. I did that.

"No." My denial comes out barely above a whisper.

The music from the string quartet continues, even though it feels as though everything should stop. Everyone in the room should be aware of what's happened but the reality is that they're all still dancing to the music that drowns out any sign that something's wrong.

Lada quickly closes the distance between herself and Dex, kneeling down to him, attempting to help him stanch the bleeding. A bright light flows out from her fingers and looks to go into Dex's wound.

I pull my eyes away from Dex to look back at Minerva. She's smiling, raising her hand again to hit the intended target this time.

I take a step closer to her, unsure of what I even plan to do, but something has to be done. Dex is injured, maybe—

Phoenix grabs onto my arm. I stumble to the side, almost falling over Dex and Lada.

Minerva releases another bolt of energy but the world shrinks away, as I'm pulled through the air, squeezed in between microscopic particles.

298

CHAPTER 32

There are carpets on top of carpets, each of varying colors. Some of them simply overlap at the corners, while others are placed directly on top of one another, the larger one beneath forming a border for the smaller one above.

There's a shiny, black grand piano in one corner of the room and a fireplace set into the brick wall.

Thankfully, there's no coffee table in the center of the room, where the four of us land when Phoenix teleports us into Gatlin's living room.

Gatlin himself is dressed today as if pulled out of the 1920s, with a knitted, gray vest over a collared, white shirt. The look is complete with a matching gray newsboy cap.

He stands over by the piano, staring at us, as we do him. I wasn't expecting to be here, either. But, he looks to adjust faster, pulling on the bottom of his vest as he straightens up. His navy eyes sharpen, taking in the situation, which includes Dex still on his knees, barely conscious, and being held upright by Lada.

"The reason," Gatlin speaks, as he walks over to look closer at Dex, "I live in the middle of the Graveyard, is to avoid house visits such as this."

"I apologize," Phoenix says, glancing worriedly between Dex and Gatlin. "I didn't have another option. At least, not a good one."

"I'm Lada," Lada tells Gatlin in a hasty introduction. "I cauterized the wound to stop the bleeding."

Gatlin nods and kneels down on the carpeted floor beside them, despite his complaints regarding our arrival.

Lada cautiously lowers Dex down so he lies on his back. Dex lets out a strained exhale, but otherwise doesn't protest, his eyes struggling to stay open. Gatlin unbuttons Dex's shirt, exposing the wound.

"He looks poisoned. What are these red marks stemming from the wound? Tell me what's happened," Gatlin orders.

Lada goes into the explanation, telling Gatlin about Chaos and her attack. Phoenix loosens his tie, unbuttoning the top couple buttons of his shirt. He stretches his neck, as if the tie had become a noose around it.

I close my eyes, seeing the bolt of energy come from Minerva's hand and strike Dex.

"You should've left me behind to face her," I tell Phoenix, my voice harsh but hushed, so to not disturb Lada and Gatlin. The latter appears busy preparing a potion for Dex, having transformed the top of the grand piano into a makeshift brewing station.

"You mean I should've left you to your death? Yes, because that seems like something I'd do," Phoenix replies, equally intense, yet quiet.

"She did this," I say, pointing off towards Dex.

Phoenix glances down at Dex and Lada, his expression softening, but when he looks back at me it's with little sympathy.

"And we'll see her again," Phoenix says, "when we're ready, but it's that kind of thinking that got us in this situation to begin with. You should never have so impulsively confronted her. You not only gave away that we know she's Chaos, but you endangered all our lives."

"Done," Gatlin announces, holding up a luminous, green potion and silencing any reply I could have mustered.

Except, I don't have anything left to say. Phoenix is right.

It's my fault that Dex was put in danger. That attack from Chaos was meant to kill me. I confronted her without a plan. I didn't even think. I just saw the chance to finally face the person responsible for making the corrupt Subject System and, most likely, making me a Subject.

The potion better save him.

Dex has given up forcing his eyes open, but his chest moves with breath, calming my rising panic. While the gash on his stomach no longer bleeds, thanks to Lada, the red veins that originate from it have spread further across his skin, nearly reaching his heart.

Gatlin hands the potion to Lada, who tilts the liquid into Dex's mouth.

We all watch him as he swallows and as nothing happens in the moment after; but then, the green of the potion spreads across the red veins, neutralizing the foreign substance within.

It's good. This is good. And yet, I can't take my eyes away from Dex, and I can't seem to let out the breath I'm suddenly holding from fear any diversion of my focus will cause those red veins to come back with a vengeance.

A hollow bang sounds from the doorway.

That breath comes out of me against my will in a startled gasp. On edge, still mentally standing in front of Chaos, expecting the next attack, I turn quickly to see something falling outside the circular window by the door, the door of this unexpectedly cozy cottage. And, Chaos doesn't know we're here.

"I'll stay with him," Lada says. "Go."

"We'll be right back," Phoenix says, walking ahead of me, but not before sparing me a warning look.

How the tables have turned. I thought I was the one that had little trust in him but now he doesn't trust me to simply act reasonably.

I force myself to count to ten like a child before following him out the door. Gatlin's not far behind, having retrieved a lantern.

He holds it up over Phoenix's shoulder to illuminate what lies on the ground.

It's Minerva's griffon, looking like roadkill, with its owl wings splayed out around it.

With a hoot, it seems to resurrect, leaping back up onto its small, furry lion legs. Immediately, it focuses on Phoenix.

"Bishop," Phoenix says, with a smile.

Phoenix holds out his arm, and Bishop flaps up to perch there, his soft tail curling around Phoenix's arm.

"Anyone else going to drop by?" Gatlin asks, petting Bishop between his pointed ears.

Bishop's eyes seem to hold my own, staring at me as if he knows Phoenix is upset with me. I don't look away, hoping they'll soften.

His eyes are perfectly round. In the dark, they look like two wells of black ink. The smooth, white feathers surrounding his eyes give him the appearance of a harmless stuffed animal. The white feathers darken into a brown, framing his face. His eyes still intensely stare into my own, and I'm reminded of the fact that the griffon sees everything that happens on Vest and Havcire.

"What do you have for me?" Phoenix asks, finally drawing Bishop's attention away from me.

From Bishop's beak, a rolled up piece of paper drops into Phoenix's hand. Gatlin holds the light closer for Phoenix to see the paper.

"Thanks," Phoenix tells the griffon.

He starts to unroll the paper but something drops out from it.

I reach for it before it can fall to the ground, my hand closing around the cylindrical object less than a second before Phoenix also reaches out to catch it. He comes to a halt, realizing I've already got it.

"Phoenix, are you getting slow in your old age?" Gatlin asks, a note of amusement in his voice. "Some of us hold up better than others over the years," he tells me.

Although Gatlin jokes, Phoenix stares at me seriously. The moment reminds me of the discussion we had after the incident with Helen, after I broke through the ice to get to her friend. Phoenix looks at me with the same expression he did then, when he questioned how my hand showed no sign of injury. Except now, there's no hint of surprise on his face.

I look away from him, focusing instead on the object in my hand. It's a cylindrical glass vile, much like the ones Gatlin uses to contain his potions. This one, however, is filled with a familiar blue liquid.

"Remember," Phoenix says.

"What?" I ask absentmindedly, still looking at the vile.

"It's what the piece of paper says. It's all it says, in fact. Very helpful," Gatlin says. "Who needs to remember, and what is it they need to remember?"

"Well, I'm sure I have things to remember. As for what, if I knew that, there'd be no need to remember."

"Fair, but who's it from?"

"Me," Phoenix says, speaking up, and Bishop lets out another hoot as if in confirmation. "It's my handwriting, but I don't remember ever writing it or ordering Bishop to bring it to us. So, clearly I have something to remember, as well."

I have at least a whole life as a Citizen to remember. I had nearly forgotten.

Bishop lets out a loud screech, and Phoenix says something quietly to the griffon that I can't make out, to which it more quietly hoots a response. At least, that's all it sounds like to me, but Phoenix obviously understands Bishop's meaning.

"Dawn, myself, and Lada are supposed to be the ones to drink from the vial," Phoenix informs us.

Gatlin lowers the lantern to his side with a shrug.

"I didn't realize you spoke bird," he says, before walking back inside his house.

CHAPTER 33

"**I** 'm good," Lada says, refusing the memory potion.

She sits beside Dex on one of the three couches adorning Gatlin's living room and looks suspiciously at the vial in my hand, as if it could be poison, which it could be to be honest.

Dex is already doing noticeably much better. He's refastened his shirt, even though it still has blood stains on it, and is able to support himself in an upright position.

"I'm the one that gave the directions that came along with this vial," Phoenix says, "and I trust myself even if I can't remember why I did any of this in the first place."

Lada looks from the vial to Phoenix and agrees, nodding her head in acquiescence.

I'm not sure how she gained such confidence in him. Actually, I'm not really sure of their relationship at all, I realize. They had seemed reluctant to deal with each other when she'd first arrived, but that was also when Phoenix still suspected she could be under Chaos's control. Since, they've worked in tandem. She trusts him, but do I?

I trust that Phoenix always has a plan, and I'm fairly certain that, no matter our history, he doesn't want me dead. So, the vial is at least not poison, in which case it is a good risk to take in case it does give me my memories back. That makes sense. Or, at least, I convince myself it does.

But, it could take away the memories I do have. Then again, if I don't take it, eventually that will happen anyway when I start another life for Max's experiment. With everything that has happened, though, is going back to being a Subject in Max's experiment even an option anymore? At this point, will Chaos still allow that or does she think the only thing left to do with me now is kill me?

Taking the potion is a risk, but every option I have now feels like a risk.

With my decision made, for better or for worse, I sit down on the couch opposite Lada and Dex. Phoenix already sits on the one between us, looking across at the fireplace.

"So, who wants to drink first?" I ask, holding up the vial, the light from the fire illuminating the blue liquid.

"You are holding it," Phoenix says, leaning back against a multi-colored pillow and earning a glare from me.

"It's good to see you've all made yourselves feel at home." Gatlin comes in from another room. "Yes, you may use my humble abode to go on a memory trip. Thank you for asking."

He leans against the doorframe, his arms crossed against his chest, as his eyes scan the room. I get up from my seat and walk over to him.

"Gatlin, we are sorry for imposing," I say, speaking to him alone. "I know you don't really know me well, except for what you gathered from those tests, but I don't take generosity lightly. I will find a way to repay you, I promise."

There's movement behind me, and I look to see Phoenix has gotten to his feet. He holds Gatlin's gaze, though, not looking at me.

Gatlin's mouth lifts into a small smile directed at Phoenix, one that makes me believe Phoenix wasn't lying when he claimed Gatlin truly is a friend of his. Still, Phoenix doesn't seem to trust how Gatlin will react to others, such as me.

Gatlin turns his attention back to me, tipping his hat in my direction.

"Payment will not be necessary, as you are fighting an enemy of us all. I remember now why I recognized your eyes. You deserve to know from where is it they come," Gatlin says. His eyes shift to behind me and again a smile creeps onto his features, and before I can question what exactly Gatlin thinks he knows... "It seems someone has chosen to be first."

I spin around to find Lada standing near the couch I'd abandoned, vial in hand. I clench my empty fists, confirming the obvious. I'd left the potion on the couch.

"What?" she asks of our stunned expressions. "Someone had to get things done."

Lada sways on her feet and her eyes flutter closed a second before she begins falling.

Dex reaches out in time to stop her from falling on the ground and effortlessly lifts her up from behind her arms and knees. It's a great relief to see he's strong enough to do as much. Ironically, he looks more like the Celestial carrying the human in the moment.

I snap myself back to the current situation. I hadn't taken the time to acknowledge that this process would involve loss of consciousness. Although, it makes sense, considering we need time to process whatever memory we stand to recover.

"Nice catch," Phoenix tells Dex, as he lays her back down on the couch, her head resting on one of the pillows.

"Thanks," Dex says, "but I recommend you two start off seated before taking your doses."

"Speaking of," I say, picking up the thankfully closed vial from the thankfully well-carpeted floor, "we should wait to take it until Lada wakes up and can tell us what happened. For all we know, it could actually end up wiping all our memories."

"You can wait, but I'm going to take it," Phoenix says, grabbing the vial from my hand.

"Are you really going to be that reckless?" I ask, my horrible British accent rearing its head again. Phoenix's brows shoot up. I groan in frustration and hesitate before continuing, ensuring my voice returns to normal. "All we have to do is wait a bit longer to find out for sure if it's safe or not."

"I'm never reckless," he says, with enough emphasis that I know he's referencing my actually reckless, or impulsive as he'd referred to them, actions from not that long ago. "I'm the one always with the plan, and I'm the one that sent us this vial. I am not going to wait any longer to get my memories back."

This *could* finally be my chance to remember everything about myself. I honestly don't know how long it's been since I've known my entire history, or if there's ever been a time in my life when that was true.

I've always waited and played along as Max's good Subject. Even in this life, where I technically cheated by knowing the rules of the game, I played the game, never considering making my own rules.

I'm that kid in those Vest experiments that holds off for more marshmallows instead of eating the one offered right away. I am the queen of delayed gratification. But, the truth is, I've never really been that fond of marshmallows, and I'm sure as hell ready to stop waiting and get the full picture of my life.

I snatch the vial back from Phoenix.

"Yeah, it's not fun to have your memories taken from you, is it?" I say.

I sit back down on the couch. Just as I'm about to drink from the vial, it disappears from my hand and reappears in Phoenix's. He sits down on the other couch with a smug smile.

"No, it's not," Phoenix agrees.

He lifts the vial to his mouth before I can move to stop him and drinks the blue liquid.

Closing the vial, he tosses it back to me, and I hasten to catch it.

"Child," I mumble under my breath, but Phoenix hears and chuckles.

I drink the last bit of the potion before resting against the back of the couch to ensure I don't fall forward onto the floor.

"Well," Dex says, with an encouraging smile, "I'll be here, making sure no one bites their tongue off or anything."

"That's great," Gatlin chimes in. "I'll be in the kitchen having a cup of joe. Sweet dreams."

CHAPTER 34

All in my head

Lightning. What seems to be hundreds of uprooted trees surround me, and that's just what I can see. The bursts of light shoot off from the branches of one long tree to the roots of another.

Except, they aren't trees. I've seen this before, not from this perspective, but I can recognize it all the same even if it seems impossible. After all this time, however, who am I to call anything impossible anymore?

Max is going to be so jealous.

I'm looking at the inside of my brain, my neurons firing at rapid speeds. This takes introspection to a whole new level.

I somehow travel between the gaps, with each burst of light revealing a new area full of bright, active neurons. I watch one stream of activity travel along a chain of neurons, hopping from one to the next, until it comes to an abrupt stop. Before extinguishing, it illuminates a void ahead, a dark space where the neurons fail to receive any messages.

Unlike the rest of my brain cells, resting in darkness, waiting for the next burst of light to come through and wake them up, this group looks as though it's been sleeping for a long time.

The chain of light starts up again but this time it is behind me. When it comes to the dead end once again, I find myself right at the point where the active neurons meet the sleeping ones. The light goes out.

The darkness lasts for longer than before. I'm in the territory of the slumbering cells.

I should panic, being apparently lost in my own inactive brain. I probably would be panicking if I could sense any part of my body at the moment but there's no heart of mine to feel pounding and no skin to feel breaking out in a sweat. Even my brain, ironically, doesn't feel like my own. It's as though I'm in someone else's dream, a mere bodiless bystander.

Suddenly, a hum of energy fills the area around me, as if the world is charging up. Simultaneously, the sleeping neurons wake up. They're blindingly bright, and I can no longer make out the individual branches and roots through the glare. There's just white light all around, and I sure hope it's not the *white light.*

I flinch away from the brightness.

I flinched! I can feel my body again. My back is pressed up against a wall. The light fades; and aside from the black swirly dots spotting my vision, I can see my surroundings again.

There's soft music, a lullaby. It comes from the crib in front of me and the mobile turning above it. But, there is no mechanical accompaniment, no quiet hum indicating an electric battery powering it. It turns because someone recently twisted it up so that it would, and the music is coming from the young woman sitting on a chair at one end of the crib.

Startled, my hand bumps into the wall behind me. She looks over, directly at me, but seems to look right through me. She turns back to the crib, unaffected.

I hold my hands out in front of me and notice that there's an odd translucency to them.

I'm not really here, of course, I remind myself. I took the potion to get my memories back, and I'm observing one now.

I gasp soundlessly, realizing that makes me the baby in the crib and this a memory from my original life.

The woman, my mother, has dark brown eyes that are fighting to stay open until the baby falls asleep and she can go to her room to do the same. She continues to hum the soothing melody as she gets up from her chair to peek over the side of the crib.

The humming stops, and she lets out a contented sigh before making her way to the door. Before closing the door, she takes one last peek into the room.

I wait till I no longer can hear her retreating footsteps to walk away from the wall and towards the crib, even though I know she wouldn't have noticed if I moved around while she was present anyways.

I look at the baby, myself, in the crib and am almost convinced that she really is asleep. But, I know that can't be true because this is *my memory after all. You can't remember something that happened while asleep.*

A few seconds pass before the baby's eyes open, and a little smile appears on her face, as if proud of herself for faking sleep. What baby fakes being asleep or even knows how to?

Her eyes, bright amber even at this age, catch on the mobile and the stars dangling from it. It has stopped turning. Without anyone touching it, it begins turning again and doesn't slow down no matter how long I stare in disbelief at both it and the baby watching it from below. As it turns, her eyes follow it around and around until they finally begin to start drooping, closing for real this time, my own vision of the room getting increasingly hazy.

The bedroom door bangs open, everything coming clearly back into focus.

I whip around to find my mother entering back into the room. Any sign of fatigue is gone, and her expression morphs her face into that of another person entirely.

The light brown hair we share is streaked through with red that I hadn't noticed before. As the door loudly slams closed behind her from the force of hitting the wall, I wonder where my father is. Was he around this night or even in the picture at all?

She's barefoot but doesn't seem to mind the fact that she steps on top of wooden splinters from the door.

The baby's eyes are open again, torn from her sleep. She stares along with me at our mother, whose face holds no sign of emotion, giving it a cold cruelty. She walks around the crib, opposite where I stand, and leans forward to rest her arms along the side. Her posture, unlike her face, suggests feelings of relief.

I make to shield the baby with my ghost-like body, knowing the futility of the act, but I can't even do that. I no longer stand opposite the woman that was our mother. I look at her from the perspective of the baby, from my past perspective.

I feel my own fear, as if I am once again living this moment. I'm helpless, unable to even attempt to escape.

I reach out to the mobile, making it sway, as my heart jumps in my chest. The mobile bounces against my mother's head harmlessly. Moonlight through the window glints off a sharp, metal object she holds in her hand.

The air is dry and cold. I'm in the Council room in the Ziggurat.

A sigh of relief escapes me. It feels as though I've been pulled out of a tidal wave, having narrowly escaped death. Except, I find the baby from the crib sitting on the floor in the center of the room, and I know we didn't escape that death. It is why we're here now.

I stand behind the baby in my ghost-bystander-form, invisible to the figments of my memory.

Barnabas, Lucifer, and Minerva sit in their respective thrones. I sit down on the marble floor beside the baby, looking up at them.

If possible, Barnabas seems even more indifferent towards the situation than usual. He doesn't even look at the baby before him. Lucifer, on the other hand, stares at her as if he despises the thing. Minerva threads a piece of silk from her throne between her fingers, concealing her thoughts by focusing on the minuscule action.

A knock echoes throughout the room, making the previous silence sound even louder in comparison.

The baby and I turn our heads to look back towards the doors.

"Enter," Barnabas says, his voice traveling across the room with strength.

The baby coos quietly. She seems to like the sound of his voice. I guess the deepness is soothing, or maybe she's just glad someone finally spoke up.

"I have a message from one of the Experimenters," Phoenix says, as he enters the room.

He notices the baby on the ground, to which he raises one eyebrow in speculation but quickly moves along to focus on the Council. I stare back at Phoenix with just as much curiosity.

I can't believe my own memory. Phoenix just respectfully knocked on a door before entering. I feel as though I should object to his actions, bringing his character into question, as if we were in a courtroom. I'm sorry, but Phoenix is clearly not of sound mind, Your Honor, evidenced by the fact that he has knocked on the door.

Not to mention, it is a little odd to see him looking identical to how he does today, while I'm no more than one year old, sitting on the floor at his feet. While I know he's immortal, it is still weird to see this situation. Like, hi there, please don't step on me. Thanks.

"Though, it isn't urgent, and I see you are busy," Phoenix continues. At this, he looks back down at the baby and waves with a smile. To his shock, and mine, she enthusiastically returns the gesture. "I can return later."

"It's nothing, just an infant that needs to be placed in Holding," Barnabas replies, motioning for Phoenix to continue.

Holding is the place in Havcire reserved for infants, where they're kept until a Citizen turns up who wants to raise a child. Normally, the infant is held for their biological parents when they, too, arrive in Havcire but not always.

The magic in Havcire is never used to merely speed up the growth process of the infant, as they would grow up physically but would lack the psychological development needed to function on their own in Havcire. As a result, humans who die as infants are placed in Holding. Magic provides for their basic needs and keeps them young until someone can raise them properly.

I can't imagine what it'd be like to be frozen at such a young age, but I may be about to remember exactly that. It would give me a whole lot of time to reflect on the few memories present in my mind as a child, including the one that would stand out above all others as traumatizing.

My own mother killed me. After all this time searching for memories of my past, I think I could've gone on without that one.

The second the thought crosses my mind, I'd like to slap my own non-corporeal body.

No matter how bad that memory was or how bad the memories to come will be, I will not regret knowing them. I might need some therapy after, if there's time, but I will not regret finally getting the answers I've been searching for.

Phoenix reports to Barnabas. While the Council members are occupied by his report, my attention gets drawn back to the baby sitting beside me. She leans forward, placing her hands out in front of her so she is supported by both her hands and knees and begins crawling forward.

I couldn't be more than six months old at this point; and yet, here I am crawling. The magic of Havcire must already be taking effect, speeding up the physical maturation before Holding can keep it constant. I didn't know it worked this fast but I've also never interacted with any infants in Havcire.

With the Council distracted by Phoenix, no one else notices the baby crawl all the way up to the foot of Barnabas's throne and push herself up to stand beside it. Well, no one else notices but Phoenix, who barely conceals a smile as he continues to report.

In the time it takes me to check Phoenix's awareness and look back towards the baby, she's somehow managed to plop herself down right on top of Barnabas's lap, pulling his attention away from Phoenix, whose face gives way to the smile.

"What..." Barnabas questions, throwing his arms out to his side, as if afraid the baby will bite.

Lucifer leans forward in his throne towards Barnabas and the baby. He reaches out a hand to her but she swats it away. Lightly, he swats her offending hand back, but she seems unbothered. In fact, she laughs.

"I like this little Vest," Lucifer says.

"How did she die?" Phoenix asks, coming closer.

Barnabas, still noticeably uncomfortable, at least lowers his arms stiffly back onto his armrests.

"Killed," Minerva responds, "by her mother."

"And her father?"

"He left before she was born," Minerva answers.

I'm not surprised it's Minerva who knows my whole life story, regardless of how little there is of it. She was always the one who ensured she had all the information, even if it wasn't necessary.

"I guess that rules out her parents taking her from Holding then," Phoenix says.

I can't quite discern his expression, whether there's some anger or even pain there. Maybe pity.

I'm limited as to what I can see now by what I had once observed as a baby. And, it's getting harder to make sense of my surroundings and the conversation, the whole place becoming increasingly out of focus.

The baby's eyes flutter, staying closed for longer periods.

I was drifting in and out of sleep. While the memory isn't as visibly and audibly clear anymore, I still get fragments of the conversation and blurry images of the Council and Phoenix.

"...keep her?" I recognize Barnabas's voice say incredulously and remember Minerva being the one to make the suggestion.

"I'll help." And then, "What? She could liven things up a bit. You know how I've been getting bored," Phoenix says.

"I support," Lucifer says.

I run along a sandy beach, my beach, towards the water of the ocean. Technically, I stand in the shade of the trees, watching a five-year-old version of myself run along the beach.

Above me is a large treehouse. This whole area is the result of allowing a toddler to decide their dream home. Naturally, I had wanted to live in a treehouse that was in a forest right by the ocean. By age two, I'd banished mosquitos from my forest and added air conditioning to my treehouse.

As the five-year-old's toes are about to touch the water rising up on the surface, a young boy, who looks to be about the same age, blips into existence behind her and pulls her away from the water.

I look up at the boy from the eyes of my past self. The light green eyes and scar through his dark eyebrow leave no question as to his identity, despite the rest of his appearance.

The accompanying knowledge of my past comes stumbling back along with the picture.

Phoenix appeared to me as the age I was as I grew so I'd see him as a peer, so that I'd have a friend.

I feel my eyebrows draw together, my mouth pulling down into a pout. It's like I'm hitching a ride in my own self, with no control over my body.

"Phoenix," I whine, "you never let me swim."

"That's because you don't know how to swim," he says, his voice unlike the deeper and smoother one I know well and much more like that of a young boy. "Do you know what happens to people who swim without knowing how? They drown. And die."

Still has the same way with words, though.

"I'm already dead," I argue.

"Still not comfortable to drown," he rebuts.

"Fine, then teach me to swim."

I'm older now, twelve years old.

I sit in my bedroom in the treehouse. It's my favorite spot - the bench beside the window with no glass to separate the indoors from out. Vines from the tree curl into the room, creating a border for the window.

Miranda, a fellow Citizen, paces about the room, book in hand. The Council assigned her to tutor me. She jumped at the opportunity to continue teaching, as she did during her life on Vest.

Miranda insisted that her curriculum cover Vestigium studies in addition to Havcire history. However, now she reads from a thick book on Havcirian natives. My eyes follow along in my matching copy.

"Minerva," she orders, testing me.

I look sidelong at her.

"Miranda, I think I know that one."

She responds merely with a stern expression. So, basically, her natural face. Miranda actually chooses to appear aged. Her natural beauty is clear in her intelligent, shining blue eyes, but her face is covered with wrinkles that betray her age as around seventy.

I sigh and relent, as I often do for Miranda.

"Minerva is a Council member. Two other examples of her from Vest mythology are Athena from the Greeks and Saraswati from Hinduism. She chose her name from the Roman interpretation. I also, personally, see her about once a week to train me in weapons and strategy."

"Good, although you know the last part was not necessary. Next page," she says.

I obey, turning the page of my text. A loose piece of paper falls out from between the pages and into my lap. I unfold it as Miranda continues reading. It's bent in half only once, but I'm afraid I'll rip the delicate page by merely straightening out the crease, it's so old and crisp.

The page is blank except for a neatly scribbled line in the center. It reads, "As Cronus was overthrown by his son, so shall Chaos be by her daughter."

"Miranda?" I ask, interrupting her mid-sentence, which she seems too surprised by to actually react. "Chaos was a Protogenoi. She was destroyed during the Firstlast War. She had no child."

"That is correct," Miranda says, eyebrows raised. "I didn't ask you about Chaos, though."

"Right, sorry," I say, nodding respectfully for her to continue.

I ask nothing else. I don't know why I don't show Miranda the piece of paper. I didn't know then why I kept it a secret from her, and I don't know now either. I watch myself hide the prophecy back inside the book.

To keep myself entertained, I'd sit in on Council meetings every so often. Barnabas would allow me to sit behind his throne on the dais. Considering the size of him and his throne and the size of myself, it was easy to stay unnoticed behind there.

I'm fifteen now and sit behind the golden throne. My thoughts wander, thinking about the trip Phoenix took me on the day before. He'd often take me across Havcire to visit Citizens in their areas. We all have our separate places that are constructed ideally for us.

I know Phoenix goes on these trips with me so I realize I'm not alone here but I have Miranda if I need evidence of that. Plus, oddly, I remember enjoying and even preferring my time spent with the Celestials. The day before, however, we had gone to an Incanter town after much insistence from me.

Barnabas's voice catches my attention, not what he says but the manner in which he says it. It's the same tone he uses when I've done something to disappoint him, and I pity whoever it is he's using it against at the moment, which is why I stop my mind's wandering to listen.

Peaking around the side of his throne, I see Lada standing tall in front of the Council.

I'd never seen her before in person but I'd seen her depicted through my studies with Miranda. She avoided the Council most of the time, I'd been told, because she disapproved of Havcire's interference with Vest.

"I've warned you before about getting involved in the Citizens' business," Barnabas is saying.

Lada rolls her eyes at him. I feel my brows lift in surprise at this, her demeanor further piquing my interest in her and the conversation.

"Business, you say. Well, it wasn't this Citizen's business to cheat on his wife. In fact, it's quite the opposite. He should be busy loving his wife, which falls into my area. Which means, I should be able to deal with him accordingly," Lada says.

I don't disagree.

"*Regardless of what you think, that's not how things work here in Havcire, and you know that. We can provide for the Citizens' basic needs, ensuring there is no conflict over such issues. However, we agreed to not get involved in their personal matters, as control over their lives is part of what makes their lives complete.*"

Barnabas makes a good point, as well. Still, I make the decision to be on Lada's side of things.

She's like a love, fairy godmother. Cinderella had it pretty tough and could have gone on struggling for the rest of her life but we don't hate the fairy godmother for stepping in and lending a helping hand, do we? Would it have been an even better story if Cinderella had managed to pull herself out of the rags and find the riches with her own strength and wits, though?

"*Yes, I'm aware of this, but the line that was drawn long ago sometimes need readjusting. After all, isn't that what you did when it came to the Subject System?*" *Lada asks.*

She watches the Council members, waiting for her solid point to get through to them, but they show no sign of relenting.

They aren't capable of acknowledging her well-made point about the Subject System, I realize, reminded this is just a memory.

This past may have been lost to me in the present, but I do know more regarding the Subject System in the present than I do at this point in time. The Subject System is out of their control.

Lada's voice pulls me back to the scene in front of me. She moves on, switching tactics.

"I don't mean to control their lives," she's saying. "I want to help the woman who has been betrayed find someone better deserving of her if that is what she desires."

Barnabas lets out an exasperated sigh.

"Lada, if you want change, then perhaps you should reconsider taking a larger role in the Council, as we have suggested before."

Lada shakes her head resolutely, her bangs ruffling against her forehead.

"No thanks," she says, and turns her back to the Council, knowing there's no more to discuss.

Lucifer clears his throat, and I glance up to find him staring at me, my head peaking out between his and Barnabas's throne.

His hand covers my face, pushing me back behind Barnabas. As he keeps an eye on me, my shoulders bend forward, playing at disappointment, until he turns his attention back towards the front of the room.

I make my escape through the hidden door behind the thrones, which Phoenix showed me a while back, and run through the halls to catch up to Lada.

"Tell me about the Subject System," I shout after her, once she comes into view around a corner.

Lada turns around, a single, perfect brow arced. Catching my breath and taking notice of her expression, I check myself.

"*Please?*" *I ask, a small smile tugging at my lips.*

"*Dawn!*" *Minerva shouts, her voice managing to sound hushed despite the rise in volume.*

Her yell distracts me further, and Phoenix sweeps my legs out from under me. I land directly on my back, the air rushing out of me in a sharp huff.

"*You're tripping yourself up again,*" *Minerva says.*

Lada smiles at me from above, as Phoenix reaches out a hand to help me back up.

The sky above them is clear with white, cotton candy clouds. The smell of the salty ocean drifts through the air on an intermittent breeze, and I regret the sand that seems to stick everywhere on my sweaty body. Maybe I'll have grass extend from the forest all the way up to the water and forgo with any sand at all.

I slap Phoenix's hand aside and lift myself up into a seated position, feeling every sore muscle ache as I do.

"*Tripping myself?*" *I ask Minerva.* "*Phoenix quite literally just tripped me.*"

"*Only because you were off balance to begin with. You must, as I keep telling you, not rest your weight too much on one leg,*" *she instructs, calmly. She's always calm.*

I force myself back up onto my feet. While Miranda took up much of my time with my studies, Minerva had taken it upon herself to consume the majority of my remaining time with training. Lucifer insisted it wasn't necessary, that I'd have no use for such skill, but Minerva spoke of the importance of knowing one is capable of fighting their own battles even if never necessary.

Generally, I agree with Minerva. Right now, I wish Lucifer had won that argument.

Today's hand-to-hand combat day. Since a year ago, when I introduced myself to Lada, she's enjoyed joining in on Minerva's lessons with me. She and Phoenix seem to have a good ole time during these sessions, and Minerva appreciates the extra challenge Lada offers by participating, as I get to fight both of them. I prefer the strategy lessons, which involve significantly less bruising.

"Okay, let's go again," I say, getting into my ready stance.

Sweat glistens on Phoenix's chest, which reminds me of the other distraction I was dealing with before Minerva's shouting.

Like me, Phoenix is sixteen years old, or at least looks that way. He explained to me when I was only three that we weren't really the same age. Still, he's kept up the illusion over the years. It wasn't until a couple years ago that I started to realize how piercing his spearmint, green eyes were; how his body had developed defined muscles; and how I wanted to run my hands through his smooth, dark chocolate hair.

Oh my god, *a part of me yells, some part that is highly aware that this is just a memory and my body is in another time and place.*

"Dawn, focus!" Minerva shouts again, pulling me out of my head.

Lada, thankfully not Phoenix, is the one to attack. A moment before her fist can connect with my face, I deflect, knocking her arm away with my own.

I grab her other arm, twisting it behind her back, and raise my elbow to hit her in the side of the face, but Phoenix comes up and kicks me in the side, forcing me to release Lada. Although the kick throws me off balance, I grab Phoenix's leg on its way down, pulling him forward and towards me. I grab his shoulder, righting myself, and bring my knee up into his stomach.

I lower my leg back down to the ground and again forget to readjust my weight in order to stand solidly on both feet.

Lada swipes my legs out from under me, and I land hard on my back.

"I know!" I shout at Minerva before she can reprimand me.

"Tell me again why we're going to see this Experimenter rather than going to see Havcire's very own Grand Canyon?"

"Because," I say, glancing sidelong at Phoenix, as we walk through the hallways of the Ziggurat, "Lada found out that this Experimenter, Max, is the one who suggested to the Council that they create the Subject System. If the Council can't give us answers, then he must be able to."

"After you," Phoenix says, holding open the lab's glass doors.

Max hunches over the papers on his desk, unkempt black hair streaked with gray hanging down around his face. He looks weighed down. He looks different.

When Phoenix and I deliberately step loudly to alert him to our presence, he barely moves, tilting his head to the side to find the source of the sound.

"Hi," I say, "I'm—"

"Dawn," *Max says, his eyes widening in recognition and surprise.*

"How do you know Dawn?"

Phoenix asks the question before I can voice it myself. He looks at me inquisitively but I shrug cluelessly in response.

Max gets up from the desk, his legs pushing the chair back. It rolls on its wheels into a table, the jolt knocking over a tent made from cards, but Max pays no attention to what must have been his creation. Instead, he comes to meet us where we stand, which is barely a few steps into the room.

"I regret what I did, or what I didn't do. I couldn't stop her. I couldn't have but I could have tried. I did think to find you after but I was afraid to draw her attention again. But, now here you are," *Max says in one exhale; and then, more slowly, like a confession,* "She killed you."

Phoenix protectively grabs onto my arm, as if there's a current threat to my life rather than the mere mention of a past threat.

"What are you talking about?" *he asks Max.*

"My mother?" I ask. "Are you talking about how my mother killed me on Vest?"

"Yes and no," Max says, looking down, seemingly confused by his own words. With a small shake of his head, he looks back up at me and continues. "No, if you are referring to your biological mother on Vest, who I believe you are. Chaos, the Protogenoi, was possessing her at the time."

I knew it. The red streaks of hair that weren't there before.

"Chaos is dead," Phoenix says. Although, he doesn't sound convinced of it himself.

"You're wrong," Max replies, with surprising conviction.

"How is that possible? How could you know of this?" I ask, mind reeling.

"Because, a long time ago, she came to me to start the Subject System."

Max makes his way back over to his desk, motioning for us to follow.

Phoenix lets go of my arm when I glance down at his hand suggestively. We follow Max.

Above his desk, on the wall, are five computer screens. They each alternate between multiple different screens. Every screen has a name at the top, with data below.

"I'd always wanted a way to test my hypotheses on Vest," Max continues. "You see, it's not the same here in Havcire. The Souls are different from how they were as humans. I came up with the idea

of the Subject System. In addition to helping me, I thought it would benefit some Subjects that had potential for rehabilitation. Chaos knew of this and told me to approach the Council with the idea. She said they needed only to be open to it for her to convince them of it completely. I didn't know she meant she would use mind control to do it."

Phoenix nods, staring at the computer screens, while I struggle to comprehend how this all connects. The pale light from the screens shadow his face, impassive as he listens to Max.

"Why did she need your help to get through to the Council if she could just use mind control?" Phoenix asks, a question which Max seems to have expected.

"She wasn't at full strength, still isn't, so she needed me to make them vulnerable by getting them to at least consider the Subject System," Max answers. "The reason I'm telling you this is to explain why it is I know what happened to you, Dawn. It was because of our deal with the Subject System that Chaos would come by my lab in the years after it got started to check on its progress. It was during one of those visits that she came in the body of your mother.

"Chaos is powered by chaotic energy. When she was defeated in the Firstlast War, the energy that had kept her alive, that stemmed from the very beginning, the so-called Big Bang, was destroyed. It wasn't until the ones who had left Havcire lost their magic in Vest and became human that she began to regain her power from the unexpected chaos that came along with the growth of the human population. But, she often had to possess humans because she didn't have the strength to manifest in her own body."

Max stalls, and I hear Phoenix's intake of breath, as he opens his mouth to further question him. I touch Phoenix's shoulder to get his attention and shake my head. Max is looking off to the side again, avoiding my gaze, but he's not done. Phoenix remains quiet.

"She was pregnant when she came to see me and panicked unlike I had ever seen her before," Max continues, still looking anywhere but at me. "She was more frightening than ever in that state, so when she asked me theoretically about if she would have ever regained her powers if it weren't for her exposure to humans, I answered without a thought as to what her motivation for needing the answer could be. It was a simple nature vs. nurture question," he says, smiling bitterly at the ground.

"She hadn't known the human woman was pregnant when she first possessed her, but it was too late by the time Chaos came to the realization. She had already passed her powers unto the unborn child," Max says, finally meeting my eyes.

"But why kill her own child, even if she had passed along her power?" Phoenix asks.

"The prophecy," I choke out, recalling the scrap of paper I'd found in the history book.

I sit in my bedroom in the treehouse, at the window seat. Phoenix sits on the other side of the bench, our backs leaning against opposite walls.

"Stop trying to distract me from my misery," I tell him.

I watch a couple of bluejays land on the branch outside the window. They hop up and down, the branch dipping as they take turns bouncing on it, making it look like they're riding a seesaw. I imagine myself in the center between them, fighting to stay in place and not topple off.

Phoenix has told me he pranked Barnabas to try to lift my spirits. I highly doubt anything can make me forget about the fact that I descend from an evil Protogenoi, who killed me and, for some reason, created an intentionally broken system. Although, on the bright side, my biological mother didn't murder me as a baby so there's that.

"By the way, we still don't know why Chaos created the Subject System, a flawed Subject System. We need to do something about that," I say.

"Well, according to you, she can't be stopped by anyone but you. So, do we have to come up with a solution or do you?"

I look away from the bouncing bluejays to glare at him, kicking my foot into his, which rests up on the window seat beside mine.

"Fine," I say, "act like you don't care."

Phoenix shrugs.

"I will, but let me get something straight. You don't want to hear about Barnabas's reaction to the news that we eloped?" he asks, a smile playing at his lips.

I try hard to hold in the laughter but a snort escapes me, which only leads to a greater desire to laugh. Phoenix smiles widely at his success.

"Funny," I say, dryly, once I've forced the laughter away. "I don't recall that happening. How'd he respond?"

"Firstly, it was a beautiful little ceremony, and you should be disappointed you don't remember it," Phoenix says, and I roll my eyes at him. Although, part of me is disappointed I don't remember the fake elopement. "And, Barnabas was ecstatic. He thinks you make me easier to deal with."

"Right, like I have any influence over you at all," I say, pulling my knees up to my chest.

The bluejays have flown away. Phoenix is quiet for once, the sound of cicadas filling the room. It's calming but Phoenix's lack of a quick retort is unnerving, so much so that I'm about to question if he's alright.

As I turn my attention away from the open window and back towards him, though, he's no longer leaning against the wall across from me. He's leaning towards me, and he brings his arms up to rest on top of my knees.

His hands are warm on my legs, a heat that travels right to my core without any such permission from my brain.

His face is only a few inches away from mine. A trace of a smile remains there but his eyes are serious, focused on me, as if there's not a single other sight in this world that'd be more important to look upon.

"I'd say you have some influence," he says.

My knees lower, allowing him to lean in closer. His hand rests on the side of my face but he hesitates to come any closer, hovering an inch away. I'm about to close the distance myself but I notice the shift in his expression, like a hidden compartment shutting back up and locking tight.

I place a hand against his chest, as much to prevent his movement as to prevent any further action from myself.

"You don't have to do this all yourself. I have a plan," he practically whispers, like a confession.

I feel a spark of hope and let my hand drop. He has a plan to deal with the Subject System and Chaos. Instead of reflecting that hope, Phoenix is impassive, his emotions sealed behind an impenetrable safe. I realize what it means.

His plan has already begun.

Before the first shred of betrayal can register in my mind and carve painfully at my heart, an unfamiliar blue liquid, shining from within a glass vial appears in his hand. The memory potion.

I'm strong from my training with Minerva but not strong enough or quick enough to stop Phoenix now.

"I hope you'll forgive me."

CHAPTER 35

The memories swim through my mind. I'm falling down the rabbit hole. But, instead of random objects floating alongside me as I fall, there are all my memories rushing back to me as I pass by each one. Chaos possessing my mother and killing me; the Council taking me in; my home in Havcire; studying with Miranda; Phoenix guiding me through Havcire; training with Minerva; befriending Lada; finding Max; and Phoenix...

I see orange through my closed eyelids. The fire. I open my eyes which feel like they've been closed for a lifetime.

My thoughts are my own, not divided by a living memory and my present self anymore. And yet, it feels different. I feel different. The memories aren't distant like many of those belonging to my past lives. They've been brought right back to the surface, and I feel them.

I remember the emotions I felt and even the physical aches. Quite literally, I especially remember the sensations from my training sessions with Minerva.

Pushing up to support myself, I manage to get into a seated position with a groan.

Lada and Dex are no longer in the room. With my feet planted on the ground, I feel significantly more oriented. In fact, my body feels surprisingly awake and alert, almost buzzing with energy.

"Dawn."

Phoenix's voice draws my attention, reminding me I'm not alone in the room. He sits up on the couch perpendicular to the one I'm on. He's just woken up, as well.

His hair is ruffled, brown waves askew, reminding me of the times I used to bother him early in the morning as a kid while he was trying to get in a few more hours of sleep.

The familiar memories come surprisingly easy to me now, bringing to mind all the years I spent with Phoenix as my closest friend, no scheme involved, no false identities.

He's kneeled down in front of me and raises a hand to my face, seemingly to examine me for any injuries, even though the only injuries one could sustain from a memory upload would be mental and invisible. Still, with the intensity of his stare, I wouldn't put the ability past him.

I reach up to touch his hand that rests against my face but stop in the middle of the action, vividly remembering the last moment we'd spent together in Havcire before my memory was erased for the very first time. Before *he* erased my memory and made me a Subject.

My hand tightens into a fist. Before he can interpret my intentions, with a speed I now know and feel I possess, I have him pinned against the wall with my forearm held against his chest, preventing him from moving even an inch. The wall I slam his back against holds, thankfully, though the sound of the impact echoes throughout the room. Despite my focus on Phoenix, I can't help but think that Gatlin would kill me if I damaged his house.

"Phoenix," I say back, the threatening tone of my voice foreign even to me. It's a far cry from the tone he'd used to say my name a moment ago.

He doesn't push back in an attempt to get out of my hold, not that I think he could, even if he tried. The realization gives me instant appreciation for my new strength.

"You should've told me the plan!" I scream at him before he has the chance to respond.

"There was no time to waste," he says, quickly and calmly before I can interrupt.

"No time to waste? What was the rush? It took no less than 400 years to get to where we are now, and you couldn't spare 4 minutes to share your plan with me?" I ask, no longer screaming, but with just as much venom laced in.

"The longer I waited to put the plan into action and the more people who knew about it, the more chance Chaos would have had to find out about it and stop it."

"Lame excuse, Phoenix. Try again," I tell him, to which I see the exasperation clear on his face, which only angers me more so

I tighten my arm against his chest, pushing him up closer to the wall.

"You need the truth? I didn't want to chance that you would refuse the plan. It had to be done!"

"I wouldn't have," I say, clearly taking him by surprise, which quickly morphs into confusion.

"Then why are you so mad at me?" he asks, piercing me with his eyes, as if trying to find the answer there rather than waiting for a response.

"Because, I thought we were in it together, and you should've trusted *me* and told me what you were planning."

I fail to keep the hurt in my voice from seeping out through the shield of anger.

I loosen my arm a bit and hear someone lightly clear her throat. I drop my arm fully, freeing Phoenix, as I turn to find Lada standing in the doorway leading from the kitchen. Dex is beside her.

"You didn't know?" I ask her. I don't doubt they could hear everything from the other room. I watch as her perfectly postured form droops at the question.

"I had no idea," she says, shooting a pointed look at Phoenix.

I rush forward to hug the friend I had forgotten I had. She lets out a startled laugh, her shoulders shaking, as she lifts her arms to return the gesture. Over her shoulder, I catch Dex's expression.

"What?" I ask him, pulling back to face him.

"Nothing," he says, unconvincingly, his brown eyes still wide with shock. "It's just, can memories give someone inhuman speed?"

I blink in confusion, seconds ticking by as I try to puzzle through Dex's observation, until I realize I must have used my speed to rush to Lada. It hadn't been my intention.

I'm going to have to get used to controlling myself, but why do I only now have this power after so many years in Vest? Assuming I… function? the same as Chaos, the reason I have any power at all, then all the time I spent in Vest, living as a human Subject should have powered me as they had Chaos after her defeat in the Firstlast War.

"The only thing that has changed after all these years," Phoenix offers up before I can voice my confusion, "is that now you finally have all your memories. I had no way to predict that the blocking of your memories would also create a barrier between you and your magic. On the bright side, the delay has conveniently kept you under the radar all these years as a Subject without affecting the impact humanity has had on strengthening you."

"Magic," Dex states, seating himself down on a couch. "In Dawn? Could someone please fill me in?"

I look to Phoenix, who now comfortably leans against the wall I previously held him against. He shows no sign of helping out.

Lada, still standing in the doorway, wears an expression of reluctance and lasting confusion.

So, that leaves me. Fine, here's my chance to show Phoenix I am capable of filling in the gaps he so unkindly kept me in the dark about. I lean against the back of the couch.

"Well, Dex, Phoenix erased my memory—"

"Actually, I erased a lot of people's memories - yours, Lada's, the Council's, Miranda's, pretty much anyone that knew you or even of you," Phoenix says, interrupting.

"Would you like to fill him in?" I ask Phoenix, not sparing him a glance.

"You're doing a great job, please continue," he says, and I can hear the mocking encouragement in his voice.

I smile, tight-lipped, at Dex and sit down on the couch next to him. It's a long story.

"I'll just start from the beginning. Once upon a time, Chaos possessed my human mother while she was pregnant with me, as Chaos was not yet strong enough to possess a Celestial or take on her true form. Her magic rubbed off on me so she killed me soon after I was born to prevent me from coming into my powers and becoming strong enough to kill her, a prophecy thing. My abilities stem from the chaos of Vestigium so being sent to Havcire ensured I'd never be strong enough to defeat her.

"Speeding this along, the Council decided to raise me; with Lada, I discovered the issues with the Subject System; and from Max we found out about Chaos and my background. She used Max to start the Subject System, along with some handy mind controlling of the Council. No, we don't know why she did this, but she sure wants me dead and control of the Council.

"Moving on, Phoenix decided to take it upon himself to erase everyone's memories and make it seem like I was never a Citizen, only a Subject, so I would be sent down to Vest as part of a field experiment and gain power to eventually defeat Chaos. With no one left with memories revealing my true identity, Chaos couldn't use possession or mind control to discover I was a threat. Phoenix, of course, couldn't exclude himself from the people who needed memory wipes, so he left Bishop with orders to deliver the potion to restore our memories when it came time to confront Chaos."

I chance a look in Phoenix's direction, unable to control my need to see if I, indeed, got everything right. I'm happy to find a hint of surprise on his face before he erases every trace of it. He nods in confirmation.

I want to tell him that I understand the plan because it was a good plan. It was, if not the only way, one of the few ways I could, without raising suspicion, spend the time necessary on Vest.

Chaos was and is a threat. She won't stop in her search for power. Control of Havcire won't be enough. Vest will be next. And, from what I've heard about when the Protogenoi ruled, I don't want to see a world ruled again by even just one of them.

The plan was necessary, even if it was I who had to pay its price. And, even though I would have accepted that if he'd only told me, he did not tell me, which leaves me holding a new grudge for the deceit that went along with the plan.

"Just so you know," Dex says, "your storytelling skills suck."

"Thanks a lot."

"I'm caught up, though," Dex says, offering me a conciliatory pat on the arm.

"Great, perfect, magnificent," Gatlin says, appearing from the kitchen.

Is he holding a broom?

"Now all you need is a present plan so to not die in the future," he continues. "I suggest an expedited planning session, that which involves the first step being your departure from my abode."

That is a broom, and he looks convincingly like a chimney sweep right out of *Mary Poppins*. I expect spontaneous singing at any moment. Or, he intends to sweep us out of here.

"Bishop's arrival and Chaos's knowledge of us means we don't have much time left," Phoenix says.

"We need to find a way to separate Chaos from Minerva. We can't fight her if she's using a Council member's body as a shield," I point out.

I can deal with all the personal, life-altering revelations later and focus on the life purpose I didn't know I had until a few moments ago instead, which might lead to my death anyway.

"Lada," Phoenix says. She stands by Gatlin, eyeing the broom, but looks to Phoenix when he calls. "You were possessed by Chaos like Minerva is now, so maybe you could work with Dex to figure out a way to separate Chaos from Minerva? Maybe there was a time when her hold seemed to weaken on you? Dawn and I can work on figuring out how exactly she might take on Chaos."

Lada nods, as if following directions from a commander even though Phoenix stated everything as a question. Dex gets up to join Lada, giving me an encouraging smile.

"Adieu," Gatlin says to me, before shifting his eyes over to the front door, where Phoenix exits.

I guess I'm supposed to follow. It's training time. I smile at Gatlin and follow Phoenix like a good soldier, saluting Gatlin before shutting the door behind me.

CHAPTER 36

"**C**an you hear me?"

I jump, startled, as Phoenix's voice seems to come from close by but he's nowhere in sight.

The trees of the Graveyard populate the area. I'd almost forgotten where it was that we sought refuge. It's still dark outside, the blue light of the moon filtered through the green leaves.

It doesn't feel like the Havcire Assembly happened this same night. I wonder how long it was that the three of us were unconscious from the memory potion. For all I know, maybe the sun did rise and set again since we lied down. I probably should have asked Dex or Gatlin about that.

For night, my surroundings are oddly visible, allowing me to spot Phoenix about a quarter of a mile away. And yet, I'd heard his voice clearly as if he had spoken directly into my ear.

"Unfortunately," I answer, and then watch him flip me off. "I saw that, too."

"Good," he says, his voice easily carrying across the distance again.

I knew their hearing was enhanced. But, this much? I had no idea. Oh my god. Wait a second.

"Your hearing is *this* good? What about all those times Lada totally was able to hear what we were talking about before she was on our side? How could you have let—?"

"I work very hard and no one appreciates it, that's how. Illusions. I make sure others only hear and see what they should. So, your hearing and vision have improved," Phoenix continues, nonchalantly. "Do you have control over your speed?"

Within the next second, I'm standing inches away from Phoenix, the leaves on the ground settling back down after being unsettled by my movement. I control my speed so I slow down in time not to run into him but store some of the energy from my momentum, shifting it to my hand as I push against Phoenix's chest. He stumbles back but remains on his feet.

"Okay," he says, regaining his balance, "you're still angry with me for not telling you about the plan."

I scoff. Even before having all my memories returned I was angry with Phoenix. He hadn't told me about how I was Citizen even when that was all he knew of my missing past. No matter what the case, this man— Celestial— whatever is always keeping something from me.

"You could say that."

"Well, maybe you should also acknowledge the fact that I was your closest friend?"

"You're right," I say, with a bitter laugh, "my friend that betrayed me."

I recognize I'm not doing the best job at focusing on the task at hand and leaving the memory fallout for after but I'm supposed to just work with Phoenix and not address my justified distrust of him?

I'm simply not capable of not bringing up topics of discussion that'd be best to avoid.

"Betrayed you?" he says, incredulously, while applying pressure to that scar running through his brow. "That's a bit harsh, Dawn, and it was centuries ago! You're really going to hold a grudge for that long?"

"I just found out about it not even an hour ago!"

"True, but the actual event you're mad at me for is ancient history."

"Really? Because in here," I say, pointing at my head, "it feels like yesterday."

"You know I did what had to be done."

"Right, and you didn't *have* to tell me about it."

"No, but I should have."

"You should have!"

And then I realize what he's actually said.

"I should have told you about the plan," he continues, "and I'm sorry that I didn't. If I've learned anything over the years, at least with you who values honesty so damn much, I should tell you the truth."

Realizing we'd been shouting, I look around the Graveyard, hoping we didn't announce our presence to any nearby Entrapped. The forest looks empty and quiet, much like my mind feels right now, even with the recent overload of memories.

I don't know if I should trust Phoenix. I just know that I want to trust him, which makes me more hesitant. My hesitancy to give in seems the only real defense I have against him and feelings I know I once had, which I'm fairly certain I never truly lost. He sounds sincere but only time can test the truth of his claims.

"Okay," I say, finally.

"Okay?"

"Yeah," I say, nonchalantly, "okay."

"So you forgive me?"

"Yeah, I'll work on it."

"You'll work on it," Phoenix repeats, contemplating my words. "Wow, thanks."

"You're welcome," I say, offering a sarcastic smile. "Now, let's get back to work. We're wasting time we don't have."

Already, the light is getting brighter, shifting from the dark teal to a purer green. Phoenix shoots me one last skeptical look before getting back to business.

"Let's just assume you have all the usual Celestial abilities and focus on what about you threatens Chaos. As in, prophecy worthy threat level."

"Maybe because I'm technically her daughter I'm her weakness because she loves me just so much."

"She killed you as a baby."

"And? Maybe that's how she expresses her love."

"That's all you got?"

"I don't know, maybe I can make her less chaotic," I answer, trying to come up with something even remotely believable.

"Helpful," Phoenix says, in such a way that suggests the opposite.

"You're the one with all the great plans. Use that trickster brain of yours to figure something out."

"And you're the smart one here. You've been through school how many times now?"

I turn away from Phoenix with an exasperated sigh and force myself to relax and think. Everything else might be complicated, but this doesn't have to be. I can think through it like a simple problem with a few factors. I start with the basics, what we know.

"I have Chaos's magic, so it should work like hers does, right?" I ask, rhetorically.

"Chaos uses disorder to give her power." Phoenix answers regardless. It's helpful, though.

"It's how she gains power from Vest. Chaos is a being of order herself so she needs the natural pandemonium of humans to thrive now."

"We believe you've been absorbing that same energy during your lives on Vest as a Subject. You should have that power stored. Give it a try."

"I have no idea how," I tell him, completely lacking any previous confidence I felt.

"Chaos wields chaos, for lack of a better term, like a weapon. So, just pull on whatever within you feels out of order or hectic. Imagine it like a sword or bullet and release it," Phoenix instructs.

I look at him doubtfully but attempt to follow his directions anyway.

I take a few steps back and close my eyes to block out everything around me, trying to focus on anything and everything inside instead. I have no idea what I'm looking for. What does chaos look like anyways? Is chaos the red, electric energy I saw almost kill Dex? Maybe I don't want to find that within myself but if it's already there hiding, I have to.

Melanie's confused face flashes across my mind. She'd asked how I broke through the ice. I just assumed it had to have been thin enough for me to do so but it wasn't thin. It took two hard punches to break it, and my hand wasn't even red. It should have been broken. I'd felt Helen's terror and Melanie's desperation, both chaotic emotions. I'd pulled from them, from the situation.

And the locker. I was trapped in the locker after listening in on Lada and Phoenix. I thought it had been faulty and opened somehow on its own but it didn't. I snapped it open after the memory of my past life, a past life where I was constantly surrounded by humans living in fear and hiding to survive. In fact, the incident with Helen and Melanie, too, came soon after another memory had returned to me.

The energy stirs inside me, not stemming from any one place. No longer dormant, it flows throughout me, traveling through my veins. I pull it out, beckoning it forward with the promise that it can be free from the prison that is my body.

Two daggers of red energy extend from my palms. They spark with power but retain the shape I've molded them into.

The hard part isn't pulling out more of the energy, but keeping it in and keeping it contained. In order to do that, I have to hold onto the memories from which the energy came from, as if keeping it on a leash, keeping ownership of them.

"We got something!" Dex yells.

I jump at the sudden sound of his voice, losing my concentration, and my hands release the energy.

The two daggers shoot out toward Phoenix. He ducks out of the way. The daggers hit the tree behind him, the red points embedding inside it before dissolving.

Where the daggers entered, there are two holes in the bark of the tree, and the dissolved energy spreads throughout the rest of the trunk, sparking with energy. The inner skin of the tree pulses like a heart before going still. Oh no.

Poor tree.

Phoenix straightens up, looks behind at the tree and turns back, eyes wide.

Dex jogs up, looking curiously between the two of us.

"Was that bad timing?"

"Not at all," Phoenix answers, sounding short of breath. "I just almost lost my head."

"All good," I say, giving Dex a thumbs-up.

Lada isn't far behind Dex. She walks up leisurely, looking comfortable to be walking in dirt and fallen leaves in heels. I'd ditched my shoes in Gatlin's house. With us all out, I wonder at the chances of Gatlin letting us back in anytime soon.

"Did Dex tell you about the Aegis?" Lada asks.

"Minerva's shield?" I ask, as Dex tells her, "No."

"I remembered once, while I was still possessed, I was summoned to the Council, and I had a brief moment of clarity while I was walking in the Ziggurat. I hadn't thought of it before because it faded so quickly."

"It was the shield?" Phoenix asks, interrupting, which earns him a peeved look from Lada.

"If you would just give me a chance to tell you," she says, haughtily.

"We don't need the whole story, Lada. Just the end result would be sufficient," Phoenix responds.

"Too bad," Lada says, before continuing. "So, I realized that it had occurred right as I walked by the hidden armory, and it was gone as soon as I passed. I believe it was the Aegis that separated me briefly from Chaos."

I recall the long, lamp-lit room Phoenix had pulled me into before starting this life. I'd seen the Aegis against a wooden, rickety chair alongside Poseidon's trident and Barnabas's Thunderbolt.

"How could a shield do that?" I ask.

"It's more powerful than an ordinary shield," Phoenix explains. "All of the weapons belonging to the Celestials are imbued with some magic to make them stronger. The Aegis doesn't just block physical threats to the bearer, but also any internal threat."

"We think, if the Aegis were to be in Minerva's possession, it would expel Chaos," Dex says, although his thoughts seem elsewhere.

Rather than looking at us, he stares at the tree I assaulted, at the charred bark surrounding the punctures created from the daggers. Is he remembering his own wound from Chaos, the one that nearly killed him? Guilt nags at me again. But, his expression doesn't appear wounded or even frightened. He looks almost reassured, as if the dead tree is a good thing. Or, maybe I'm just reading him wrong.

"Sounds like it could work," Phoenix says, confidently, and I pull my attention away from Dex. "Shall we go take down Chaos?"

Not a second after the words leave his mouth, a now-familiar sensation hits. My surroundings disappear as the world moves around me. I close my eyes against the force of it, barely able to expand my chest with all the pressure. When it stops, or I do, I open my eyes.

The Council is before me.

CHAPTER 37

"A bit hasty, don't you think?" I whisper to Phoenix, the end of the question leaving my mouth with an accent. Under this pressure, with the Council in front of me, including Chaos posing as Minerva, it's impossible to hold back my nervous habit. And yet, it's at this type of moment that I wish most it didn't exist. Phoenix looks too puzzled to register it, though.

"This wasn't me," he whispers back, before walking forward towards the Council.

I glance at Lada standing by my side. Dex isn't anywhere in sight.

We could have planned our attack, how and when exactly we wanted to confront Chaos. We needed to get the Aegis. Now, Chaos is here, and we're the only ones who seem to have not gotten the memo about dropping by.

With no other choice, we follow Phoenix forward.

I remember Lucifer tossing papers to me with information about new souls arriving in Havcire. He was meant to read them to prepare for the meetings with the new souls, welcoming them into Havcire, but he found them to be boring and long, so I'd read them behind his throne and summarized, reciting the highlights for him. Now he stares at me like a predator, and there's no doubt I'm the prey who's fallen into his trap.

I remember Barnabas helping me design my home in Havcire when I was a child. I liked hearing rain in the forest, the drops pattering on the leaves, but I didn't want my treehouse to get wet. He made sure every night it rained in the forest but not near the border, where my treehouse was and the beach began. As I meet his stoic stare, I know all he sees in me is a Subject who's caused increasingly more trouble over the years. He's not wrong.

Chaos, looking through Minerva's eyes, isn't as good at masking her emotions as Barnabas. Barely concealed fury lies beneath the surface. I avoid her gaze.

Bishop is noticeably absent from the room.

"Dex finally pulled through," Barnabas says. "I send two Celestials to get a job done; and while you both failed, the Siphoner delivered."

I feel I should be surprised; and yet... Dex finally, for the first time, completely makes sense to me.

All the little things that didn't add up about him, why he always seemed to be playing a role, keeping a straight face, feigning formality, while his eyes laughed at whatever ridiculous thing I did or stupid, bad joke I made.

Dex is a Siphoner, not a Subject. He is the one who teleported us to the Council, using Phoenix's ability.

And, while it's a crazy guess, I may have finally figured out who exactly he's always reminded me of. Why I naturally trusted him.

"Now, you three are not supposed to be working together," Barnabas continues. "Don't attempt to lie your way out of this, Phoenix, because Dex has reported everything back to us about how you have been attempting to disrupt the Subject System.

"Phoenix, you had your role to play in this Subject's life, as assigned by Max. Of course, we didn't trust you because you are who you are so we sent Lada to keep an eye on you. But, we didn't trust that Lada would prioritize our interests. It didn't matter, however, because we'd also sent Dex to report directly back to us about everything going on—"

"It probably would have been more efficient to just send someone you trusted to begin with," Phoenix suggests, interrupting, which earns him a scowl from Barnabas.

"My point is," Barnabas continues, disregarding Phoenix, "there is no point in denying anything."

"Then you know that—"

"Then you know how unfair the Subject System is and that you should correct it," I say, interrupting Lada before she can continue.

It doesn't add up. One, that Dex would truly betray us. I do recognize the fact that he's lied to me this whole time about who he really is. I'm realizing, however, that lying is complicated and multi-layered.

Two, that Barnabas would choose to focus on our minimal interference in the Subject System rather than our main focus, Chaos, if Dex had reported everything about us back to them.

I see Lada glance at me curiously but I keep my focus on Barnabas, hoping she'll trust me.

"The Subject System is fair, as it was designed to be," Barnabas says.

"You think it seems fair that after all this time it's been in effect, there has never been a Subject who has gained enough points to become a Citizen?" I ask.

"If there hasn't been a Subject to do so, then there hasn't been a Subject worthy of becoming one," Barnabas argues.

"And you know that for a fact?"

I'm met with empty expressions from both Barnabas and Lucifer, who had been sharpening his nails on the blades of his armrests. He has no interest in Barnabas's scolding, merely the outcome. Except, now he stops and stares at me along with Barnabas.

I've hit the wall, triggered Chaos's mind control. There's no point in continuing to prod them. I won't be able to get through, but I'm stalling, to what end I'm not quite sure yet.

"Do you remember organizing the Subject System, figuring out how it would work?" I ask, continuing. "You don't, but you remember everything else you've done in detail. The details regarding the Subject System seem so hazy because you didn't create it. Someone manipulated you into it."

"And, who would it be that you're referring to?"

Minerva's voice cuts in, and I force myself to face her. No more avoiding it but it feels like resisting the urge to cover my eyes before the most terrifying scene of a movie.

Barely lifting a finger, she summons her power to the surface in the form of a red wave crackling with energy. Still dazed from Chaos's influence, Barnabas and Lucifer don't see it coming. It flows through and past them, like a wall of mist. No physical harm seems to be done, but they are left unconscious on their thrones.

Not sparing them a glance, Minerva keeps her eyes on the three of us. A smile creeps onto her face.

She stands up from her own throne, and Phoenix inches closer to my side, as if he expects I'll need protection or, at this point, maybe even restraint. I'm not rushing into anything this time around, though.

While the body is still Minerva's, the way she carries herself is distinctly different from how Minerva would. She stands tall, yet looks relaxed, as if preparing to pounce.

Minerva focuses in on me, her eyes like microscopic telescopes. When was the last time she blinked?

Perhaps my nervous habit of acquiring an accent is a result of the past lives I lived in other countries and on other continents, accents I once had slipping in like muscle memory. That, or maybe I really am just outright weird. After all, the British accent that comes out of my mouth so often is quite rubbish.

She blinks, thank god, and I let go of my random thoughts. Mind control powers require an ability to get inside another's mind, which means it's reasonable to infer that Chaos can read minds.

She was attempting to read my thoughts. No longer focused solely on me, she scans us all.

"You were referring to me, were you not?" she says. "Well, unfortunately for the rest of the Council, they had no idea what you were talking about. Of course, the credit for that goes to me, as I ensured that they would never question the Subject System. In fact, I ensured that everything would play out beneficially. That is, except for the part where you came into existence."

At this, she pauses again to look at me specifically, but it only lasts a second before she continues on in a lilting voice.

"I took care of that, too. I killed you, and you were supposed to stay that way and, most importantly, out of my way—"

"Sorry," I say, interrupting. I'm grateful she's too stunned to kill me on the spot. "Before you finish what you started at the Havcire Assembly, would you mind at least explaining why you began the Subject System?"

Phoenix loudly clears his throat, forcing Minerva to switch her attention to him.

With the moment reprieve, I take notice of my sweating palms and trembling fingers, my body reacting to the dire situation even if my brain refuses to allow panic. I wipe my hands against the silky skirt of my dress, wishing it were of a more absorbent material, and clench my hands into fists to stop the shaking. I can have a panic attack when we're safe, *if* we're safe.

"Everyone loves explaining their well laid out plan," Phoenix says, thankfully supporting me. "I should know."

"I remember you," Minerva says, her eyes boring into Phoenix.

For a second, I think it's really Minerva looking at him and not Chaos because she looks at him with such familiarity, not characteristic of two strangers who may have once faced off against each other in an ancient war. A smile slightly lifts the corners of her mouth, but it's gone so fast I think I might have imagined it.

"I remember both of you," she continues, shifting her gaze from Phoenix to Lada. "You understand power. In fact, Lada was so self-righteous after the Firstlast War that she believed herself ready to give up her magic and live in Vestigium."

I turn to Lada, who stands frozen beside me, surprise written on her features, along with what might be a hint of shame.

"How flattering, Lada," Phoenix says. "Did you know at the time that even a dead royal held an interest in your life?"

"I had not," Lada answers him, trying for the flippant air that Phoenix so easily projects.

"Life and death," Minerva scoffs. "It's all so black and white to you people. You could not kill me. I was weakened, yes, forced back into my elemental form, but the moment you continued to squabble, even after your proclaimed victory, my return was inevitable. Chaos was inevitable.

"As for Lada, I had little to do then but listen and observe. The fun point I am making about Lada is that she backed out of her plan in the end, too afraid of what she'd be without her power. You want to know why I started the Subject System," she states, as though amused by our interest.

"Vest and Havcire were separating physically, drawing further apart the more years that passed with no communication between the two. Soon, there would have been no portals left. As it was, there were only two remaining by the time I got the Subject System running. The Subject System was just the idea of an overly ambitious Experimenter. I merely used the idea to reconnect Havcire and Vest. How was I to rule the world if it was left fragmented?"

"And the corruption?" I ask.

"Well, I didn't want to actually help some worthless Subjects get a second chance at becoming Citizens," Minerva responds, as if this should have been obvious.

"Of course not," Phoenix says, voice dripping with sarcasm.

Before I can consider another ploy to distract her further, Minerva's stepped down from the dais, and she extends her arm out towards us. Another wave of red electricity pushes forward.

It's easier to find the reservoir of energy within myself this time, and it instinctively comes to my aid, forming a barrier. It spreads from me to cover Phoenix and Lada also, shielding us before the threatening red wave can hit.

It's difficult to tell where my red barrier begins and where the matching, assaulting red wave hits up against it.

More waves follow the first, pulsing against the shield. I feel each attempt to break through, as if my body itself forms the barrier, but it doesn't hurt. I feel the pressure of the waves but not the pain that would result from actual contact.

I meet Minerva's gaze. If she's surprised at all by my display of our shared power, she doesn't show it.

"Nice trick," she says, "but you don't actually believe you're strong enough to hold me back, do you?"

I didn't even know I could form a shield with this energy until a second ago. I thought it was only good for some tree-killing daggers. And yet, I can feel the power of the waves fighting back against me. I know I can't keep up the shield forever.

"I may not be able to hold you back for long but I can fight you," I say, extending the shield of red an inch further out, trying to bolster my words.

But it's complete false bravado. Even if I could fight Chaos, I can't, not until she's out of Minerva's body.

A breath of air hisses out of me as I feel a painful sting on my arm. It feels as though a flaming dagger has sliced my arm, and I look to find a large cut on my forearm surrounded by irritated, red skin.

Some of the red lightning got through my barrier, and more holes are forming increasingly fast. Lada shifts out of the way inside the bubble I've created to avoid another streak of lightning that makes its way through.

I can't hold her back. It's like arm wrestling with a bodybuilder, when I've only just started weight training that day.

My energy continues to drain, as if it's leaving me directly through the cut in my arm, and I realize it is. Chaos's matching energy calls to my own, pulling it out of me like a magnet now that its exposed. The power inside me has no allegiance to me. I've taken it from others, from their chaotic feelings born from chaotic situations. It leaves me for Chaos with no regrets, pulled to the one who has years of practice on her side.

The shield falls. As it disappears, I fall to my knees, the energy in me completely drained.

I hear words escape from Phoenix in haste but my ears are ringing, and then he and Lada are hit by the red lightning and sent flying backwards.

I can't hear the scream that rips from my throat, as I see Phoenix and Lada slouch against the far wall of the Council room, infected as Dex was by the red lightning. But, I feel the burn in my throat and regret the lack of air left in me.

I'm hauled to my feet but my legs fail to hold me up, so Minerva drags me by the arm.

We pass Lada and Phoenix by the doors and exit into the hallway. I don't have energy left to resist, and I know any action would be futile anyways. Still, I weakly try to grab my arm out from her tight grip, even though it's the only thing keeping me upright. I tried stalling, and it didn't work. Maybe I was wrong about Dex after all.

"I will admit this to you," Minerva says. "I expected more from someone with my magic flowing through her veins. You disappoint me."

"At least there's that," I spit out.

"Bye."

A bitter smile tugs at her mouth and then she releases me, pushing me backwards, into a portal that depicts the open sky. As the bare skin on my arm touches the wall, it ripples, letting me through.

CHAPTER 38

I'm tumbling through the air. I try to control my limbs and focus on one direction but I wasn't prepared to skydive.

Minerva pushed me through off balance, and now I turn uncontrollably as I plummet surely to my death. I catch sight of the hard ground below. This is the end.

Where's my life flashing before my eyes? Is my brain sick of always remembering my past lives, so much so that it refuses to recall them now?

The air is cold, or at least it feels that way falling through it at this speed. My body feels tight, as I attempt to resist the dropping sensations.

A sharp scream escapes me when something hits me from behind, someone I realize, when arms wrap unexpectedly around my waist.

I fall faster with the added weight. And then, the world stills as I parachute up and the descent slows.

I'm closer to the ground now, the sandy ground. Having slowed, I'm able to see exactly where I am.

Pyramids are not so far off in the distance, but they don't look like the ruins that exist on Vest. Instead of sand-colored rugged sides, the pyramids are of a pure white that reflect the light of the sun, making them almost too bright to look at. The tops are made of gold.

A flash of bronze distracts me from the scene, as a pair of large wings beat the air around me. They're made of bronze feathers and look to have a wingspan of at least ten feet.

"You have wings!"

The words leave my mouth, as if on their own accord, the moment I see who caught me and to who the wings belong.

Phoenix glances down at me, hair windblown and cheeks flushed, most likely from the dive through the air he had to take to catch up to me before I reached the ground.

I'm alive. I'm alive!

I look down and see his arms wrapped around my waist. My back is pressed up against his chest. I have to tilt my head at an odd angle, up and to the side, in order to see him behind me.

His arms around me loosen but, before I can panic, he quickly readjusts, shifting one arm under my back and swinging my legs up so his other arm rests under my knees. Reflexively, my hand shoots out to steady myself, flattening against his bare chest. I pull back, as if scorched, awkwardly placing my hand in my lap.

Why is he shirtless, I question, before taking note of the wings once again. They rise up behind him, pressing against the air enough to lower us slowly and safely down to the ground. I guess it's hard to sprout wings with a shirt in the way.

"Why didn't you tell me you had wings?" I ask.

"Seriously?"

We reach the ground, and he releases me, his arms sliding away from behind my back and knees. My feet land on the soft, yellow sand.

"No?" I say, unsure whether it comes out as a question or not.

I continue to stare at his wings, much like those of an angel.

I remember the Havcire Assembly performance, the depiction of the Firstlast War. There had been one Celestial in the fight that had been shown sprouting wings and charging through the air at the Protogenoi.

With one powerful thrust that lifts grains of sand into the air around us, the wings disappear back behind Phoenix's back.

"No," I say again, meeting his eyes. "We have to get back."

I reach out for his arm, intending for him to teleport us back to the Council Chamber. Lada's still there with Chaos. She was injured, they both were.

The realization floods through me along with sudden and profound relief over the fact that he's clearly okay.

"How are you all right?" I ask. "Minerva, or Chaos, she—"

"It was an illusion. Lada and I were never really hit," he says, brushing off my concern. "We helped Barnabas and Lucifer, and the three of them are holding Chaos off, but they can only do so much, as they don't want to actually harm Minerva."

"Okay," I say slowly, still trying to register that Phoenix and Lada weren't really harmed by Chaos. "Then why are we still here?"

"Because," Phoenix says, his white button-down shirt from earlier appearing in his open hand, "you already almost died."

"Almost dying is better than dying."

I thought Phoenix *had* died. He's here. Not dead. He works his arms through the shirt and focuses on rolling up the sleeves to just above his elbows. Still unbuttoned, the shirt's ends play in the dry breeze of the desert, flitting away from his body.

"Well we'd better come up with a better way not to do either," he says.

What have I been waiting for? Whatever was holding me back, I really don't care anymore. I just know I am really glad Phoenix is not dead.

"I'm going to regret this if we somehow survive."

Phoenix's focus shifts from fastening the buttons on his shirt up to me. By the time he's met my eyes, I've closed the distance between us, and my lips meet his.

Despite the sudden need I'd felt, I kiss him slowly. Unsure, like testing the waters, I gently move my lips over his. I feel his lashes brush smoothly against my cheek as his eyes close, and then he's kissing me back. The second he does, the softness is gone, despite the incredible softness of his lips. There's an urgency manifested both from lifetimes of holding back and an uncertainty of the future.

I reach my hand around the back of his neck, twining my fingers through the silky hair at his nape. He grabs me around the waist so our bodies collide. His hands press up against the silk skirt of my dress, and I can feel him through it. He gathers the material in his hands, bunching it together. The silk slides smoothly up, baring more of my legs, before he lets the skirt drop back in place.

The absence of him is too much so I hook my leg around him, drawing him back closer. He lifts a hand to the back of my head, which tangles through my hair, and my head tilts back at the sensation.

Phoenix breaks away to kiss the curve of my neck, teasing. I want to pull him back in but I force myself to pull back instead. It feels not unlike ripping myself apart.

A gold spark passes between us, like static. I think I imagine it but I see it reflected, too, in Phoenix's eyes.

Phoenix steps back, creating a normal amount of distance between us again, except it doesn't feel normal to me anymore. His fingers work quickly to finish fastening up the remaining buttons of his shirt.

"Sorry," he says.

"For what?" I ask, relieved to hear my voice come out normal and free of any abnormal accent, even though him uttering that word after what just happened fills me dread.

"I'm afraid you'll have regrets, as we're not going to die. I've realized something, sparky," he says, with a half-smile.

I restrain a sigh of relief because, right, I had said *I* was going to regret it if we somehow survived.

"Chaos needs to pull power from humans because she feeds on their chaotic energy, but you *are* human. You were born and have lived twenty-seven separate lives as one. Your power is your own."

Phoenix stares at me, expectant. Does he expect some sort of spontaneous breakthrough on my end? I wish I could deliver.

What he says makes sense. For the whole of my lives, I've lived thinking I was fully human. I was born to a human, even if I absorbed Chaos's magic within the womb. Does that make me physically human? Even if it didn't, there's no denying my humanity, the lives I lived and struggled through. I lived without the use of any magic.

I think of my doubts, my questions, and confusion. I think of the anger I've always had to direct at one person or another in order to have someone to blame for the lack of control I feel over my life, but maybe that's not the point. Maybe, the point is that life is naturally out of control. It's what you choose to make out of the chaos that matters. I even told Helen as much. I wanted to believe it true then but now I know it's true.

There is no clear answer to nature versus nurture, nor any complex matter of humanity. Humanity lives within chaos and learns to thrive within it, as I did.

My hand tingles like it's fallen asleep, itching to move. Phoenix's gaze shifts down to my hand. I follow and find sparks of golden energy dancing between my fingers. They hop from finger to finger almost playfully before disappearing.

"Time to go," Phoenix says, grabbing onto my other arm.

CHAPTER 39

The first thing I notice when we arrive back in the Council Chamber is the noise. It sounds more like an indoor thunderstorm than a small battle, which makes sense when I spot a large thunderbolt strike out towards Minerva. It comes from Barnabas, who stands up on the dais beside Lucifer.

The thunderbolt meets a red bolt shot from Minerva's hand. They collide, creating an explosion of white and red light that spreads out to either side, including where Phoenix and I now stand.

I face Phoenix, using my body as a shield against the splintered red energy that heads our way.

I don't pull on the reservoir of stolen energy as I did before. I don't think of other people's experiences and emotions. Rather, I pull on my own memories, and I imagine my mind as I had before, with my neurons firing frantically. I imagine they fire golden lightning, like I'd seen dance between my fingers. I pull on it, drawing it through the rest of me and out. It responds eagerly, familiarly.

The red energy hits.

My own gold energy pulses around me like an aura in response, neutralizing the red energy. The red dissolves harmlessly. The gold power naturally returns back to me, a part of me.

No one else notices what's happened, still absorbed in their throwing of blows.

Lucifer, the second Barnabas's thunderbolt fails, throws his bident at Minerva, while Barnabas lets off another bolt of lightning. With both to fend off, she only has the time to stop the bolt and must twist to avoid the airborne bident.

"I guess this wasn't the best place to enter," Phoenix says.

As if attuned to our voices, Minerva's eyes shift to focus immediately on the two of us.

Phoenix steps out from behind me but he doesn't dare go so far as to step in front of me. I wouldn't allow it, and he's smart enough to know it. Minerva's eyes narrow as she sees me. If I can trust my vision, they seem to flash red with anger.

Lucifer's bident flies back to his hand like a boomerang, hitting Minerva in the shoulder on its return. It throws her off balance but does little harm. It's clear the two of them wish only to distract Chaos and not harm Minerva.

She shapes her energy into bullets, shooting off an array of them toward Barnabas and Lucifer, which they busy with deflecting, while Minerva uses the distraction to make her way towards me.

With her first step in my direction, Phoenix disappears from my side.

She charges, not willing to put off killing me any longer. I can't blame her. She's tried and failed at it at least three times now.

A sword of vibrant, red energy forms in her hand, and I make a matching one of gold in my own. It comes automatically this time, much more easily than it had been to summon the red energy.

The change in color doesn't stall her at all. In fact, she barely seems to register the change at all, thinking nothing of it.

Her sword comes down hard on my own, forcing me to lunge back to help absorb the power from the hit. I slide out from under it, twisting to the side and out of the way.

She turns quickly to face me and once again takes the offense before I can, bringing the sword down from high, forcing me to block it above my head, leaving the rest of my body vulnerable. With her free hand, she punches me in the stomach, a move I hadn't expected. I double over, my arm weakening above me.

Lada appears out of thin air at my side, holding a familiar-looking golden spear, ornamented on one end with a pair of wings. She thrusts it in between me and Minerva, forcing our swords up and apart.

Before Minerva can retaliate, Phoenix is grabbing onto me and Lada and teleporting us away. We reappear directly behind Minerva. Catching her by surprise, Lada stabs the spear right through Minerva's thigh.

"Thanks," Lada says to Phoenix, pulling the spear out and tossing it back to him, blood dripping from the end.

Phoenix catches it without taking his eyes off Minerva. I assume he's looking on with concern over having injured her but, when I follow his gaze, I realize the wound is not the problem. Rather, it's the lack of wound.

We'd been so focused on not harming Minerva but it seems a side-effect of having a Protogenoi possess you is that it's not so easy to bring about such harm. The wound on Minerva's thigh stitches itself back up, the red lightning weaving across the opening like stitches until it's completely closed.

If we can't even wound her enough to incapacitate, how will we defeat her in Minerva's body without killing Minerva?

Even Lucifer and Barnabas seem to have stalled in their attack, watching Minerva's nonexistent wound.

The three of us back up slowly. Phoenix readies his spear. Two throwing stars, shaped like the sun, each ray coming to a sharp point, appear in Lada's hands. And I've got...

Nothing.

Static shocks my hand. A golden spark dances between my fingers again. Of course, I forgot. I have powers I barely understand. It's almost as if the golden power was offended my thoughts.

"Lada!"

Dex's voice travels through the room, even though he's nowhere in sight.

"Close your eyes," Lada warns.

I don't hesitate. From behind my eyelids, I still see the brightness that suddenly fills the room, like the sun dropped down from the sky and into our laps. Even the temperature seems to rise, heating the cold marble floor against my bare feet.

The light disappears, and I don't wait another second to reopen my eyes. As I do, I see Dex sliding across the floor. He closes the few inches of distance that remain between himself and Minerva and rises to his feet, pushing the Aegis against her chest.

"Surprise," he says, a smile lifting his lips.

Minerva grabs onto the shield. As she realizes what it is she holds, she urgently attempts to pull away, but it's too late. The leather strap on the back of the Aegis has already tightened around her arm, attaching itself to its true wielder, Minerva, not Chaos.

Dex, having made his delivery, retreats. He comes to stand beside us and focuses on me even though the threat is still close and very much so still a threat. His expression is an odd mixture of regret and pride.

"It was the only way to catch her off guard," Dex says, by way of an explanation.

"You took your time," is the response I muster.

I don't dare move, keeping a close eye on Minerva. As if she were a projection, Chaos is pulled out from Minerva. The force from the separation sends Minerva flying backwards. The Aegis still attached to her arm, she collapses on the ground unconscious.

Barnabas and Lucifer rush forward to pull her further away from Chaos, who is quickly becoming more corporeal.

Separated from Minerva, Chaos no longer wears the white clothes of the Celestials. Instead, as her own body forms, at last strong enough to exist without another's energy, she forms her own clothing. Seemingly made from pure chaotic energy, a tight black bodice appears with red lightning flowing throughout, patterned like the veins of a leaf. From her hips, the lightning continues to form a long skirt. Where the skirt touches the floor, it shoots off sparks.

Hair that matches the color of her lightning falls in loose curls past her shoulders, and I remember the streak of red hair that had appeared on my human mother's head when she'd returned to my room that night. I'm not surprised to see her irises are of a matching, unnatural red. They have the same eerie quality as my own but are even brighter. They glow. Although she isn't as tall as either Minerva or Lada, her presence demands attention and she radiates pure, unbridled power.

I can feel it. Now with it unconfined, I recognize it like a familiar song or routine, but it feels tainted by anger. Some of the anger belongs to Chaos herself but most of it belongs to the energy that was stolen, as if it maintained some memory of the humans it once belonged to and provided for. She lacks its full allegiance, just as I had.

Her power wants to be free of her, while mine is a part of me. I had been fighting fire with fire when I had water at my disposal.

Having pulled Minerva to relative safety behind the dais, Lucifer and Barnabas charge at Chaos. The energy I feel coming off Chaos isn't only solidifying as she does, but I realize it's also building in on itself as if preparing to—

"Wait!" I shout, but it's too late.

CHAPTER 40

Chaos's energy explodes around her like a bomb, extending out towards all of us. It's not a wave like before, but thousands of deadly bolts shooting out in every direction.

I don't know if I'm capable, or if it's even possible, but I summon my own power, attempting to pull it not only out of me but to separate it completely from me, to work independently. I imagine it traveling to each person in the room and the energy forming a dome around each of them to block the impact. I don't bother imagining one for myself.

Multiple bolts of red lightning strike me hard, forcing me backwards and onto the ground.

Phoenix, the closest to me, I see remains standing beneath a golden dome. It worked, at least it did for him, and I can only hope it did for the rest, as I'm unable to gather the strength to check. But, if it did, it's too suspicious and dangerous for them to be left standing, unaffected.

I collapse the golden dome I can see, and the rest I assume exist, into those they were meant to protect, knocking them unconscious as Chaos's wave had before to Lucifer and Barnabas.

It all happens in a matter of seconds. The last of the assaulting red bolts fly by. With their disappearance, all traces of my gold shields are gone, leaving behind only the visible wreckage from the explosion.

From where I lie, I can see Dex, Lada, and Phoenix on the ground with no sign of movement.

Sparks of red electricity rain down from above, the excess from the bomb that is Chaos.

I breathe through the pressure that comes with all the energy I absorbed. It's not easy to contain but it also doesn't pain me. I bite down on my cheek, as I feel it pulse against me from the inside, like a separate heartbeat.

I force myself over onto my back to face Chaos, even though my head spins from the weight of the energy. A spark falls and hits my cheek, splashing like a rain drop. It absorbs into my skin. I'm not sure how long my body can hold onto everything, if I can contain it all. I push up onto my elbows.

"I should have known not to trust a prophecy," Chaos muses. "The only true power they have is that of self-fulfillment."

She kneels down next to me, her dress pooling around her, and grabs my face roughly in her hand. Her grip is strong, and I tighten my jaw against it, almost afraid it might break against her strength. Her crimson eyes stare into mine, evaluating.

"Why do you want this?" I ask, before she can continue. I have to strain to make my mouth work. "Why is it so important for you to rule over everything?"

A spark passes from beneath my skin to her hand, shocking her. She flinches slightly from the sensation, but tries to pass the expression off as disgust. She releases my face harshly, tossing me to the side as if she can't stand to touch me for a second more.

Chaos rises from the ground to stand before me.

"I ruled once because I was among the most powerful beings, and it was taken away from me. I deserve my rightful place returned."

"So it's about what you deserve? You never deserved to rule in the first place."

The energy pulses inside me, threatening to get out and break through me if I won't release it myself. I grimace against its force, searching for my own energy amongst the onslaught of displaced energy.

Chaos surges toward me in anger. It's not smart to be egging her on but it's hard to concentrate on the right thing to say to an unstable megalomaniac while my own body is threatening to fall apart from the inside out. I speak up again before she can end me.

"Thank you."

I say the words in a rush but they give her pause.

"What?" she asks, the word wielded like a blade.

"You deserve my gratitude," I continue. "I, too, thought I deserved better, especially when it came to the lives the Subject System put me through. But, it turns out I'm grateful for a lot of the experiences. It wasn't all bad, and it gave me time to become who I am. You created the Subject System so I must owe you some gratitude, as well. In fact, it is somewhat your fault that I ever came into my powers. You unintentionally provided me a way to live again."

Something like a growl escapes from Chaos at my words. She raises her hand, and the sparks that continue to fall like rain to the ground gather to form a whip in her hand. She brings it down, where it loudly hits the floor, sending off more sparks that fly in my direction. I turn my head, flinching away, both to hide the fact that they, too, absorb into my skin and because they sting painfully when they make contact.

"That's enough," Chaos says. "You have the power of a Protogenoi. Stand up and face me like one!"

"That's what I've been trying to tell you," I say, lifting myself up from the floor.

I feel weighted, at least double what I normally am, but I've located the pure energy within myself. As I rise to my knees, bracing myself with a hand in front of me on the ground, I see my hazy reflection in the marble floor.

My eyes glow a brighter amber than they ever have before.

"I'm not like you," I tell her. "I'm not a Protogenoi."

I release the golden energy.

The lightning flows out, forming one long rod in my right hand, just as Chaos aims her whip at me. Eager to be free at last, the red energy I stored races out of me, drawn to the golden lightning rod I've formed.

Chaos's whip follows the same path, breaking apart to dissolve into the rod.

The remaining falling sparks swirl in the air, changing direction to head for the rod.

I lighten as the red energy continues to release from me, and my own power strengthens.

Chaos throws more of her power at me but each time it's absorbed by the rod until it's gained enough energy to draw the power out of Chaos herself. It absorbs the rest of her stolen chaos like a magnet, leaving her with no energy left to heal herself. The power leaves her in waves of red, sparking with electricity, but turns to gold as it stabilizes in the rod.

Shocked, and with no power left, Chaos falls to her knees.

I hit the bottom of the lightning rod on the ground, and it breaks apart. Most of the energy returns to me in its golden form. But, some remaining sparks, energy that retains memory of whom it once belonged to, go elsewhere. I suspect the energy will be returning to Vest, where it belongs.

I look around the room. Everyone else is still unconscious but none of them show any sign of the poisonous lightning, as Dex had when he was truly hit. My barriers must have worked.

I send off small, golden sparks, much like the one that had harmlessly passed between Phoenix and I earlier, to Lada, Dex, and Phoenix to wake them up.

With all of Chaos's energy gone, she's drained of all color, the red no longer highlighting her irises or radiating from her hair. It has faded from her clothes, leaving behind a plain dress, the remaining lightning letting out a few last sparks, as if gasping for oxygen. She leans against the dais, struggling to stay even in a seated position.

"She looks almost human," Dex says at my side, startling me.

Turning around, I almost bump into Phoenix who stands right behind me. Lada stands beside Dex.

I knew I'd woken them but I hadn't expected such a subtle approach on their end. Phoenix lifts his arms to steady me, which I would normally brush off, but the reabsorption of all the energy has left me feeling a little unstable, as if I've just stepped off a rollercoaster.

"Is everyone all right?" I ask, looking between the three of them.

"Are *we* all right?" Lada asks, eyeing me skeptically.

"Yeah," Dex says airily, "we're good. Right?" He looks between Phoenix and Lada with a smile, all the while nodding encouragingly.

"You have no idea what you've done."

Chaos's voice has a silencing effect on all of us. Phoenix walks around to my other side to see her. We all turn our focus back to her. Despite her threatening tone and words, I fail to see any sign of danger.

"What do you mean?" Phoenix is the one to ask.

"My death by the hands of my descendent wasn't the end of the prophecy," she says, her voice weak. "By killing me, you've released a greater threat to yourselves. So, while my death wasn't part of the plan, it also doesn't mean my defeat."

"What greater threat?" I demand.

"You've released them," she says.

A weak smile fights its way onto her face.

She takes her final breath.

CHAPTER 41

We burned her body, not even bothering to move to another location.

Lada directed her light, amplifying it with enough heat to catch fire. I was tempted to trap the ashes and smoke, rather than let any remnant escape out the high windows of the Council Chamber. She'd risen once before.

She was never truly defeated after the Firstlast War, only weakened. Still, I had to repeatedly remind myself of that as I watched the last of her escape into the air.

By the time the Council members had awakened, every last trace of her was gone.

I promised the Council I would return once I finally changed out of the dress I'd worn to the Havcire Assembly, and I intend to keep that promise. Eventually. I hear there's a lot of traffic in my part of the forest at this time of day so I'm waiting it out from the comfort of my old Havcirian home.

The gentle breeze drifts in through the paneless window, smelling of salt and sand. I close my eyes and inhale. I don't know what's coming, but I'm going to take the win for now.

⚜

"You're a Siphoner, half Vest and half Celestial, with the ability to use any Celestial's power within a certain distance from you," Lada states.

"Someone listened in Havcire Demographics 101," Dex says.

"Havcire is my life," responds Lada, "but Siphoners are rare to come across, considering there was an agreement for Havcire and Vest to have no interaction. Apparently, there are a lot more exceptions to that than even I was aware of."

"You both are here upon the Council's request," Barnabas cuts in.

He sits back on his golden throne. None of the three Council members show any sign of injury nor any hint that they were involved in the battle that took place in this very location.

Bishop is back in usual position, perched on Minerva's throne. Her arm rests comfortably next to the griffon. All back to normal.

Dex and Lada look up at the Council members, as if they had forgotten their presence.

"Now that I have your attention," Barnabas continues, his voice holding authority, "I might ask how it is that three Celestials were sent to Vest to accomplish a job and absolutely none returned having accomplished any part of it."

"Half Celestial," Dex corrects.

"Had they merely followed instructions," Minerva chimes in, "we would currently be overtaken by Chaos."

"Minerva, that is so not the point here," Lada says, her words glossed in an airy sarcasm. "We must dwell on our inability to follow strict instructions."

Minerva, letting go of her regularly serene and emotionally void expression, smiles at Lada. Barnabas doesn't acknowledge Lada's mocking tone.

"Of course, this is true," he admits. "It does not mean we cannot acknowledge the present company's disregard for authority."

"I feel Phoenix should be here for this lecture, as well, if that is the case," Lada says, reasonably, any hint of facetiousness gone from her tone and expression.

"Phoenix is supposed to be here, as is Dawn," Barnabas says.

"Well," Dex says, "then this seems like a waste."

"I would have to agree with the Siphoner on this one, Barnabas," Lucifer says.

"All done. All memories returned to their rightful owners."

"You make it sound like you personally delivered each lost memory. All you did was give everyone you'd once stolen memories from the same potion we took to return them. It was the least you could do, really," I tell Phoenix, turning away from the window to find him standing in the doorway to my bedroom.

I notice his change of clothes. He's not wearing the usual Celestial white even though we are back in Havcire now. Instead, he wears a gray hoodie and some ripped blue jeans, always presenting himself in the finest.

"Perhaps," he says, coming over to sit beside me on the window seat, "but I did it nonetheless."

I shake my head at him and feel my ponytail brush against my neck from the motion.

Finally, I got to shower, taking off all the makeup, which had not held up great after everything, and I pulled my hair up completely out of my face as I prefer it.

"And now that the Council knows about the Subject System? What's their plan?" I ask, somehow eager to know something's being done to fix it and too exhausted at the same time to hear the answer.

"Okay," Phoenix says slowly, looking up from his sweatshirt's strings, which he'd been fidgeting with, to meet my eyes with his own seemingly pleading ones. "Please let me finish explaining before you say anything."

I force back a smile at his sincere concern. He looks cute, weary of my tendency to jump in with questions. I nod my head and listen.

"The Council has decided to keep the Subject System in place but they will be ensuring that the point system is no longer corrupt. The Subjects will have a fair chance to become Citizens."

"But the Experimenters—" I interrupt, quickly shutting my mouth, as Phoenix raises his eyebrows in a silent plea for me to shut up.

"The Experimenters will be watched more carefully, and there will be rules in place. They'll still be able to observe the Subjects but they won't be able to manipulate them into doing anything that would directly set the Subject on the wrong path. And, if you would like, you have been offered the job of reviewing the Experimenters' plans to ensure that they do follow these new rules." Phoenix pauses, searching my face for any reaction. "Okay, now I'm done. Any questions?"

So many.

I'm not even sure there's a word for what I am.

I'm human, a native Vest, born with the powers of a Protogenoi. Still, for the majority of my life I believed I was a Subject. As much as I hated the Subject System, it had given me hope that I could become more.

Phoenix told me why he chose his name. *I wanted to be able to aspire to something.* If done right, that's what the Subject System could offer.

Minerva's silvery voice fills the Council room.

"You are not here for a lecture," she says, "but you will have to inform Phoenix and Dawn of what we discuss. The four of you successfully uncovered Chaos's plan and defeated her. We have come to the conclusion that it would be best if you were the ones to also investigate the threat she issued before her death. Of course, this time we would expect to be kept informed of any progress."

As always, Lada stands poised before the Council. Still, she manages to hold herself taller at Minerva's words. The Council's offer is genuine and entrusts Lada, along with the others, with a matter of importance.

"We'll have to consult with Dawn and Phoenix but we will consider this and get back to you," Dex says, speaking up before Lada can.

She turns to him, surprise written across her face. She's not the only one who looks at him in such a way.

Barnabas and Minerva match her expression, while Lucifer lazily raises a black eyebrow.

"What do you think you're doing?" Lada asks him, under her breath. "You're speaking to the Council."

"That is fair," Minerva says, cutting off any response from Dex and also Barnabas, who had noticeably opened his mouth to speak.

With that said, Minerva nods her head once in a dismissal. Barnabas, too, raises his hand up from the armrest of his throne to dismiss Lada and Dex. With a last glance at the Council, they leave the room.

The hallway outside is calm, the portals closed off for now, the walls and floor displaying nothing but white marble. Their footsteps echo hollowly as they walk from the Council Chamber, until Lada stops after a few steps down the hall and pulls Dex to a halt, as well.

"You can't just say no to the Council," she says, her tone more confused than reprimanding.

"I don't see you treating them with the upmost respect either," Dex counters.

"That's different," Lada says, shaking her head, her blonde bangs ruffling against her forehead, while retaining their perfect style. "I never outright refuse them. No one does."

"Right, we just scheme behind their backs," Dex says, his mouth curving into a smile. "Maybe it's time we tell them what they need to hear."

Lada nods her head but it's not in agreement with Dex. Instead, she looks as though she's made sense of the puzzle, her confusion lifting.

"You didn't grow up in Havcire, did you?"

"I grew up with my human mother on Vest," Dex answers, and continues on down the hallway. Lada follows.

"Also, my name isn't actually 'Poindexter.' It's just Dex. That was just a little addition Max thought would be a good idea to make me more believable, or so he said." Dex rolls his eyes, thinking back to Max's involvement in crafting Poindexter as a Subject. "Still," Dex continues, "my not being a native Havcirian doesn't mean I'm wrong about the Council, Lada."

"Maybe," Lada says vaguely, her narrow eyes sliding sideways to look at Dex. "So, we are going to agree to look into this new threat, aren't we?"

Dex's smile returns.

"Definitely."

"And you're sure?" Phoenix asks. "It means you have to stick around."

"Yes," I tell him, not sure why he won't just accept my answer. "It's not like I'm the type of person to carelessly make decisions. I mean, most of the time. I'm sure, okay?"

"I'd just hate for you to have any regrets," he says, the hint of a grin playing on his face.

He says the last word as if announcing checkmate. I feel my face heat. The memory of my mouth pressed against his intrudes on my mind.

I stand, pretending as though I need something from my nightstand to have an excuse to hide my unwelcome reaction. I walked right into that.

I had almost died and thought I was about to die. I wasn't thinking straight, and it can't happen again.

I'm not the same person I was when I lived as a Citizen here. At that time, I may have even loved him but I didn't know him as I do now. Neither of us are the same as we were then. So much time has passed, so many lifetimes. With each one, I learned over and over again not to trust him. And still, when it's really counted, he's always been there for me, and I can't deny I still have strong feelings for him, that he might be the most important person in my life, which is exactly why I need to be cautious.

I have time now to discover exactly how much I can trust him. And, I'm only one half of this potential equation.

I couldn't even begin to guess what Phoenix thinks of me. I'd been a pawn, practically entertainment for him during my life as a Subject. I don't know what I meant to him when I was a Citizen. I really have no idea what he's felt for me at any point, *if* he's ever felt anything... for me, that is.

I'm sure he's had feelings at some point during his long life. But, whatever, it doesn't matter. My focus needs to be on determining whether he will stick around as an ally against this new threat or become a part of the threat.

All that sits on my bedside table is an alarm clock, a notebook, and a pen. I choose the pen, tossing it in my hand. I hear Phoenix get up from the window seat behind me but I keep my back to him, the heat in my cheeks still cooling.

"Don't concern yourself with my regrets," I say. "My whole new thing is not dwelling on the past."

I face him, plastering on a smile. He leans against the wall by the window, arms crossed against his chest, looking so very comfortable. He never looks awkward or bothered.

"How very enlightened of you," he says, looking convincingly happy for me. "But, before you forget completely about the past, there's something you should see."

I see a piece of paper held between his fingers. He uncrosses his arms and walks up to me, holding out the paper.

"I found the prophecy where you left it hidden."

I smile to myself. I used to hide everything in the same place, underneath Barnabas's throne. I had liked the idea of keeping whatever was secret right under his nose, or at least I had when I was a kid. It became habit later on.

"But we already know what the prophecy says."

"We *knew* what the prophecy said, but it's changed. When Chaos mentioned it, I figured it was worth taking another look. Some prophecies are only visible to those it directly refers to. Or, at least that is the case until the person dies. At that point, the magic that keeps the prophecy secret is erased and it can be viewed by anyone."

Phoenix holds out the familiar piece of paper toward me.

Chaos had never intended for anyone to find this prophecy, even when it was partially concealed. She'd hidden it in an old history book she suspected no one would actually read. She didn't know Miranda.

It's the same yellowed, old piece of paper I remember laying eyes on long ago.

The first part is what we know, referencing the story of Cronus from Greek mythology. The last line, however, is new.

When Chaos perishes, the Protogenoi will rise from their prison and once again be free to rule.

Acknowledgements

Thank you to my parents who read everything I write and are willing to have in depth conversations about fantasy worlds whenever I like, which is extremely often.

To the rest of my family, I love you, and thank you for always inspiring and motivating me.

To my friends, thank you for supporting my delusions, I mean fantasies; for being Yorick; and for being there.

Vic Gonzalez, thank you for being able to interpret my ideas for the cover when I can't even draw a stick figure. The cover art is amazing.

Lastly, thank you to the readers. Every single one of you helps bring this world to life.

Molly C. Gross grew up in Boca Raton, Florida and then decided to switch coasts and move to another equally warm place, Los Angeles. Molly studied criminal justice, psychology, and creative writing in undergrad, before going on to get her masters in screenwriting. The idea for *Myth Dawning* came to her while driving Florida's Turnpike in college. What if a dead criminal was given the chance at redemption through a psychological experiment that puts to test the question of nature vs. nurture?